The Beginning of Once Upon a Time

KRISTY DIXON

MEEGORE PUBLISHING, LLC

To Amanda Thomas

For igniting a love of reading in the future generation.

Chapter 1

Izla peeked around a large sycamore and smiled. Ruben and Emmie were locked in a tight embrace. She knew she couldn't take all the credit, but she had encouraged the couple more than once. If there was one thing in life Izla could see, it was a good match, and Emmie and Ruben were definitely that.

"Spying on mortals again?" came a voice from behind.

Izla spun around and glared at her brother. "Shhhh! Look how cute they are."

Thane shook his head and grinned. "One of these days, you are going to regret meddling in people's lives."

"Today isn't that day," she said, running her hand over her long green dress. "And it isn't meddling." She turned and walked deeper into the forest. She would not let Thane or anyone else ruin this victory. Two people were happy, and she was at least partially responsible. It made her feel warm inside.

Thane rushed up beside her. "The people in that village might find out you are a fairy and then you will need to avoid this area. Then, how will you amuse yourself?"

Izla tucked a strand of long red hair behind her ear and smiled. "People like fairies. I doubt they would care."

"Yes, but they will all swarm you asking for gifts. That happens every time. At least give it a break. Let people find love for themselves."

Izla tilted her head and studied her brother. His neat reddish brown hair fell over his forehead, and he had gotten tall. He had always been taller than she was, but now she had to crane her neck when she looked at him. He was also getting strong. His muscles weren't as well defined as their father's and other brothers' were, but they would be soon.

"The villagers are all too busy to see what is in front of their faces. They work too much and play too little. If I don't interfere, no one will. They need me."

"Do they, though?" Thane asked, tripping over a branch. Izla grinned. He may be getting taller, but he was still her clumsy older brother.

"It's my calling in life. I was meant to be a matchmaking fairy."

"That's not a thing."

"It is now."

Thane leaped over a small stream of water, and Izla followed.

"So, who is your next victim?"

Izla giggled and pushed her hair over her shoulder. She knew Thane was more like her than he wanted to admit. "Not victim. Beneficiary."

He rolled his eyes. "Alright, who is your next beneficiary?"

"I'm thinking Snow. Do you know of her?"

"The princess from Denholm?" he asked. "Of course I know of her. I know about all the royal mortals."

"She lives with that horrid stepmother. I'm sure she could use some happiness in her life."

"That won't work. She isn't allowed to leave the castle unless her stepmother is with her."

"Yes, but I can be sneaky. I've never met Snow, but I've observed her. I think I can pull this off from the shadows. She'll never even know I was involved."

Thane laughed. "I'll believe that when I see it. You do nothing quietly."

"I've helped people without them knowing."

"Sure you have. You like people to know. I can't believe Father lets you mess with people the way you do."

Izla frowned. Was Thane serious? She had helped so many people find love, and what was better than that? Her father must believe in her. He'd never tried to stop her, so he must think she was doing something worthwhile. She supposed it was possible he didn't know what she spent her days doing. He was the king of the fairy realm and had a lot on his plate. He wasn't always aware of the things his children did.

"What if you make things worse?" Thane asked.

"What do you mean?"

"Snow doesn't have a good life. What if you interfere and make life worse for her? There are whispers about the evil queen being a witch. You might turn her stepmother's wrath onto her."

"Then, I'll just have to be careful. If the queen is a witch, I'll figure it out and let Father know. Evil witches should not be ruling kingdoms. As for Snow, I'll find the perfect person for her. Someone who will cherish her and take her to his kingdom." Izla was bubbling with excitement. She was going to make all of Snow White's dreams come true.

"So, a prince?"

"Of course a prince. She is a princess."

"People are going to avoid you."

"I don't care what people think. My path is clear."

"Everyone cares what people think, especially you."

"People adore me. I'm not worried. This will be the greatest match ever. Just you wait," Izla said, running away from her brother. She didn't need to spend her time with a downer. Maybe Thane couldn't comprehend her vision because he had never been in love. That gave Izla something to ponder. Perhaps her own brother would benefit from her matchmaking skills someday. Then, he would understand and stop trying to stifle her gift.

Thane watched Izla disappear into the trees. Arguing with her never went in his favor.

"I do not know what to do with that girl."

Thane jumped and spun around to face his father. King Henan stood at his side, staring at the place Izla had disappeared.

Thane focused on getting his heart under control. "I wish you would make more noise when you appear. You frightened me near to death."

King Henan gave his son a half-hearted smile and rubbed his hand over his neat brown beard. "Would you prefer I appeared with a large plume of pink smoke like Izla?"

Thane shook his head from side to side. He hated the way Izla couldn't do anything simply. She liked all eyes on her.

King Henan sighed. "I am too busy to keep Izla out of trouble. I need you to watch out for her. Help her with her projects."

Thane groaned. "You mean with her silly matchmaking adventures? I am sure there is someone else much better suited for that job. What about one of her friends?"

The king arched his brow and gave him a pointed look. "You think those girls can have any sway with her? I wouldn't trust them to feed my dog, let alone meddle in people's lives."

"I don't see how I can keep her in line. Can't you command her to stay out of other people's business?"

The king looked up at the blue sky and frowned. Thane knew it would be best to give up now. King Henan was a wise and caring leader, but he had one enormous flaw—he believed his youngest child and only daughter should be allowed to do almost anything she wanted.

The king placed a hand on Thane's shoulder and looked into his eyes. "Izla does not get to rule like you and your brothers do. She needs purpose, and this matchmaking scheme she has come up with means a lot to her. She enjoys seeing people fall in love. It is your job to help her. She is compulsive, and she could get herself into trouble."

Thane's mouth turned down, and he nodded. Izla was spoiled, but she was his sister, and he wanted her to be happy. It would solve everything if the king changed the laws and let Izla rule her own part of the land, though. King Henan's oldest five sons were all settled into their own kingdoms, ruling under their father's guidance.

"I'm sure she's going to get into trouble. The question is just *when*."

"You realize I would not need to put you in this position if you were prepared to take your own kingdom?"

Thane stepped away from his father and resisted the urge to kick at a rock on the ground. "I'm not sure when I'll be ready." There were requirements that Thane must achieve before he could rule. One of them was getting married, and he was not ready for that.

The king crossed his arms over his chest. "I would say to take your time, but you already are. Until you're ready to take up your crown, you are to stick with your sister. If nothing else, it might encourage you to come to terms with your responsibilities."

Heat creeped up Thane's neck, and he tried to ignore it. He hated when his father implied he was being irresponsible. Getting married wasn't something he would jump into without thinking. Besides, he was still young and had things he wanted to do. Perhaps when he got closer to two hundred. He still had years until then.

He glanced at his father and tried to look respectful. "Did you hear what Izla said? She wants to interfere with Snow White. If rumors about the queen are true, she might be taking on more than she can handle."

King Henan nodded. "I have little to do with the kingdom of Denholm, but I have heard the talk. I'm sure Izla will be fine, especially if you are with her."

"Helping royalty might draw attention," Thane protested. "When Izla helps the villagers, it doesn't cause a stir, but Snow White is a public figure—or she was until her father died. Eventually, Izla is going to draw attention to the fact she is a fairy. Where will we be when that happens?"

"I understand your concern, Thane. I do. If I thought Izla's talents would cause problems I could not fix, I would stop her."

"Every time a village learns Izla is a fairy, we have to deal with that many more people coming and asking things of us."

"The people all know where our castle is. Anyone from any place could find us."

"Yes, but when Izla befriends them, they all feel entitled to our help."

"There are worse things."

Thane clenched his teeth together to keep from disagreeing. His father would only put up with so much.

The king shifted and glanced back up at the sky. He always looked at the sky when he didn't want to admit he was wrong. "Izla won't have time for Snow White for a while, so you do not need to worry at the moment. In two days, it will be the celebration of Princess Rosamond's birth. Izla has been invited to be a fairy guest of honor."

"I don't have to go, right?" Thane hated those celebrations. They lasted forever, and the babies were too young to appreciate them. They usually ended with a wailing baby and a rattled queen.

"Not this time. They only invited twelve delegate fairies to keep things on a smaller level."

"Twelve?" Thane asked, frowning. "If they only want a small group, they should still invite thirteen. If they leave out one of the thirteen delegates, someone will not be pleased."

King Henan tilted his head and studied his son. "Yes. It is careless of them. With hope, the fairy they left out is not one that will be angered."

"Perhaps you should speak to the king."

"No. I cannot direct the mortals in everything. If I stop them from making mistakes today, what is to stop them tomorrow? I can see you disagree with me."

"You are the king," Thane said, bowing his head.

"I am. One day, you will have daughters, and you will understand."

The king disappeared, and Thane took a calming breath. His father was wrong. He would never let his children run around messing with other people's lives. They would have rules. Rules that would benefit them and the world.

He ran a hand through his hair. Thane couldn't picture himself with children. If he had children, that would mean he had a wife, and Thane wasn't good at talking to women. It scared him more than he would ever admit. Whenever he talked to them, he came off gruff or sarcastic.

He wouldn't worry about it now. There was plenty of time to figure out his future. Right now, he needed to focus on Izla and keep her out of trouble.

Chapter 2

Izla's eyes ran over the elaborately decorated palace, and she smiled. The king and queen of Thurin knew how to host a party. Blue, green, and pink lanterns lined the walls, and the tables were covered in blue cloth. Izla would have preferred pink, but blue would do. Pink was Izla's favorite color, but she couldn't wear it as it clashed with her red hair.

She glimpsed her reflection in a large mirror that was lined with gold trim and tried to admire herself without looking obvious. Her eyes glittered back at her. It wasn't hard to see that she was the most beautiful woman in the room. The thought was vain, and she knew it. It wasn't fair to compare herself to mortals. Even the ugliest fairy was prettier than most humans. She straightened her green sleeve and moved toward the head of the large room. The table for fairies was always the most elaborate. Gold plates and utensils lined the table. Izla frowned. Something wasn't right.

"Iz!" a familiar voice exclaimed.

Izla turned around and smiled as her three friends made their way to her. Ava led the pack in a shimmering red dress. Her brown skin glowed, and delicate white flowers decorated her waist length black hair. Zina was close behind in a burgundy dress that boasted puffed sleeves. Her corset must be too tight again because she looked near to faint. Her blonde curls framed her face and bounced when she walked.

Lily brought up the tail. Her brown hair was wet and hung limply down her back. Her yellow dress was rumpled. Izla hid a smile behind her hand. She wouldn't be surprised to see Lily's dress buttoned unevenly. Lily valued reading over all else and often left preparations until the last minute.

"This place looks lovely!" Zina said, catching Izla up in a hug. "It's been a long time since we've been invited to one of these events."

Lily sighed. "It's a pity they did it so early in the evening. One more hour, and I could have managed my hair."

"If you had stopped reading sooner, you could have managed it," Ava said, crossing her arms and giving her friend a slight smile.

Izla pulled her thin wand from her pocket and waved it over Lily's head. Her brown hair dried, and another swirl of the wand had it twisted into an attractive knot with soft curls falling at the sides.

Lily touched her hair and smiled. "Thanks, Iz. I wish I had the magic you do. If I try anything like that, I'm more likely to start a fire than make anything presentable."

Ava nodded. "Iz has always out done us with magic. It's a good thing she is our friend or I might fear her!"

The others laughed, and Izla tried to look stern, but her lips turned up at the corners. "Just don't do anything to anger me and we will all be fine."

"Um... do you all see what I see?" Zina asked. Izla turned to look at the table Zina was pointing at.

"No, what?" Lily asked.

"There are only twelve plates at the table."

Izla pursed her lips and tried to ignore a wave of panic. "Perhaps someone couldn't come?"

Ava gave a small smile, but her eyes held fear. "That's probably it. The king and queen wouldn't exclude anyone."

"I hope not," Izla said, scanning the gathering crowd. Most of the people were mortals, but she saw four fairies in the mix. Her friends were scanning the crowd as frantically as she was.

Zina gripped the fabric at her stomach and turned to her. "I don't see Nassandra," she whispered.

Izla swallowed hard and searched the faces again. Zina was right. No Nassandra.

"Oh dear," Lily said, rubbing the back of her neck. "Should we leave?"

Izla gazed over the people, searching for the king. "No, there must be a mistake. I'll go talk to King Fredrick." Izla grabbed the bottom of her dress and weaved expertly through the crowd. King Fredrick stood speaking to someone. His blond beard was neatly trimmed, and he wore a long brown cape lined with white fur.

She should wait until he finished his conversation, but this was a serious matter, and as a fairy princess, she outranked him.

"Excuse me," she said with authority.

The king turned to her, and an enormous smile broke out across his face. "Princess Izla, so good of you to come. How may I help you?"

"I haven't seen Nassandra, and I'm wondering if she will be coming?"

The king's smile slid from his face. "We were short one of our gold plates. We didn't want to offend any of the fairies by giving one of them a different plate, so we decided it would be best to not invite one."

Izla choked back a bitter laugh. "So, instead of offending with unmatching dishes, you left her out? Have you ever heard of Nassandra? She is not forgiving."

The king cleared his throat. "We didn't invite a large group, so I don't think she will even know it happened. Even you have to admit that of all the fairies, she is the most unnerving."

Izla fought back the urge to give the king a tongue lashing he wouldn't forget. Of all the fairies he could have left out... The man was a fool. She nodded at him and stomped back to her friends.

"Is she coming?" Ava asked.

"She wasn't invited."

Lily fanned her face with her hands. "Oh dear."

"Yes. This won't end well."

Zina sank into a chair and rubbed her temples. "If we are lucky, Nassandra will be too busy to take notice."

"Nassandra notices everything," Ava said, joining her friend at the table. "I wonder if we should leave so we don't have to witness anything unpleasant."

"What to do?" Izla said, tapping her lip with a finger. It would be better to be prepared. Izla's magic was strong, but she wasn't sure it could outdo Nassandra. Ava, Zina, and Lily would help, but their magic was unpredictable and nowhere near as powerful as hers.

The king and queen stood together, and the queen held baby Rosamond. The king gathered everyone's attention and gave a brief speech. Izla didn't hear any of it. She was too busy fretting over Nassandra. She drummed her fingernails against the table and tried to come up with a plan. It was possible Nassandra wouldn't realize she'd been slighted, but she wouldn't count on it.

The other eleven fairies sitting around the table all wore unsettling expressions. Some whispered back and forth to one another, and Izla could only assume they were all wondering where Nassandra could be. The people at the other tables were all fixated on the king, none of them realizing the situation they might all be in at any moment.

Ava leaned toward her, her deep brown eyes filled with worry. She whispered, "Why would they slight Nassandra? Everyone knows she has a temper."

Izla didn't answer. The stress of the situation was overwhelming. Ava was right. Any other fairy here would be forgiving. Offended, yes, but they would get over it. There were stories that circulated about Nassandra and the people who had upset her. They never ended well.

Servants entered the great hall and passed around roast chicken and vegetables. It smelled divine, but Izla had to force herself to choke it down. She told herself there was hope when the meal finished without interruption. All that was left was the gift giving ceremony.

"Oh dear," Zina whispered. "I forgot we were supposed to bring a gift. I've only been to one of these, and I was young and with my mother."

"I forgot as well," Ava muttered.

Lily's eyes were wide. "As did I."

Izla rolled her eyes. Her friends were not very imaginative. "They are expecting something magical from the fairies. Come up with something quickly."

A petite fairy with soft brown eyes and curls stood. She carried a large metal shield with a bird etched onto the front. She smiled as she handed it to the king. "This shield holds the magic of the old kings. I present it with love to Princess Rosamond. Guard it well, and it will be a protection for her."

The king and queen smiled and thanked the fairy. Another stood and presented the little princess with a magic sword. One by one, the fairies gave their gifts and returned to their seats. Ava, Lily, and Zina were squirming in their chairs. Ava was next, and from her expression, she hadn't come up with any ideas.

Izla leaned toward her friend and whispered, "Give her a spell."

"You know I'm not that good at spells," she whispered back.

"Look at the king and queen. He is handsome, and she is beautiful. Give her the gift of beauty. It's almost guaranteed to come true. Wave your wand around and no one will be the wiser."

Ava's eyes lit up, and she grinned. "Thanks, Iz. I never would have thought of that." She got to her feet and made her way forward.

"What about me?" Zina asked.

Did Izla really have to do everything around here? "The king is said to possess a magnificent voice. Tell them you give her the gift of music."

Ava returned to her seat, and the king and queen were beaming at her. Ava smiled and mouthed, "Thank you," to Izla.

Zina stood and waved her wand in the air. "To the princess, I give the gift of music. May her voice forever fill the air with beauty." She pointed the wand at the baby, and everyone clapped. The king and queen looked ecstatic.

It was Izla's turn. She smiled and came to her feet, gracefully bowing to the king and queen. She waved her wand, and a spinning wheel appeared. Everyone in the room looked at the wooden device in confusion. They were expecting something different. Izla smiled to herself.

The queen gave her a forced smile. "Thank you, Princess Izla. I am sure she will enjoy it."

"That is no ordinary spinning wheel," she said with a smile. "This spinning wheel can spin straw into gold." There was a collective gasp among the small crowd.

The king's eyes lit up. "Straw into gold? How extraordinary."

"There is one catch, I'm afraid," Izla told him. "The spinning wheel only works when it is used to help someone else. The person spinning cannot use it to get rich. It will teach the princess to be industrious and compassionate."

"What a lovely gift!" The queen's smile was genuine this time.

Izla smiled and sat down.

Lily was the last fairy to give a gift. She stood nervously, and Izla's smile became forced. Lily must have some plan, or she would have asked for an idea like the others.

Without warning, the ten large windows in the great hall blew open, and the lanterns went out. It was still light, but that didn't stop a chill from crawling up Izla's spine. She shared a concerned look with Ava.

A gigantic cloud of black smoke swirled into a window and settled in the middle of the room. Izla stood and pulled her wand from her pocket, ready for anything. Nassandra appeared as the smoke faded. Her long golden hair sparkled against her black cloak. Her black dress went down past her feet.

Nassandra's eyes were lined with black, and her lips were an unnatural red. Izla wondered what she had done to produce that color. The fairy slowly scanned the crowd until her gaze landed on the king and queen.

The queen held on to the king's arm and bit her lip.

Nassandra smiled. "Sorry for the entrance, but I am in a hurry. My invitation must have been lost. I can't believe you wouldn't invite me. That would be foolish."

The king's jaw was set, and the queen looked down at the floor.

"Well, this is awkward. I guess you didn't invite me. I know my presence can be... overwhelming."

Ava leaned forward and whispered, "That's because she is a freak."

Nassandra's eyes jumped to her, and she smiled as Ava gulped. Her eyes took in all the fairies and stopped when they landed on Izla.

"Hello, Princess," Nassandra said, glancing at Izla. "No need to hold that wand so tightly. I'll just give Princess Rosamond my gift and be on my way."

Izla took a step forward. "You may leave without giving a gift." Perhaps she could turn any anger the fairy might have on her so she would leave the others alone.

"But my gifts are coveted," she said, pulling a wand from her pocket. "It will only take a moment."

Izla bit the inside of her cheek and tried not to fidget.

She smiled, her eyes flashing with excitement. "I give the princess the gift of curiosity."

Izla let out a slow breath. Curiosity wasn't so bad.

Nassandra waved her wand in the air. "I give her the gift of curiosity, the gift to question everything. When she turns seventeen, she will find a spinning wheel. Curiosity will cause her to touch it and prick her finger on the spindle—and die."

"NO!" the queen yelled, dropping to her knees.

"Take it back," Izla demanded, pointing her wand at Nassandra.

The woman threw her head back and laughed. "Never." Smoke swirled around her, and she disappeared. The hall was silent, then the queen began to cry.

"All is not lost," Izla said, raising her voice over the queen's sobs. "Lily still has a gift to bestow. Perhaps she can make it right."

The queen looked up, her eyes pleading with Lily. "Please help us."

Lily swallowed twice and reached into her pocket, pulling her wand out with a shaky hand. "The princess will prick her finger on a spinning wheel," she said nervously, "but she will not die. Instead, she will fall into a deep sleep of a hundred years."

"A hundred years?" the queen asked.

"Yes," Lily said, waving her wand. "Or until she is kissed by one who would love her." A flash of light shot from Lily's wand, and everyone closed their eyes at the brightness. All in attendance sat in silence.

The king stepped forward and raised his voice. "All spinning wheels in the kingdom will be destroyed!"

Izla snapped her fingers and made the spinning wheel she had presented to the princess disappear. Making a spinning wheel that could produce gold was not a simple thing to do. She wouldn't have the king destroying it.

The fairies disappeared one by one until only Izla and her friends remained.

Sweat ran down Lily's face, and she wore a defeated frown.

Izla put her hand on her friend's shoulder. "Come, let's meet in our spot in the woods."

She spun her wand and took herself to a small clearing in the forest. She watched as her three friends appeared. Lily sank down to the earth, her yellow dress puffing up around her. She placed her hands over her face and shuddered.

Izla, Ava, and Zina shared a look and joined their friend in the dirt, forming a circle.

"You did the best you could," Zina said.

Lily wrapped her arms around her knees and rested her chin on top. "That was awful! I couldn't think. I cannot handle that type of pressure. Izla should have been the last one. She would have thought of something."

"At least you gave them hope," Izla said. "Still, a hundred years? Why not one? Or five minutes?"

Lily stared at her feet. "A hundred years isn't so long."

"It is when you're a mortal. When Rosamond wakes, everyone she knows will be gone."

"Yes, but I said she could wake with a kiss from someone who would love her."

Izla's mind began turning, and she smiled. She hadn't processed that part at the palace. It was possible this could become a wonderful love story, after all.

Ava scrunched her nose. "But Rosamond will only be seventeen. What if she hasn't fallen in love?"

Izla tapped her lip. "Lily said, 'Someone who would love her.' It doesn't have to be someone that *does* love her. That could be several people."

"That's right!" Lily said, a slight smile on her face. "I am sure we can fix this. Especially with Izla's help."

Izla's mouth turned down. "You three are going to have to deal with this one without me."

Zina's eyebrow raised. "Us? Without you? You are the expert in things like this."

"And you three always want to help. This is your chance. I have so much planned these days. I don't have time to wait around for a baby to grow up. You three need to stay in Rosamond's kingdom. We can't be sure Nassandra won't cause more trouble."

Ava sniffed. "Stay in the kingdom? For a hundred years?"

Izla cocked her head as she studied her friends. "Yes. The kingdom will need protecting, and so will Rosamond. Once she pricks her finger, you must be ever vigilant. Guard her until she is awakened."

"Perhaps she won't prick her finger," Zina said. "The king did order all the spinning wheels to be destroyed."

"When has a plan Nassandra made ever been ruined? Never. Don't let yourselves think for a moment that it might not happen. Instead, plan on how to make sure it is reversed."

Lily nodded. "We will do our best. Can we call on you if we need help?"

"Of course." Izla hoped they wouldn't need her. At least not until the princess was grown. She would enjoy helping with part of a love story, but she wasn't one to sit idly while grass grew beneath her feet.

Ava twisted a small purple wild flower between her fingers and let out a long breath. "I suppose I am up for it. You do know the three of us are the worst fairies for the job? We bungle things up more than all the others put together."

Zina wrung her hands. "Ava is right. I'm always surprised you chose us as your friends. You are one of the most skilled in the entire fairy realm."

Izla shrugged and pushed back a wave of guilt. She liked her friends, but sometimes she wondered if she unconsciously picked them because they made her look good. Ava was right. If there was someone who was going to mess up a spell, it was these three. Still, Izla cared about them, and she knew they had potential.

"You will all do wonderfully, I'm sure. Keep the royal family safe. I will tell them you are assigned to them. They will find that a great honor and a comfort." Izla was sure it was true. People liked fairies. It was just the way things were. That was why Izla only told select people she was a fairy. If everyone knew, there would be no peace.

Chapter 3

Thane paced across the throne room of his father's castle and tried to control his temper. King Fredrick was a fool. No one in their right mind would neglect sending Nassandra an invitation to anything. The kingdom of Thurin would be under Thane's rule someday, and he would inherit their troubles. If his father had his way, it wouldn't be too far off.

Thane had more reason to want to avoid Nassandra than some people. He had memories of her that he had never told anyone about. Dealing with the fairy would be more awkward than anything, and he hoped to have no part of it.

"I'm sure my friends will handle it," Izla said. She was sitting on her father's red and gold throne, rubbing her hand over the elaborate gold flowers etched into the arm. She was the only one that didn't get in trouble for sitting there.

A bitter laugh slipped from his mouth. "It would be the first time they handled anything."

He tripped over the long red carpet that ran from the door to the throne and righted himself. He hated this room. People were allowed to come in on one day a week and tell their problems to the king. The throne and the carpet were the only things occupying any space. King Henan didn't want it to distract people from their purpose. One hundred people could stand in the room, without crowding the king. The walls were covered in red and gold trim, gold sconces holding bright candles were spaced every five feet.

Izla straightened the small silver tiara on her head. "They have seventeen years to work it out, and if worse comes to worst, Rosamond will wake after one hundred years."

"How comforting for her parents," Thane said, letting the sarcasm hang thick.

"You are acting like I am responsible."

He sighed. "I know you aren't. I'm just upset it happened. It will not improve anyone's relationship with Nassandra. I wish our father would call her in and put her in her place."

"I always thought father wasn't afraid of anything. I think she makes him nervous, though."

Thane sneezed and cringed as the sound echoed through the room. "I hate it in here."

Izla rose from the throne and walked toward him. "Really? I've always loved it. Remember when we used to run and slide across the floor with our stockings on?"

He grinned. "What do you mean, used to? I still do it when no one is looking, and I bet you do as well."

Izla's eyes sparkled. "I'll never admit it. Come. Let's speak of something less gloomy." She linked her arm with his, and they began strolling toward the door.

"Such as?"

"Snow White."

Thane groaned. "I hoped you had forgotten about that."

"Never. Are you coming with me?"

He wanted to make excuses, but he remembered his father's words. "I'll come."

She squeezed his arm. "It's going to be so much fun!"

He shook his head. At least one of them would enjoy it.

Izla straightened her long brown dress and glanced behind her. Thane was hidden in the bushes to the east of Snow White's castle. She could make him out, but only just. Her shoes were with him. It was easier to scramble around barefoot.

The large gray castle seemed to climb up to the sky. Dense fog made it impossible to see the castle's towers. Izla felt the fog was a blessing, as it would help hide her. She could use magic, of course, but doing things without it made it a bigger challenge and more fun. A light gray fountain stood between her and the castle. The sound of the water splashing from a stone statue of a woman with a vase would hide any small sounds she might make.

Izla dropped to the ground when she heard footsteps coming quickly from the side. She crawled to the opposite side of the fountain and sat with her back against the cool stone. Her heart raced, and she smiled. This must be how robbers felt.

A sobbing nearby caused her smile to slip. Getting onto her hands and knees, she raised herself until she could peek over the fountain. A young girl, no more than sixteen, sat across from her on the edge of the fountain. Her hands covered her face, and her shoulder shook. It had to be Snow White. Her shiny black hair fell over her shoulders in soft waves, and Izla would almost bet that if the girl put her hands down, she would have beautiful red lips. It was what she was famous for, after all.

Something touched Izla's side, and she bit back a shriek. She turned to see Thane down on his knees next to her.

"What are you doing?" she whispered. "You were supposed to stay back."

"Yes, well, I don't want a lecture from Father for letting you get in trouble."

"What trouble?"

"With you, I am afraid to guess."

Izla rolled her eyes. She rarely got into trouble. She was an expert at avoiding it.

"Do you have a plan?" he asked, glancing over at Snow White.

"I'm going to speak with her."

"No, Iz. You said you could do this from the shadows."

She narrowed her eyes. He never understood the need to improvise. "She needs someone to talk to."

"What makes you think she will talk to you?"

"I don't see why she wouldn't."

"Hello?" came a soft, melodious voice. "Is someone there?"

Izla pointed at Thane. "Stay here." She hopped to her feet, and Snow White jumped to hers. The girl was pretty, just like the rumors said. Of course, her eyes were red and swollen, but she was lovely, especially for a mortal.

"Who are you?" Snow asked, taking a step back.

"A friend," she said. If she gave her name, the girl would immediately know who she was.

"Friend? I've never seen you before."

Izla walked carefully around the fountain and stopped in front of her. "I would like to be your friend. You look as if you could use one."

Snow pulled a white cloth from her blue dress and wiped at her nose. "I am not supposed to talk to people."

"No one needs to know. Why are you crying?"

"Do not concern yourself with it."

"But I want to help."

"Why?"

Izla kept a smile on her face. "Because that is what I do. I help people."

Snow frowned and took a step backward. "I am fine, but thank you."

When people knew Izla was a fairy, they poured all their troubles out to her, but she wouldn't tell. She would prove to Thane and herself that she was persuasive without using magic.

"Your stepmother is not the nicest person. Is that why you were crying?"

Snow's eyebrows met, and she took another step back. "You should watch what you say. You do not want to incur her wrath."

"I'm not scared of the evil queen."

"I need to go," the girl said. She turned and ran around the side of the castle, leaving Izla standing with her mouth open.

"Great job," Thane said, getting to his feet.

She put her hands on her hips. "I wonder why she wouldn't open up to me."

Thane chuckled. "Why would she? She doesn't know you."

"Yes, but people usually confide in me."

Thane lifted his brow. "Do they?"

Izla crossed her arms and stuck out her tongue. Sometimes Thane was annoying. Still, she would rather have him at her side than any of their other brothers.

"Think about it, Iz. If you were upset and a random stranger wanted you to talk about it, what would you do?"

She shifted her jaw from side to side. He had a point.

"Even if she wanted to talk to someone, what makes you have any authority in her mind? Does she really want to tell someone her own age, with little experience?"

"I am much older than she, and I have a lot of experience."

"Older in years, but in fairy years, you are about the same. Perhaps a year or two older."

Izla arched her eyebrow. "Are you saying I should have appeared to her disguised as a grandmother?"

He chuckled. "It might not hurt."

"Did you hear that?" she asked, straining her ears. "Someone is coming." They both ducked back down behind the fountain and peeked over the edge.

Snow came rushing back from around the corner. A middle-aged man with a dark goatee and ponytail followed behind her. He wore a black leather coat and boots. Over his shoulder was a bow, and he carried a small hunting knife.

"Why would the queen ask you to take me for a walk?" Snow White asked, rushing toward the woods. If she kept going straight, she would walk right over to Izla's shoes.

"The queen worries about your safety," the man's baritone voice responded.

"I always walk on my own. I prefer it."

"No use arguing with the queen."

Snow sighed. "I suppose not."

"Follow them," Izla whispered. "I'll catch up in a minute."

Thane scrunched his nose. "Follow? Why?"

"I don't trust him. Hurry, before you lose them." She watched as he reluctantly headed after them. She stood and walked toward the castle. It was time to find out what Snow White's stepmother was all about.

Thane was growing bored, and he was more than a little tired. He had been trailing Snow and the queen's man for over an hour. Every time Snow suggested they return to the castle, the man would tell her to go a little further. Thane had nothing to prove, so he turned himself invisible so he could follow them without sneaking. As long as he took careful steps, no one would be the wiser.

"I am quite fatigued," Snow said to the man. "I feel we should turn around."

The man sighed and ran a hand over his face. "I suppose this is as good a place as any." Thane's eyes narrowed as he watched the man glance from his knife to the girl.

"So, we can return?" she asked, a slight tremble in her voice.

"I'm afraid not," the man said, taking a step closer to the princess.

Her eyes widened when she saw the man hold his knife in the air. "W-what are you doing?"

"I was ordered to kill you," he said, his voice void of emotion.

She stumbled back. "No!"

"I'm afraid so. I hate to be the one to do it, but I fear punishment."

Thane walked quietly up beside the villain and prepared to act.

"Please spare me," Snow pleaded. "I will run away and never return, I swear it!"

"Where would that leave me if you were to return?" he growled. "I shudder to imagine what would happen to me."

She held her chin high. "So, you are a coward? I always believed the queen's huntsman to be a brave man, full of honor."

The man flinched. He might make the right decision, but Thane would not count on it. He grabbed a large rock near his feet and, in one smooth motion, knocked the man unconscious. Snow yelped and jumped back.

The huntsman laid on the dirt, blood running from his head. Thane became visible, causing Snow to let out another small squeal. He didn't know what to say to girls, so he ignored her and bent down to press his handkerchief to the unconscious man's bleeding head.

"How did you do that?" Snow asked, holding a hand to her chest. "You appeared out of nowhere."

"If I were you, I would run," he said, not looking away from the huntsman. He muttered a spell that stopped the man's bleeding, but left him with a large purple and blue bump on the side of his head. Perhaps a reminder would be good for the man.

"Run? Where?"

Thane glanced up and sighed. "Anywhere. Just stay away from the castle and your stepmother."

"Do you have magic?" she asked, leaning forward to see what he was doing.

"Yes, now go."

"What kind of magic?"

He had heard the princess was shy and rarely spoke. That was obviously a lie.

She kneeled down, so she was at his level. "Are you a wizard? Perhaps a sorcerer?"

"I'm a fairy."

She let out a small giggle. "No, really."

He stood and crossed his arms over his chest. "I am a fairy. Now get out of here before your stepmother realizes you are still alive."

"You cannot be a fairy. Fairies are small, and they have wings."

Thane pursed his lips. Why did Izla get him into these ridiculous situations? He could shrink himself down, sprout some wings, and fly away, but Thane hated wings, and he hated being small. Wings at regular height looked ridiculous. Once he ruled over this land, he would have to help people get over their common misconceptions about fairies.

"The queen tried to have you killed and you want to stand around arguing about whether I'm a fairy? You should be worried about more important things."

She stood and raked her hand through her black hair. "Like what?"

Thane blinked. "Like where you are going now? You cannot return home. The queen will probably continue trying to get rid of you."

"I wonder if he was lying," Snow said, glancing down at the huntsman. "I cannot imagine why my stepmother would want to kill me."

"Perhaps because she wants to continue ruling?"

"I know she doesn't like me. She's rather cruel, to be honest, but she doesn't seem like a murderer. I do not think she cares about ruling. She spends most of the time admiring herself in her mirrors."

Thane gestured at the huntsman. "He told you the queen sent him to kill you. It cannot be more clear than that."

Snow's eyes studied Thane, and he tried not to squirm. "He did not say the queen sent him, only that he was sent. Even if she did, I will become queen once I marry. That would stop the guilty party."

"Great. You find someone to marry, but for now, run before the queen sends someone else."

"It would solve the problem if I were to marry now," she said, taking a step closer to him.

Thane's eyes grew wide, and he threw his arms up in the air and took a step back. "Not me."

"Why not? You would get to rule the kingdom. I wouldn't interfere. I have no desire to rule."

What was wrong with this girl? "I told you. I'm a fairy. Not only that, but my father is the king. I'm not marrying a mortal."

Her eyes narrowed, and her lip came out in a pout. "You want me to believe the fairy king's son is out in the forest? I don't believe it."

"You know what? Just go back to your castle. I don't care, I'm leaving."

"She can't go back," Izla said, popping in at his side. Snow took a step back. "If she does, I am almost sure she will be killed. I overheard the queen talking to one of her advisors. It seems she is jealous of Snow and has no kind feelings toward her."

Snow's lip quivered. "So, I have to spend the rest of my life hiding in the forest?"

"No," Izla said. "The easiest way to get you on the throne is to get you married."

"Yes, I was just telling this gentleman that."

Thane frowned. "I am not going to marry you."

"But—"

"No," Izla said, putting her hand up to silence the girl. "He is not the one for you."

"But he is very nice to look at. The people would obey him. He has a commanding presence."

Thane scowled and ignored the heat running across his face and neck. Who was going to obey him? He couldn't even get this one girl to listen to him.

Izla shook her head. "We need to find you a prince. That isn't important right now, though. You need to get away from this place before the huntsman is missed, and the queen sends someone out here. Go. Hide somewhere, and I will find you soon."

Snow crossed her arms and glared at Izla. Thane had heard rumors over the years about Snow White, and so far, they didn't seem very true. She was said to be quiet and passive, but the flames in her eyes as she looked at Izla would never be described as passive.

"Why are you still here?" Izla asked.

"I do not see why I should obey you. You could be lying about the queen wanting to kill me. I have never seen you in my life, and you want me to trust you?"

Izla's eye twitched, and Thane wondered if his sister was going to give the princess a lecture.

"You know, the queen sent the huntsman for you," Thane said. "He said it himself."

Snow shifted from one leg to the other. "I suppose."

"There is no *suppose*," Izla said. "You need to hurry."

Snow sniffed. "I don't feel like hurrying, but I will go." She spun, her black hair swaying behind her, and walked away at a leisurely pace.

"Oh, no, you don't," Izla muttered.

She pulled her wand from her pocket and waved it over her head. In a flash, a gray and black wolf came leaping out from the trees. He bounded toward Izla, wagging his tail. She knelt on the ground and ran her hand over his head. Animals were drawn to fairies. Thane liked them well enough, but Izla loved them all. This wolf was one of her favorites. She even let him sleep in the castle.

Izla whispered something to the wolf, and he turned and ran at Snow. She shrieked and bolted into the trees.

Izla rolled her eyes. "Thane, you should probably go. I'll deal with this."

"Thank you," he said.

He popped back to the castle before Izla could change her mind. Thane rushed down a long gray hallway, ignoring all the servants and nobles he passed. When Izla had a plan, she rarely deviated from it, and if her plans were going to include him, he needed to get more sleep.

"Where are you off to?" King Henan asked, grabbing Thane's arm as he tried to hurry past.

Thane came to a stop and sighed. "Bed. Izla's endeavors wear on me."

"Did she return with you?"

"No."

The king frowned. "You are supposed to stay with her."

"All the time?"

"Well, no. But I want you with her when she is working on her projects."

Thane looked over his shoulder to make sure no one was listening. "Her *projects* are painful."

The king's eyes narrowed. "To whom?"

"To everyone she involves, and to me. I don't understand her need to help Snow White. I mean, the girl needs help, but probably not matchmaking."

"It might do you well to meet some princesses."

Thane stifled a yawn. "I've met plenty."

King Henan's eyes lit up. "I have heard Snow White is quite beautiful."

"I suppose," Thane said. "I find her annoying."

"Annoying? She is said to be shy."

"She didn't seem shy," he muttered, trying to ignore the awkward time he'd spent in the girl's presence.

The King smiled. "Oh?"

"Izla needs to find her someone with sense. She can't see what's right in front of her, and that isn't good for ruling a kingdom. That reminds me. You should probably do something about Snow White's stepmother. She tried to have the girl killed."

The king's smile left his face. "I have heard rumors. I had hoped the people of that kingdom would band together and do something about it. If I interfere, it could cause problems."

Thane wouldn't share his opinion. Getting into an argument with his father was the last thing he wanted to do right now. There was no doubt Izla would wake him bright and early the next day, and he needed his sleep.

"May I be excused?"

"Yes, but I want you to be committed to your sister. Do you understand?"

Thane kept a straight face as he nodded.

The king clapped him on the back. "Good. Now get some sleep. You look tired."

Chapter 4

"Thane, wake up," Izla said, shaking her brother. The sun had been up for over an hour, and he was still in bed. She was always amazed at how much he could sleep. Any sleep over four hours was too much for her.

"It's too early," he moaned, rolling away from her. She sighed and glanced around his neat room. Everything was in its exact place. Dust wouldn't dare show itself in Thane's room. He didn't allow servants to clean after him, he did it all himself. What was the fun of being royal if you didn't take time to enjoy the perks?

Izla wasn't messy, but she was nothing like Thane. Even his dark blue quilt that covered him was neat. The bed almost looked made with him in it. There was a small bedside table with one book on top. It looked like he had measured to make sure the book was in the exact center of the table. She was almost sure if she were to open the large hickory wardrobe, she would see his clothing perfectly lined up and pressed to perfection.

"Snow needs us," Izla said, pushing his book just enough to make it crooked.

He sat up and rubbed his eyes. "She needs something."

Izla grinned and crossed her arms, a sparkle jumping into her eyes. "She seemed to like you."

He groaned. "I hope you aren't getting any ideas."

"Of course not. She needs a mortal prince. I have a few in mind. I'm not sure if I should wait until the queen is dealt with first, though."

Thane leaned over and straightened his book. Izla smiled. When they were young, she would sneak into his room and move things just to see how long it would take before he noticed and fixed them. It was never long.

He yawned. "Did you follow Snow? Did your wolf eat her?"

She frowned. "Of course I followed her, and Axel would never eat anyone. I only called him to get that girl moving. She was a bit more stubborn than I had expected."

"Did she find shelter?" he asked, throwing his legs over his bed.

"Yes. There was a little cottage in the woods. She knocked on the door, waited about five seconds, and let herself in." The princess had surprised Izla. Entering a strange house could be dangerous, but Snow didn't seem to care.

"Who lives there?"

"The cottage belongs to seven men. They own a diamond mine close to the cottage."

Thane got to his feet and grabbed his robe. "I've heard of them. They keep to themselves."

"Yes, and they don't seem to be dangerous. I'm not sure what happened, but they didn't throw her out when they got home."

He arched his brow. "You didn't go invisible and spy?"

"I wanted to do this with as little magic as possible, just to show you I can. It isn't going the way I planned since you told her you were a fairy. Since I was with you, I'm sure she realizes I am as well."

"You appeared in front of her. You can't blame that on me."

He was right. She hadn't even realized her mistake. Izla walked to the door and glanced back at him. She wouldn't be surprised if he fell back into bed. "Meet me in front of the castle in fifteen minutes."

"Fifteen?" he groaned, running a hand through his hair. "Thirty, at least. I need to get dressed and eat."

She sighed. "Twenty-five."

"Fine."

Izla pulled the door open and rushed out. She wasn't sure what she should do first. Searching out an acceptable prince was a must. Getting Snow to understand her situation was also important. There was also the evil queen to deal with. It was unfortunate her father wouldn't interfere in that situation.

She bounced down a long, dimly lit stairwell and out the front door. Axel ran to her, and she dropped to her knees and rubbed his soft fur. He wagged his tail and closed his eyes when she rubbed his head.

"You are such a good boy," she said. "Thank you for driving that silly princess in the right direction. I thought she would be a lot more cooperative." She didn't like to encourage people to fear animals, but sometimes there were advantages.

She sat on the dirt, and Axel sat beside her, resting his head on her lap. "Snow didn't seem to trust me," she muttered, running her hand over his fur. "People usually trust me. She seemed ready to marry Thane on the spot. That shows an error in judgment. Not that there's anything wrong with Thane, but why trust him and not me? She must not be thinking past his pretty face. Isn't that always the way? That means we can't find her a prince that is unattractive. She might be a bit shallow. That eliminates a few kingdoms right there."

"Is Axel giving you good advice?" Ava asked, appearing at her side.

Izla startled and placed a hand on her chest. "Ava! You scared me."

Ava pushed her long black hair behind her ear and smiled. "It's about time. You scare me all the time when you appear. I don't know how you appear without making any noise. I still make a small popping sound, but you must have been too engrossed in your conversation."

It was hard to sneak up on Izla. She would have to be more careful about being distracted. "Talking to Axel helps me work out my problems. Sometimes hearing them out loud makes things more real. Shouldn't you be watching over Princess Rosamond?"

Ava squatted and patted Axel's head. "Everyone calls her Rose. She really is the sweetest little thing. We don't all need to watch her every minute. She has a large following of guards at the insistence of the king and queen."

"Were they happy to have the three of you watching over the baby?"

Ava nodded. "Oh, yes. They are so worried about Nassandra. They feel a lot better knowing we are there. We were given rooms in the castle so we can stay close."

"Wonderful."

"What are you up to?" Ava asked, standing and brushing off her blue dress.

"Do you know of Snow White?" she asked, joining her on her feet.

"Yes. Don't tell me. You are going to save her from the wicked queen."

Izla shrugged. "In a roundabout way. I'm planning on making a match for her."

Ava giggled. "I should have guessed."

"Thane is helping me. Against his will, of course."

Ava's eyes widened. "Thane? Where is he?"

"He will join me in a few minutes."

"Oh. Well—I guess I should go then," Ava said, wringing her hands.

Izla's eyes narrowed. Why did Ava look nervous? "You can stay until he comes. He doesn't bite."

"Who doesn't bite?" Thane asked, popping in next to her.

Izla jumped. That was the second time in less than five minutes. Perhaps she should stop popping in on people the way she did. It was unsettling when you weren't expecting it.

"Axel," Ava said, pointing at the wolf. "He doesn't bite."

Thane rubbed the wolf's chin. "Everyone knows that. He probably thinks he's still a puppy, the way Izla treats him."

Izla crossed her arms and glared at her brother. "I'm not the only one."

Thane nodded. "Good to see you, Ava."

Ava swallowed and nodded. "I better go. You two have a lot to do."

"You can join us," Izla said, studying her friend with new-found interest. Did Ava have a thing for Thane? Surely, Izla would have noticed before. She did pride herself on things like that. She would have to think about it later.

"Oh, no," Ava said, taking a step back. "I better go back to the castle." She gave a little wave and disappeared.

Thane shook his head. "Have you noticed Ava has started acting strange around me?"

"Strange?" Izla asked, holding back a smile. Thane wasn't usually observant about things like this.

He frowned. "Your friends are the only girls I've ever been able to talk to. For the last few years, I feel like Ava has been avoiding me. I wonder if I offended her somehow."

Izla rubbed her lips together and tried to think of what to say. Since she had only noticed Ava's behavior a moment ago, she hadn't had time to analyze it. "She's said nothing to me about it."

"Hm."

"Shall we go?" Izla asked. She didn't want to have this conversation until she thought about it some more.

"Alright," he said, still frowning. "But you would tell me if she ever said anything?"

"Of course."

Thane tried to focus on whatever it was Izla was saying as they hid behind some bushes next to the cottage Snow White was in. He was having trouble paying attention. He must have insulted Ava. Zina, Lily, and Ava had been friends with Izla for a long time. He had spent his fair share of time following them around at the insistence of his father.

The four friends had been inseparable. Thane used to tease them when he was in an annoying mood or join in with them when he was feeling friendly. He thought of his sister's three friends as his own friends on a certain level. He figured Izla had adopted them into her circle because she liked to show off, and Zina, Lily, and Ava were impressed with everything she did.

It annoyed him sometimes, the way they thought Izla was so perfect. Still, he had good times with them. He would never admit it, of course. Ava learned a lot from Izla. The other two tried, but failed more often than not. Thane had never known any fairies that had so much trouble with simple magic.

Even if Ava was angry with him, he shouldn't care. It wasn't like he didn't have his own friends. He wouldn't have spent any time with any of them if his father hadn't been so insistent. Still, it bothered him.

Izla fixed him with a hard stare. "Are you listening to me?"

"We're waiting until the miners leave and then we talk to Snow."

Her lips formed a tight line. "The miners just left. Where is your mind? They made enough noise to wake the dead."

Thane didn't have any other guesses. "So..."

Izla sighed. "I'm going to the cottage. You stay here." She stood and made her way to the small dwelling. It wasn't the most sturdy looking structure. The thatched roof sagged on one side, and the white paint adorning the door and window shutters was almost completely gone. It would be a complete eyesore if it weren't for the purple wildflowers growing all around the cottage.

"Why am I even here?" he muttered, making himself invisible. If Izla thought he was going to sit obediently in the bushes all day, she had a surprise coming. He followed behind at a safe distance and stopped when she knocked on the cottage door.

The door opened a crack, and Snow peered out. "You again?" She flung the door wide and crossed her arms. "What do you want?"

Izla ignored the girl's hostile expression. If there was one thing that could be said about Izla, it was that she did not get intimidated easily. She didn't lose sight of her quests, either, even when she should.

"I'm here to help you," Izla told Snow.

"Why would a fairy help me?"

"What makes you think I'm a fairy?"

Snow narrowed her eyes. "I'm not stupid. The man you were with said he was a fairy. You appeared out of thin air, so I assume you are the same. I didn't believe him at first, but I thought about it last night, and I suppose it makes sense. He made the huntsman stop bleeding, and it seemed magical."

"I want to help you. That's what I do. I help people."

"Well, can you get me out of here?"

"You should stay here until the problem with the queen is resolved."

Snow stomped her foot. "You want me to stay here? You should look in this cottage. It's small and dirty, and it smells worse than anything I've ever encountered."

Izla tilted her head and glanced inside the cottage. "That is unfortunate, but it is the safest place for you right now. If the men who live here will let you stay, I think you should stay."

"They won't let me stay for free."

"Oh?"

Snow looked up at the sky and shook her head. "They said I can stay if I clean their house and cook for them."

Izla nodded. "That sounds reasonable."

Snow snorted. "Reasonable? I am a princess."

"As am I," Izla said, folding her own arms. The two stared at each other with identical glares. Thane didn't know Snow, but he knew Izla. She would not back down. "Not only am I a princess, but as the daughter of the fairy king, I outrank you."

Snow's arms dropped to her sides, and her eyes widened. "Your father is King Henan? Then, you are the sister of the man I met yesterday?"

"Yes."

"Do you think you might bring him here?"

Thane grimaced. He was glad to be invisible.

"Why would I do that?"

"Well, if you are trying to help me, he might want to help as well."

Izla laughed. "I might get him to come. As for now, you should get to work cleaning the cottage."

Snow sighed. "Even if I wanted to, I don't know how."

Izla pushed past her and entered the cottage. "I rarely clean, and even I can figure it out. How hard is it to pick something up and put it away? It's not like they are asking you to tame dragons or anything."

Thane followed them inside and held a hand over his nose. Snow hadn't been wrong. It smelled like something crawled into the cottage and died. He would have to be careful. It was a disaster, so it would be hard to walk quietly.

Chairs were on their sides, and that was only the beginning. Old food and broken pottery littered the floor. Clothing was draped on every surface, and the fireplace was full of half burned garbage.

Snow pushed a strand of hair behind her ear. "You said you came to help me. Are you going to help me clean?"

Thane smiled as he watched his sister try not to twitch as she studied the mess.

She cleared her throat. "Clean? Me? Of course."

Snow clapped her hands. "Wonderful. Where do we start?"

Izla wrinkled her nose. "Well, I suppose we should start by straightening up the things that are easy to figure out. Like picking up the tipped chairs and gathering all the garbage. We should probably scrub the spills on the floor."

Snow and Izla both glanced around the room. Neither one of them moved. Thane smiled and tried to guess who would start first.

"Alright, I admit this is ridiculous," Izla said. She pulled her wand from her pocket and turned to Snow. "Don't tell my brother about this."

Thane's smile grew. He leaned against the far wall and watched with amusement. He knew Izla couldn't work without magic. Izla swung her wand, and the chairs tipped back to their feet. With another swing, the broken pottery mended and flew into the other room.

Snow squealed with delight. "Amazing!"

"If you liked that, watch this," Izla said, pointing her wand at the fireplace. Sparks flew from her wand and burned up the garbage. After the flames licked up the mess, they disappeared, leaving a sparkling clean fireplace. It looked like it had never been used.

"I'm sorry I wasn't accepting of you when we first met," Snow said. "It's always hard to know who to trust, and I find it difficult to converse with people like you."

Izla's brows rose, and she waved her wand, causing all the clothing to gather in an enormous pile in the middle of the room. "People like me?"

"Well, women. I find most women are jealous of me, so I don't trust them."

"Like the queen?"

"She's been envious of me since we met. It's hard to be beautiful. I'm sure you understand."

"I do," Izla said.

Thane rolled his eyes. There was too much vanity in this room.

"I admit I was nervous when I met you. I mean, you are exquisite, but I suppose that is to be expected since you are a fairy. You are a bit intimidating."

"Don't be intimidated by me," Izla said, waving the wand and cleaning the clothing.

"Can fairies change their appearances?" Snow asked, tapping her lip with a finger.

"Of course."

Snow tilted her head and watched Izla work. "If you want to get people to confide in you, it might be better if you look different."

Izla lowered her wand. "What do you mean?"

"You are so young and pretty. Anyone would be intimidated by your shiny red hair and sparkling green eyes. If you appeared as an older woman, people would open up to you."

"Hm. I'll have to think about it," Izla said.

Thane rolled his eyes. He would bet Snow wanted Izla to appear different to make herself look better. Snow was said to be very beautiful, and she was, but a mortal could never compare to a fairy.

"It looks wonderful," Snow said. "Should we do the kitchen next? Then, when it is clean, perhaps you can help me with dinner."

"Of course," Izla said, following Snow from the room.

This was ridiculous. Thane didn't think of Izla as someone that was easily manipulated, but that was what appeared to be happening. And what about him? How long did Izla think he was going to hide in the bushes? She'd probably forgotten all about him.

Izla flopped down on her cozy feather bed and let out a long sigh. She was exhausted. It had been a long time since she had used so much magic in one day, and she was drained. She wasn't even going to take time to brush her hair out. She smiled. Snow wasn't as bad as she had thought she was going to be. The two might be friends if Izla had the patience to befriend mortals.

The seven miners had been impressed when they came home to their sparkling clean cottage and a delicious dinner.

She might have overdone it when she replaced the roof and paint. It would be hard for Snow to impress them after today. With luck, she could keep it tidy now that she had a clean start.

Izla was content with the way the day had gone. She hadn't expected to spend the day cooking and cleaning, but it could have been worse. Sure, she had used more magic than she had planned to, but she would do better tomorrow, and Thane wouldn't ever have to know.

"Thane!" Izla said, sitting up. She'd left Thane in the bushes! He was going to be angry.

The door opened, and Thane poked his head in. "Thanks for forgetting about me."

"I am so sorry," she said, frowning. "I got distracted and forgot to have you come."

Thane crossed his arms and leaned against the doorframe. "I didn't come to talk about that. I came to tell you I can't come with you tomorrow."

He didn't look mad. She would be mad if she'd spent all day hiding. "Why not? I won't forget you again."

"Father has to go meet with some important people. He's put me in charge."

"Well, better you than me." Izla hated staying at the castle when her father was gone. Her father spent a day every week listening to people's problems. When the time was over, he spent the evening trying to fix those problems. Izla found it boring. People's problems were usually tedious things that they should be able to fix themselves.

"Are you going back to the cottage tomorrow?"

"No," Izla said, lying back on her pillow. "I'm not sure where to start. Snow will be alright for now. I might go see the queen, or I might go search for a prince."

"Don't do anything dangerous when I'm not with you."

"I'm surprised you aren't angry. I completely forgot about you. How long did you sit in the bushes?"

Thane grinned. "Two minutes." He turned and left, shutting the door behind him.

Izla's brows came together. Two minutes? She wouldn't expect him to sit there all day, but two minutes? She would worry about it tomorrow. Right now, sleep was all that mattered.

Chapter 5

Izla ran up the path to the cottage in the woods. A servant had woken her early this morning. One miner had come to the castle searching for her. Something had happened to Snow. It had been a month since Izla had been to the cottage, and she regretted her absence. She blamed herself for neglecting the girl while she searched for a suitable prince. She had thought it would be easier, but several princes were already betrothed, and some just didn't feel right.

The door opened, and a short man with white hair and a short beard peeked out. Izla pushed past him. "Where is she?"

"Here," the man said, leading her through a small hallway and into a bedroom.

Snow laid eerily still on a bed that barely fit her. Six more beds occupied the room, and seven small wardrobes. Izla scanned the girl, looking for an injury. Six almost identical men stood watching her. The seventh had to travel back from Izla's castle. She should have brought him with her, but she had panicked.

"What happened?" Izla asked.

One man scratched his head. "We don't know. We got home, and she was on the ground."

Izla leaned over Snow and watched her chest for any sign of breathing. "How long has she been like this?"

"Two days."

Izla touched the girl's face. She was still warm. "She looks like she's sleeping. Why is she wearing a corset over her clothes?"

"What's a corset?" one man asked.

"This thing around her middle." Izla studied the tight contraption and frowned. "Why didn't you take it off? It's really tight."

The men all looked at each other in confusion.

"Never mind," Izla muttered, pulling a knife from her pocket. She cut the strings of the corset and pulled it open.

Snow's eyes fluttered, then she took a deep breath and sat up. "What happened? I feel so dizzy."

"She's alive!" one man yelled. They all cheered.

Izla grabbed the corset and held it in front of Snow. "Where did you get this?"

Snow frowned. "Oh no! Did you cut it? It's so pretty."

Izla frowned. "It almost squeezed you to death. I'm almost certain it's magic."

Snow reached for it, and Izla held it away from her. "I got it from a nice old woman. She was selling things, but she gave it to me for free."

Izla walked to the fireplace in the corner and tossed it into the center. Blue flames billowed from the fireplace, and they all stared in silence.

"Blue flames. That means magic." Izla looked into everyone's faces. "Could the evil queen know Snow White lives?"

"How would she know?" Snow asked. "The huntsman would tell her I'm dead rather than risk her wrath."

Izla paced in the small area between the door and the bed. "I would guess she knows. I bet the old woman was the queen in disguise."

Snow rubbed her ribs. "If it was, I should be safe now. She must think I'm dead for sure."

"Perhaps," Izla said. "You must be careful. She may come back to make sure you are dead. Don't talk to anyone. Stay inside."

Snow nodded.

Izla raised her brow. The girl didn't look as concerned as she should. "This is serious. If she keeps trying to kill you, she will succeed eventually. Do not open the door for anyone."

One man took Snow's hand. "You've only been with us a short time, but you've made a place in our hearts. Please be careful."

Snow smiled. "I will."

Izla motioned to the door. "Let her rest."

"I think she's had enough rest," one man said. Izla glared at him, and he hurried out the door after his brothers.

The men all filed into the kitchen and took seats at the table. Izla scanned the kitchen. It wasn't as clean as it had been when Izla left, but it wasn't a monumental disaster, either. Snow must have at least tried to keep up with things.

She stood at the head of the table and leaned forward, resting her hands on the wood. She thought about asking for names, but the men looked so similar she was certain she would never remember who was who. None of them were making eye contact with her.

"How did you know to send for me?" she asked.

One man swallowed hard and glanced up at her. "Snow said you were friends."

"You all need to help Snow understand how dangerous life can be. She's been very sheltered, so she doesn't know how to do a lot of things."

"Snow is great at cleaning," one man said. "She worked a miracle in this place. She got it cleaner than it's ever been."

Izla stood tall and sighed. "Yes, well, that won't keep her safe."

"Snow is not so good at cooking," another man said. "She made a pretty splendid dinner that first time, and it's been a disaster ever since. She burns everything."

"These are not things that matter right now. What matters is that she is in danger. Keep her safe. Do you understand?"

They all nodded.

Izla looked into each of their faces. "I will hold you all responsible if anything happens to her. Any questions?"

They all shook their heads.

"Good." Izla pulled her wand from her pocket and waved it, causing herself to disappear.

Thane stifled a yawn as he listened to people's problems. King Henan was gone again, and so it was up to him to listen to the complaints. It was the only time he was allowed to sit on the throne. He straightened the gold crown on his head and focused on looking interested.

Thane liked to help people, but most that came before him had petty problems. One had complained about his neighbor singing too loud. One thought the town should pitch in and have his house painted. A woman had been upset that the cows next to a church were too smelly. He didn't know how his father did this all the time without going crazy.

The only problem that had actually needed immediate help today was when one man Snow White was staying with had come in and said Snow was in a deep sleep that seemed almost magical.

The man standing in front of him now appeared nervous. He wore a ratty old button-up shirt and trousers. His dark hair stuck out in all directions, and he held a straw hat that he was turning around in his hands.

"How may I serve you?" Thane asked, trying to appear interested.

The man looked around the room. No one was there except the man, Thane, and Levnor. Levnor was the man who brought people before the crown. King Henan believed people should feel comfortable and not have to worry about others judging them for their problems. That was why they came one at a time.

"Feel free to speak," Thane said, when the man only stood there.

"It's about my daughter," the man finally said. "I fear I have accidentally put her life in danger."

Thane leaned forward. "What do you mean?"

"The king of Glovem stopped at my mill when he was traveling the countryside. I'm a miller, you see. He asked for a meal, which we eagerly gave him. It isn't often a king stops in on the humble."

"Go on."

The man's eyes were fixed on his hat. "I wanted to impress the king. I told him that my daughter Otelia could spin straw into gold."

Thane's eyes narrowed. "Why would you tell him something that could be so easily disproved?"

The man wiped his nose on the back of his hand. "I panicked. All I could think about was impressing him."

"The king didn't believe you, did he?" Thane asked. If the man's daughter could spin straw into gold, the man wouldn't be dressed so shabbily.

"I'm not sure. He took my daughter."

Thane felt tired. This wasn't a problem that could go unaddressed. "Took her?"

"Yes. To his castle. He said if she can't spin a room full of straw into gold, he will have her put to death."

"Why would you tell such an obvious lie?"

"It was the first thing that popped into my mind. Everyone has been talking about how Princess Izla gave Princess Rosamond a spinning wheel that could make straw into gold. Everyone was impressed. I figured the king would be as well."

"Who wouldn't be?" Thane mumbled under his breath. His father wouldn't be back for two more days, so this was up to him to fix. He wished Izla was here. She would tell the man what was what.

"I've tried to think of a way to convince the king to let her go, but in the end, your family was my only hope. Can you help me?"

"I will help," Thane said, turning to Levnor. "Levnor, this is a pressing matter. Tell all the others to come back on a different day."

"Yes, Sire," the tall man said, walking to the door.

He looked at the miller. "As for you, there will be a fine. For now, go home, and I will deal with it."

The man nodded and slunk away.

Thane pounded his fist against the throne, then leaned back. He ran a hand over his face and sighed. He needed a plan, and he needed a good one. The king of Glovem was not his friend. They clashed every time they met. He needed to deal with this without having to speak with King Dan. His name wasn't really Dan, but his real name was so long, Thane could only guess how to say it.

This was something Izla would enjoy dealing with. She would somehow manipulate the king into marrying the miller's daughter instead of threatening her. Thane wouldn't feel good about that outcome. None of this was Otelia's fault.

Gold wasn't precious to fairies. They used it, but they could make it with magic so it wasn't rare for them like it was to mortals. It wouldn't be hard to make a pile of gold pop into the room with the miller's daughter. It wouldn't look spun, though, and King Dan would be suspicious.

Thane didn't respect King Dan, but the man wasn't stupid. He probably took the girl to teach the miller a lesson. Thane got to his feet and tossed his crown on the throne. He needed to fix this without letting anyone know he was involved. The only question was how.

The door opened, and Thane looked up, prepared to see Levnor. He was surprised to see Ava. She entered, her long blue dress swishing around her ankles. Her black hair fell in long curls over her shoulders, and her deep brown eyes landed on him.

He shut his mouth when he realized he was staring at her like a little schoolboy that had never seen a beautiful girl before. He shook his head. Why was he thinking odd things every time he saw her lately?

Her eyes widened. "Oh. Hi, Thane. Do you know where Izla is?"

"She had to go fix a problem. I'm not sure when she will be back."

"Alright, thanks," she said, turning to leave.

Thane took a step forward. "Wait."

She glanced over her shoulder. "Yes?"

"I have a problem, and I need some help. Do you think you could spare some time for a good cause?"

Ava turned, and a small smile appeared on her face. "I have time. What do you need?"

Thane explained the miller's problem, and Ava listened with concern.

"What do you need me to do?" she asked.

"I'm not sure. I need to fix this without letting the miller's daughter or the king know I'm involved. We don't need problems with Glovem."

"You could change your appearance."

"I suppose. I don't want to appear and scare the girl, though, and I can't walk into the castle without raising questions."

Ava looked thoughtful. "I think it would be better to appear in the room. It might scare her, but she's probably scared already."

"Can you change my appearance?" he asked. "I have a hard time keeping a different form when I do it to myself."

Ava rubbed her arm and frowned. "I can try. I'm not as good as Izla, you know."

"That's alright. Just do your best."

Ava took a deep breath and closed her eyes. She pulled her wand out and waved it in the air and pointed it toward him. He felt a small breeze and the feeling of falling.

"Did I shrink?" he asked, looking at his hands. His fingers were long, red, and slightly gnarled. He was definitely closer to the ground.

"Oh my," Ava said, covering her mouth with her hand. "I turned you into an imp."

Thane let out a small laugh. "That's excellent. I never would have thought to do that."

Ava dropped to her knees in front of him. "I didn't mean to do it. You look a bit terrifying."

Thane reached up and felt two horns on his head. His skin felt tight and itchy, and when he rubbed a hand over his face, it was rough. "This is perfect. No one will ever suspect it's me."

"I could try to change you," Ava said, looking concerned. "You can't be over three feet tall. It might make things more difficult."

"No, this will work. Do you want to come with me?"

Ava's brows came together as she thought.

"If you shrink down small enough, you can observe and make sure I don't do anything stupid."

She bit her lip. "Alright." She waved her hand over her head, and before Thane could blink, she was the size of a mouse. Of course, she didn't look like a mouse. She looked like her, but with silvery wings. Not having wings when you were that size was a hazard, and no one wanted to chance doing it without.

"I like your wings," he said, feeling awkward.

Ava bowed her head and smiled. "Thanks." She flew to his shoulder and landed gracefully on it. Her nose wrinkled.

"What's wrong?"

"Um... I... I think—I don't know," she stuttered.

"Just say it," he said.

A small giggle escaped her. "I didn't just make you look like an imp. I made you smell like one, too."

Thane smiled. "Then, I guess you did a thorough job."

Chapter 6

Trusting people was not a strong point in Izla's life. The men would probably watch over Snow, but they worked long, hard hours, and she spent a lot of time on her own. How could they watch her if they weren't there? Izla thought one of them would stay behind and keep guard, but all of them, minus the one that was still traveling home, had left the house the next day.

Izla stayed back away from the cottage with Axel. He had joined her the night before, and she was happy to have his company. She was resting against a tree, and Axel was asleep with his head on her lap. She ran a hand over his fur as she thought.

This would all be easier if her father would banish the evil queen. She hated that he rarely interfered with the mortals. He thought they should solve some of their own problems, and he didn't want to give off the impression that he wanted to take over. He let them rule to the best of their abilities.

Axel raised his head and looked into the trees. Izla paused and listened. Someone or something was coming in their direction. It couldn't be the miners. They had gone a different way.

"Go, puppy," Izla whispered to Axel. "I'll take care of this." She rubbed behind his ears and kissed the top of his head. Axel wandered lazily away as Izla made herself invisible and watched the woods.

An old woman stepped into her view. A black cape and dress swayed behind her, and her gray hair hung limply to her shoulders. She held a walking cane, but she wasn't using it. She ambled past Izla without slowing down. Once she got near the cottage, she hunched over and used her cane.

Izla's eyes narrowed, and she shrunk herself to fly quietly after her. This had to be the queen. With luck, Snow would keep quiet and stay away from the door. Even if she opened the door, she would have to be wiser than yesterday.

The queen crouched down in front of a window and waited. Izla landed on the ledge of the window and watched. She wondered how long the woman would stay. It didn't matter. Izla could be patient.

In only a few minutes, Snow's voice floated through the window. The queen sucked in a breath, and Izla sighed. Snow had no common sense. She was singing loud enough to carry through the walls even if the window wasn't open.

"Blast that girl," the queen croaked. She stood and hobbled a few feet to the door. She knocked, and Snow's voice cut off. Izla crossed her arms and watched. The queen rapped on the door a second time.

Snow poked her head out the window, and Izla pressed herself against the side of it.

"Hello, my dear," the woman said, standing in front of Snow. "Do you have a moment to spare?"

Snow squinted and studied the woman. "I can't talk now."

"Can't talk? You have no time for a poor old woman?"

"I talked to a poor old woman the other day, and she nearly killed me."

The woman put a hand to her heart. "How dreadful! You poor thing."

Snow tilted her head and studied her. "Thank you for stopping by, but I have things to do."

The woman held out a small comb decorated in gems. "Here. Let me give you this beautiful decoration. It will look lovely in your hair."

"I have no money."

"I'll give it to you for free."

Snow crossed her arms. "Why?"

"I believe in doing good deeds. Here. Take it."

Izla rolled her eyes. Nobody was going to be fooled two times by the same type of trick in one week. Snow leaned out the window and took the comb. Izla shook her head. What was the girl thinking?

"Thank you. Now you must go."

"Of course," the woman said, turning and hobbling away.

Izla flew in the window and became visible and her normal size. Snow stepped back, and Izla grabbed the window and slammed it shut. "You aren't supposed to talk to strangers."

Snow studied the comb. "I only talked through the window, so no harm was done."

"You took something from the evil queen."

Snow laughed. "That wasn't the queen."

Izla held in a sigh. "Of course it was."

"If the queen was the one who gave me the corset, then that woman who just came was not her. She looked nothing like the other woman."

"Everyone says the queen is a witch. I'm sure she can change her appearance."

Snow shrugged. "But she couldn't change it twice."

Izla clenched her teeth. "Why not?"

"I don't know."

Snow lifted the comb to her hair, and Izla screamed. She grabbed the girl's arm and knocked the comb to the floor.

"What are you doing?" Snow demanded.

"Keeping you from getting hurt. Don't take things from strangers! Don't you have any sense?"

Snow folded her arms, and her lip came out in a pout. "You are being overly cautious."

"That is better than the alternative."

"I wish you would stop coming around."

Izla was fuming. This girl couldn't be this naïve. "I saved your life yesterday. Do you wish I hadn't?"

The door opened, and the miners filed in. Izla turned to greet them, then spun around when she heard a thud. Snow White laid on the floor, the sparkling comb glittering in her hair.

"Oh no!" one man said, as they all gathered around the girl.

Another one put his hand in front of her mouth. "She isn't breathing."

Izla ground her teeth so hard she was surprised they didn't break. She bent down and pulled the comb from Snow's hair. Snow took a deep breath and started coughing.

"She's alive!" one man exclaimed.

"Oh my," Snow said, placing a hand on her head. "I feel faint."

Izla made the comb disappear. "I am very busy. I cannot keep saving you. This is ridiculous."

"It won't happen again," Snow said, getting to her feet. She wobbled and grabbed one of the men's shoulders to stabilize herself. "Now I know I can't trust anyone."

Izla shook her head. "It's impossible to estimate the time it will take to fix your problems. Stay in this cottage, and do not answer the door for anyone." She turned and stomped out the door. She could disappear, but sometimes stomping was more satisfying.

Thane looked up at the castle in front of him. It might be impressive to someone not accustomed to seeing castles, but as far as castles went, this one was small.

"I doubt this castle can hold over two hundred people for a party," he said, counting four balconies and two towers. "Still, it looks well built."

Ava grinned from her spot on his shoulder. "You sound conceited."

He rubbed the back of his neck. "What? No, I'm just...uh..."

"Stalling?"

Thane let out a sigh. "Perhaps."

Ava swatted at a fly. "I detest bugs when I'm this size. I'm sure you'll do fine."

"Izla is better at these things. She enjoys it, at least."

"This seems straightforward. Spin the straw into gold, save the girl, and go home. What could go wrong?"

"Talking to women—it isn't my strong point."

"I've seen you talk to plenty of women."

"Yeah, well, I always end up sounding rude or sarcastic."

"You've talked to me, Zina, and Lily for years. I never noticed you having a hard time."

He rubbed one of his pointy ears. "Yeah, but that's because you're my little sister's friends. That makes it different."

Ava didn't respond. With her on his shoulder, he couldn't see her expressions to guess what she was thinking. He didn't want to tell her he was having trouble talking to her as well. He was going to rule over a kingdom someday, and he didn't want her to think he was completely incapable.

"It shouldn't be hard," she finally said. "You don't have to impress her. You look like an imp. No need to spout poetry."

Ava was right. If he didn't look like himself, that would make it a lot easier. "Let's get it over with."

Thane took them both to a medium-sized room in the castle. There were bars on the windows, and the room was full of straw. A girl was draped over some of the straw, sleeping. That must be Otelia. Her long brown hair was covering her face, and her brown dress was wrinkled. An old, wooden spinning wheel stood against one wall.

"Wake her," Ava whispered. "I'll hide over there." She flew off his shoulder and out of sight.

Thane walked toward the girl and swallowed. He imagined what he must look like with his pointy ears and horns and felt better. She wouldn't know who he was, and he was supposed to be an imp. Nothing good was expected of an imp.

"Hey! Wake up!" he said, trying to make his voice high. He'd never spoken with an imp, so he wasn't sure what one sounded like.

The girl moaned and rolled to her side. Thane waited for her to open her eyes, but she didn't. He moved closer and put his boot on her shoulder and shook her gently.

The girl sat up and yawned. She glanced at Thane, and her eyes widened. "Oh my." She jumped to her feet and moved to the far wall, never taking her eyes from him.

"Don't be scared. I'm here to help you."

"Help me?" the girl asked. "An imp?"

"Do you see anyone else here?"

"Why would you help me?" she asked. Thane didn't know what to say. Imps were not helpful. He'd never heard of a single good thing one had done.

He put his hands on his waist. "Does it matter why? Do you want to get out of this mess or not?"

"I do," she said, pushing a stand of hair behind her ear. "The king says he will kill me if I don't spin all this straw into gold. My father likes to brag. He told the king I could do it, but I can't." A tear ran over her cheek, and she brushed it away.

"I'll do it," Thane said. "But if I do, you must give me your bracelet." He figured he better demand some payment. No one would suspect an imp of doing something from the goodness of its heart.

She held up her arm and looked at her bracelet. "It isn't worth anything. It's only colored glass."

"And that is what I want. Do you agree?"

"Yes, of course."

"Alright. Stay out of my way, and I'll have it done."

The girl lowered herself to the ground and leaned on the wall. She pulled her knees in and hugged them to herself. Thane went to the ancient spinning wheel and took a seat. It would be easier to make the straw disappear and zap in a pile of gold, but that would be cheating. He grabbed a handful of straw and shook his head. He supposed this whole thing was cheating, but here he was. If nothing else, it would make a good story to add to some of Izla's.

Thane snapped his fingers and caused some of the straw to fall on Otelia. While she was pushing it off herself, he made the spinning wheel disappear and replaced it with the one Izla had fashioned for Princess Rose. It was in better condition than the other one, but with hope, the girl wouldn't recognize the switch.

Time inched by, and the pile of golden thread grew into a large mound. It was tedious work, but not difficult. The straw was almost gone, and Thane's fingers were aching for relief. The miller's daughter had fallen asleep and slept through most of it.

"There is something satisfying about watching the straw turn to gold," Ava said, landing on his shoulder. "It does feel like we've been here for ages, though. I wonder if you've been missed."

"Missed?" Thane asked, focusing on the last handful of straw.

"You didn't leave a message telling anyone what you were doing."

Thane smacked himself in the head with his hand. "Oh no! Normally, it would be fine, but my father left me in charge. I am going to be in serious trouble. We better go back quickly. If I'm lucky, my father won't be home, and everything will be running smoothly."

"Someone is coming," Ava said, flying behind the spinning wheel.

Thane made himself invisible and waited. The sound of a key turning in the doorknob made him hold his breath. He stood and moved closer to the wall. King Dan entered, his long blue cape swishing behind him. He wore a crown much too big to be comfortable and too decorated to be humble.

Otelia woke up and got to her feet. She brushed at the wrinkles in her faded dress and tried to smooth down her hair. King Dan glanced around the room, his mouth hanging open in awe. The golden thread was heaped into piles, taking up most of the space. Thane had to admit it was a sight to behold.

King Dan leaned down and picked up a handful of the thread. "Amazing," he muttered. "I never would have believed it. This is truly magnificent." He glanced over to Otelia and smiled. "You've done well."

Otelia kept her eyes on the floor. "Thank you, Your Highness."

The king rubbed his chin. His eyes were alive with something Thane could only call greed. "I am still not convinced. It could be a trick. I will have more straw. We will fill this room to the brim. If you can spin it all into gold by tomorrow, you will live."

The girl's lip trembled, and Thane frowned.

The king rubbed his hands together and smiled. "I will have a hearty supper brought to you. I'm sure the task is tedious, but indulge me this one more time." He turned and left the room, locking it behind himself.

Thane reappeared as Otelia burst into tears. "Don't cry," he said. "King Dan is an ogre."

She sniffed. "Why must my father brag so?"

"There are some things I need to deal with. I'll be back when the straw is refilled. I will spin it for you if you give me your ring."

Otelia nodded and pulled the metal band from her finger. He felt guilty taking anything from her. The bracelet and ring weren't worth money, but they might be sentimental. He would make it up somehow. He was sure she didn't own many things.

Thane grabbed the ring and took himself to his room. He hoped Ava would follow. He couldn't say anything to Ava or the miller's daughter would know she was there.

"Ava?" he called.

She appeared full sized next to him. "That king is ridiculous. That was enough gold to last him more than a lifetime. Why does he need more?"

"I've found that the more a person has, the more they want."

"I wanted to put a curse on him right there. I would have if I could count on it working correctly."

Thane looked down at his gnarled hands. "Can you change me back before I go search for my father? He's going to be mad enough without seeing me like this."

She took a deep breath. "Um—right." She spun her arms above her head and pointed at him. Nothing happened, not even a small breeze. "Drat. You should have gotten someone else to change you. I've never been good at things like this."

Thane held out his arms. "I can't stay like this."

Ave bit her lip. "I'm sorry. I don't know what to do."

"Can you go find my father? Or Izla?"

She nodded.

"Make sure you warn them. My father rarely acts rashly, but if he comes in here and sees an imp, there is no telling what he might do."

A pounding at the door made them both jump. "Thane!" his father called. "Thane, are you in there?"

"Yes," he called back. "Can you give me a minute?"

"I will not give you a minute," King Henan growled, turning the knob. Thane jumped behind his bed and ducked down. He heard the door creek open. He couldn't believe he was hiding behind his bed. This day wasn't getting better.

"Ava," the king said in surprise. "What are you doing here?"

"Well... I... the thing is..." she stuttered. "I turned Thane into an imp, and I can't change him back."

"What? Where is he?"

Thane stood, and his father's eyes rested on him. The king stared at him for a moment and then he burst into laughter. Thane ground his teeth together and frowned.

Ava twisted her hands around each other. "I'm sorry."

The king smiled. "I don't know why Ava would do this to you, but it's better than any punishment I would have come up with."

"I'm sorry I left today. There was a problem that needed immediate attention, and I left without thinking clearly."

The king's smile faded. "I was informed about the miller and his ridiculous situation. I assumed that was where you went, but you still should have made sure someone around here knew they were in charge."

"Yes, sir."

"I am assuming Ava changed you so you could deal with King Danivonalin?"

"Yes."

"Is the situation resolved?"

Thane frowned. "Temporarily. I spun the straw into gold, but I need to go back. The king demanded she do it again."

"I hope you have a plan. You cannot go every day if that is what the king wants. I've always known him to be greedy."

"I don't have a plan, but I'll think on it."

"Do you want me to go back with you?" Ava asked. "I don't think you will stay an imp forever. My magic usually wears off, so you might need me to do it again."

"Yes, thank you. I really hope it wears off eventually. If not, I'm going to have to go into hiding."

Ava nodded. "I'm sure Izla could help."

King Henan shook his head. "I doubt she could undo a spell cast like this. You must be the one to undo it if it doesn't fade."

Thane looked at Ava's troubled expression. It didn't inspire confidence.

Chapter 7

The evil queen liked purple. Izla stood before her throne and tried not to be distracted by the room. The carpet was purple, as was the material on the throne. Lavender ribbons adorned the candle sconces that lined the wall. That had to be a fire hazard. If she wasn't mistaken, the glass in the two large windows was tinted purple. A small table sat next to the throne, and it held a vase filled with lilacs.

The queen sat tall on the throne, her brown hair flowed over her shoulder and ended at her waist. She wore a floor-length amethyst dress with long black sleeves. A tall golden crown adorned her head and matched her necklace and bracelet.

The queen wore a half smile as she gazed at Izla. She drummed her long violet fingernails against the arm of the throne. Izla refused to appear intimidated. She stood before the queen wearing her best green dress and her favorite silver tiara that was decorated in small diamonds.

"Princess Izla, what a pleasure," the queen said, not standing. Izla would let it go this time. Any other royalty would stand and bow to her as the daughter of King Henan. "To what does our humble kingdom owe the honor of your presence?"

Izla raised her brow and tried to mimic the way her father stared at people when he wanted to intimidate them. "I have come to tell you to leave Snow White alone."

The queen arched her own brow. "Snow White? The girl ran away some time ago. We could not find her."

Izla took a step toward the queen. "I know you found her. I am not here to solve a mystery, but to give you a warning. Step down, and stop trying to kill the girl."

The queen smiled. "Why would I try to kill her?"

"I didn't come to guess at your reasons. Do you not know how succession works? You should not be ruling, only guiding Snow. You are not royal through blood but by marriage. Even if Snow were eliminated, you should not be the law. There are relatives of the White family that would take the throne."

"What power do you have over this kingdom?" the queen asked. "What makes you the authority on what should happen here?"

"Would you rather I send my father?"

The queen shifted, but kept her face passive. King Henan was a kind ruler, but when he decided an injustice was committed, he could be frightening.

"I don't see why you are here accusing me. All I've done is guide the child. If anything, you should find her and teach her how to rule a kingdom. The girl is vain to a fault and incapable in every way. Letting her rule in her current state would be irresponsible on everyone's part."

"You have been overheard speaking of your jealousy toward Snow."

The queen shrugged. "I don't hide it. Who wouldn't be jealous of her? She does whatever she pleases, and everyone else takes care of things she should."

Izla studied the queen. She didn't appear to be lying. "You aren't jealous that her beauty puts yours to shame?"

The queen's eyes narrowed. "You think Snow is more beautiful than I?" She got to her feet and walked briskly toward Izla, her purple dress flying behind her.

Izla swallowed and kept her chin up. She wouldn't let this woman intimidate her.

When she was a few feet away, she turned slightly to the side, passing Izla. "Follow me."

Izla turned and walked hesitantly behind her. She could be going into anything. Could she have mistaken the queen's motives? It was true Snow White was beautiful, but so was the queen. They left the throne room and walked down a long, bright hallway. Izla forced herself to focus on the queen and not all the purple decor.

The queen stopped at the end of the hallway and rapped on the stone wall. Izla's brow raised as the wall opened, and a spiral staircase twisted upward. The queen began the climb to the top, and Izla followed, her heart pounding in her chest. If this was a trap, she was walking right into it. She stuck her hand in her pocket and gripped her wand.

At the top of the stairs was a small, round room. They must be in one tower of the castle. Gold mirrors lined the walls, making it possible to see all angles of a person. Izla tried to seem unimpressed as she examined the layout.

"These are my magic mirrors," the queen said.

"Alright," Izla said. "I don't understand why we are here."

The queen smiled at her reflection. "The mirrors always tell the truth."

A chill ran over Izla's arms, and she resisted rubbing them.

"Watch," the queen commanded. "Wonderful mirror that I see. Are there any fairer than me?"

Izla felt a slight urge to giggle, but she held it in. The mirror clouded and different shades of purple swirled on the surface. Izla had heard of magic mirrors, but this was the first time she had ever seen one.

The outline of a person appeared in the swirls, and a deep voice came from the mirror. "Queen, your beauty is more than rare, but one with more beauty stands right there." The person pointed at Izla and she felt herself blush. Thankfully, the queen's attention wasn't on her.

The queen placed her hands on her waist, and she sighed. "Blast, you wretched thing," she muttered. "You know what I meant." She turned to Izla. "The mirror only responds to things that rhyme. It's annoying, to say the least. I've gotten better, but rhyming isn't one of my gifts."

Izla only nodded.

The queen turned back to the mirror. "Magic mirror on the wall. Who is the fairest mortal of all?"

"You, oh Queen, are the fairest of all, especially after Snow White's fall."

Izla's eyes widened. "Snow White's fall?"

The queen shrugged. "I don't know what he means."

Izla pulled her wand out and pointed it at the woman. "What did you do to her?"

"Nothing. The mirror will tell you if I can come up with a rhyme."

"Rumors say you are a witch. An old woman tried to kill Snow twice. Once with a corset, and once with a poisoned comb."

The queen's perfect lips made an o shape, and she put a hand to her head. "It must have been my mother."

"Your mother?"

"Yes. If anyone is a witch, it is her. She has destroyed her enemies with poisoned items before."

"Why would she attack Snow?"

"We were poor when I was growing up. When I married the king, it changed her life. She doesn't want to lose that."

Izla was wasting time. The mirror said Snow White's fall. She needed to go to her. Waving her wand, she appeared at the miner's cottage. She ran to the door and pounded. No one answered. She pushed the door open and ran inside.

Snow laid on the floor, not moving. Izla dropped to her knees and rolled the girl onto her back. She searched her for any poisoned objects, but she found nothing. She glanced around the room, and her eyes spotted an apple with a single bite missing.

She hopped up and spun around when the door flew open, and the miners filed in. Two of them held onto the arms of an old woman with wild gray hair. She had a large purple bump on her forehead. She didn't look like the woman from before, but if she was a witch, she might be able to change her appearance. The hag glared at all of them.

"Princess Izla!" one man said. "We found the witch that poisoned Snow."

"Fix her," Izla demanded.

"I cannot," the woman croaked. "This time I made sure you couldn't, either." She laughed, and Izla shuddered. "The girl will not be missed. There are few that can tolerate her presence."

Izla glared at the woman and raised her wand. With a simple swish, the woman froze where she stood. She must not be a very good witch, or she wouldn't have been captured by the miners.

"Now what?" one man asked. Izla shook her head. She couldn't see anything that might be a magical object touching Snow. It wasn't often that Izla didn't know what to do. She had the men carry Snow to the bedroom and place her on a bed.

She touched Snow's cheek and frowned. "She's still warm. I would bet there is magic involved. If that apple on the floor was poisoned, I would think she would be dead. Someone burn the apple so no animals come across it."

Thane would wait and worry about his appearance later. There was plenty of time to stress after he finished helping Otelia.

"Are you coming back with me?" he asked Ava.

She chewed her lower lip. "Yes. It's not like I'm actually helping with anything, though."

King Henan put a hand on her shoulder. "It's always a good idea to take someone with you when you are working with people. You never know when you might need someone's opinion or guidance."

Thane nodded. "I might need you if I change back into myself. How would I explain that?"

Ava sighed. "I'm sorry I'm not better at magic."

"This is fine," Thane said, glancing down at his red hands. "No one will ever suspect it's me. Should we go?"

Ava opened her mouth to answer, but before any words could escape her mouth, Izla appeared in a puff of pink smoke. Beside her was an old woman with frizzy gray hair. The woman wasn't moving.

King Henan arched his brow. "Do I want to know?"

Izla pointed at the old woman. "This is the evil queen's mother. I'm not actually sure if the evil queen is evil after all. She's vain for sure, but I don't think she's a killer. That would be her mother. She poisoned an apple, and Snow ate it. This woman needs to be locked in a cell that blocks magic."

"What has become of Snow?" the king asked.

Izla frowned and looked at the ground. "I don't know. She appears to be dead, but she's still warm. I'm not really sure what to do."

The king rubbed his chin. "You go back to her. I'm sure you will figure it out. I'll take care of this witch."

Izla nodded and vanished.

"It sounds like you have a long night ahead of you," the king said. "Go. I'll deal with this."

Ava shrunk down and landed on his shoulder. "You were up all night last night. Will you be able to make it two nights in a row?"

"Sure. You've been awake just as long. Will you be alright?"

"I slept while you were working."

Thane nodded and took them to King Dan's castle. They went right to the room Otelia occupied. She was sitting on a pile of straw. The king had not exaggerated. The room was so full of straw there wasn't much space to move.

Otelia stood. "You came back! I was worried."

"No need to worry," Thane said, making his voice higher. "I'll just get to work." He sat at the spinning wheel and grabbed a handful of straw. Ava flew off to hide.

"You have a fairy?" Otelia asked.

"Um... I don't have her... She's... a friend," he stuttered.

"Is there some way I can help? It is really boring here."

Ava stepped forward at her full height. "Since you already know I'm here, maybe we could visit?"

"You are the fairy?"

"Yes."

Thane wasn't sure Ava should have shown herself, but it was already done. "Don't tell anyone about meeting either of us. It will bring bad luck."

Otelia nodded. "Of course."

Ava and Otelia sat on the straw and started talking. It distracted him for a moment, but there wasn't a lot of thought that had to go into spinning straw. He had secretly hoped Otelia would fall asleep so he could use magic. After all the monotonous work he did the night before, he had decided it would be alright to magic some gold thread into the room. If Ava kept her awake and talking, there was little chance he could manage it.

The longer he spun, the more irritated he felt. Otelia's father was a fool. Once Otelia was safe, he would make sure the man knew the trouble he would be in if he ever put his daughter in danger like this again.

With luck, King Dan would let her go after tonight. Thane wouldn't be surprised if he demanded more gold. His greed had already manifested itself this morning. They needed a plan so it didn't keep happening.

This was going to take forever. He glanced back and saw Otelia and Ava in deep conversation. He pointed his finger at a pile of straw and made it disappear. In its place, a pile of gold thread appeared. It was almost as nice as what he'd spun. He looked back at the women. They hadn't noticed. He smiled. He might be able to take care of a lot without Otelia being any wiser.

"Amazing," King Dan said, running his hand through the gold thread. "You have done well, Otelia."

"Thank you, Your Highness," she said, bowing her head.

Ava and Thane were invisible once again, watching the exchange.

"I don't like the look in his eyes," Thane whispered. "He's not going to let her go."

"Probably not," Ava agreed quietly.

"May I speak, Your Highness?" Otelia asked, not daring to look up at the king.

"Of course."

Her hands trembled at her sides. "Tomorrow is my birthday."

"Oh?"

"My nineteenth birthday."

The king tilted his head as he watched her. "Is that significant?"

"Yes, Sire. My gift of spinning gold ends on my nineteenth birthday. After today, I can never do it again."

"Clever," Thane whispered. Maybe Otelia could save herself after all.

King Dan frowned. "How unfortunate. Still, you have today. I have already had a larger room next to this one filled with straw. If you do not spin it, you will die. If you manage it this third time, you will be my wife."

Otelia's eyes widened. "That is unnecessary."

"You do not need to feel beholden to me. You are very beautiful, so I have no objections to marrying you. Come, follow me to the next room."

Thane and Ava followed quietly behind. A man picked up the spinning wheel and carried it after them. They had to hurry to avoid him running into them. That would be hard to explain.

King Dan hadn't exaggerated. The room was at least three times larger than the one they had just left. Straw covered the floor and reached the ceiling. Thane wanted to sit on the ground in defeat, but he couldn't do that to Otelia. He needed sleep, and he wouldn't mind a bowl of something. Fairies could function with very little sleep, but he had always enjoyed it more than others.

"I'll have breakfast brought to you," the king said. "After that, you can get to work." He shut the door, and Thane sighed as he slumped down onto the seat near the spinning wheel.

"It was smart the way you told him you couldn't spin after today," Ava told Otelia.

She shrugged. "I knew this couldn't go on forever, and my birthday really is tomorrow. It was the only thing I could think of. The only problem is... I have nothing else to give you."

"Well, I will not do it for free," Thane said, folding his arms. He would do it for free, but no self-respecting imp would.

"If I must marry the king, perhaps I can give you something later?"

"Of course," Thane said. "Once you are married, you must give me your firstborn child."

Otelia sucked in a sharp breath. "That is a steep payment."

"But it is for your life. The choice is yours."

Otelia paced for a moment, and Thane forced himself to remain glaring. Inside, his mind was a mess. Her firstborn? What had he been thinking? Perhaps he had been an imp too long, and it was affecting him, or maybe he was just exhausted. He looked at Ava. She was glaring at him.

"Alright," Otelia finally said. "I don't see that I have a choice." She sat on the floor and covered her face with her hands.

Thane sat down and resisted the urge to yell. He was going to avoid straw for the rest of time.

"It will all work out," he heard Ava say.

"I don't see how," Otelia sobbed. "This is a steep price to pay. My entire life is going to change for the worse."

"Your father is a poor miller, and tomorrow, you can marry a king. That's got to be an improvement," Thane mumbled. He rubbed his eyes and reached for the straw.

"I detest the king," Otelia cried. "Why would I want to marry someone who threatened to kill me? Not only once, but three times. I do not see how we will have a good life together."

She was right. King Dan was abominable. Thane shoved the straw at the spinning wheel and watched it fall to the ground. His eyes were blurring, and a headache was creeping up on him. He waved his hand, and a piece of warm bread appeared. He devoured it while the women stood by the door speaking quietly.

The bread helped rejuvenate him for a while, but he was tired. He had gone about this entire situation wrong. He should have commanded the king to release the girl, and that would have been that. His father wouldn't have approved of that method, but it would have been fast and painless.

The hours passed slowly, and Thane wasn't sure how much more he could take. He figured it was about time for a break. When he turned to speak with Ava and Otelia, he found Otelia asleep on the straw, but Ava was nowhere to be seen.

"Ava?" he asked softly. There was no response. She wouldn't just leave him here, would she? He stood and stretched his back. It wasn't easy in this form Ava had given him. His back had a curve to it that was uncomfortable.

If no one was watching, Thane felt free to finish this job. With a few waves of his hands, he had all the straw turned into gold thread, except the small pile under Otelia. He smiled. That saved hours of work.

Ava appeared in the room with a small smile on her face. "You finished? I was only gone for ten minutes."

"I couldn't take it anymore. Where did you go?"

Ava's smile grew. "I had a thought. What would Izla do in this situation?"

Thane rubbed a hand across his face. "Oh dear. What did you do?"

"Nothing bad. Well, I made the king fall asleep, but it was for a good cause."

"What good would that do?"

"I gave him a dream." Her smile faded. "At least, I think I did. I'm not sure if it worked, but I have hope."

Thane cocked his head and tried not to notice how pretty Ava's dark brown eyes were. "What kind of dream?"

The sound of keys near the door had them scrambling. Ava shook Otelia awake and pulled her to her feet. Thane waved his hand at the straw she had vacated, and it became gold. He grabbed Ava's arm and made them both invisible right as the door opened.

King Dan and his brother Prince James entered the room. Thane preferred King Dan's brother to him in so many ways. Prince James thought before he spoke and had good ideas. Even Izla and their father admitted he had a good head on his shoulders. It was always shocking to think the two men could be brothers.

"You see?" King Dan said to his brother. He gestured around the room at all the gold. "We will be some of the wealthiest rulers in the world now."

James's eyes were wide as he studied the golden thread. "It is amazing, but we don't need it. Think of the good we could do with it."

Otelia stood there, her eyes glued to the floor.

"I assumed you would say something like that," the king said. "I will give you a third. You can do what you wish with it. I will also give you the girl."

Otelia's eyes jumped up to the king. She took a step back but didn't speak.

"What are you talking about?" James asked, running a hand through his wavy brown hair.

"I had planned to marry her myself, but I had a strange dream just now. I believe it was a warning that I would be cursed if I married her. In the dream, a fairy told me to have her marry you instead."

Thane grinned. Ava must be responsible for that. James would make a much better husband than Dan.

James shot his brother a scathing glance and then walked over to Otelia. "I am sorry you have been forced into all of this. I always knew my brother would choose who I married, but it isn't fair to you."

"Don't apologize," Dan said, rolling his eyes. "This should be the best day of her life. Now she won't be forced to marry a pig farmer. I don't have time to be bothered with the details. We will have a wedding before the week is out. Now, if you will excuse me, I have things to do." With a swish of his cape, he left the room.

James walked to the door and closed it, leaving him and Otelia in the room. He turned and leaned against it with his hands in his pockets. "I will do my best to help you have a happy life," he said. "I would appreciate it if we could always be honest with one another."

Otelia glanced at him. "I try to be honest."

He nodded. "I know you didn't turn that straw into gold. If you had that ability, you wouldn't be living in such humble conditions."

Thane should probably leave. It wasn't nice to spy on people, but he wanted to make sure the girl would be taken care of, and he didn't know where Ava was.

A tear ran down Otelia's cheek, and she brushed it away. "I... I don't know what to say."

James moved away from the door and came to stand in front of her. He gently lifted her chin with his finger. "You do not need to fear me. I am not my brother. Who spun the straw for you?"

"It was me," Thane said, appearing before them.

James dropped his hand and blinked in surprise. "An imp?"

Thane put his hands on his hips. "Yes, an imp."

"Oh no," James said, looking at the girl. "What did you promise him? Imps never help people for free."

"I had no choice," she cried.

James glared at Thane. "What did she promise you?"

"Her first-born child."

James' eyes bugged from his head. "Take something else. I can give you gold."

Thane scoffed and pointed at the piles of gold. "Do you think I need gold? Ouch!" he called out as something pinched the back of his arm. It must be Ava. It was good he brought her to bring him back to reality.

"I will let you keep your first-born, if you can guess my name."

James rubbed the back of his neck. "How many guesses do we get?"

"As many as you care to make. You may create a list if you wish. I will come back in two days. Agreed?"

James looked at Otelia, and they both nodded.

Chapter 8

Thane threw himself onto his bed and pulled his blanket up to his chin. His bed had never felt so cozy. He was going to sleep until noon tomorrow, possibly longer. He closed his eyes and then opened them when he heard someone clear their throat. Turning, he saw Ava standing by his bed, her arms crossed, and her toe tapping against the floor.

He squinted up at her. "I'm exhausted, Ava. Can this wait?"

"Wait? What were you thinking?"

"During which part?"

"Taking her first-born? What in the world would you do with it? Do you realize how much work a baby is?"

"I don't know what I was thinking," he admitted. "I didn't really plan on following through. Don't worry. I'll make them guess names for a while, eventually pretend they guessed it, then they can get married and live happily forever, or whatever Izla calls it."

"Happily ever after."

He yawned. "Right."

"This whole thing was a little messy. I think Izla would be happy with the way I tricked the king into letting his brother marry Otelia. Prince James has an excellent reputation and is well liked. She will be a lot better off with him."

"I hope you don't begin matchmaking like Izla. There isn't enough room on this planet for another Izla."

She smiled. "It won't be my obsession, but I am pleased with how it turned out. They might actually be happy together."

"I'm sure they will, but for now, can I sleep? I'm so tired I'm seeing things that aren't there."

"I suppose. I won't be satisfied until Otelia no longer fears she owes you anything and I get you turned back into yourself."

Thane rolled back over to face the wall. "I hope you figure that out as well. I'm not sure how well the people will respect me if I remain an imp." He closed his eyes. He wasn't sure if she answered or not. Sleep had overtaken him.

Izla stood next to the miner's cottage and watched at a distance as the men all stood around Snow White's coffin. No one had the heart to put her in a real coffin, especially since she still looked so lifelike, so Izla had fashioned a glass coffin to place the princess in. She couldn't hear what the men were saying, but she assumed they were reminiscing about their time with Snow.

Izla smoothed her light blue dress with one hand and looked at the gray sky. It would rain soon. Izla had refused to wear black. That felt like giving up, and she had not given up. There had to be a way to wake the girl. She just hadn't discovered it yet.

The first drop of rain hit Izla's face and ran over her cheek. She wiped it away and swallowed a lump in her throat. She wouldn't cry. There was no reason. This would be fixed. She didn't know how, but she was determined.

A walk through the woods might clear her mind. The smell of rain would either calm her or make her feel worse. It was anyone's guess. She turned and disappeared into the trees, pulling her blue cloak tighter and adjusting the hood. The rain turned from a drizzle to a downpour, but she ignored it.

People might see this as her fault. She had helped the princess, after all. People wouldn't know that if it hadn't been for her, the huntsman might have killed Snow earlier. It was best that hadn't happened. If it had, no one would have realized the queen's mother was behind it.

If Izla had been faster at meeting with different princes, this might have been avoided. She had only gotten around to five, and none of them seemed to be a good match for Snow. Prince Klevin of Torlin had reminded her a bit of Snow, but that seemed like a terrible idea. One person in a relationship needed to be qualified to rule, and Izla couldn't picture either of them taking the initiative.

Axel came bursting through the trees and dashed toward her. She fell to her knees and opened her arms. The wolf put his paws on her shoulders and licked her face. Izla gave a small laugh and rubbed his smelly, wet fur. The laughter quickly became a sob.

"This is all my fault," she told the wolf. Tears ran down her face, blending in with the rain. "I should have hidden her better. After the first sign of danger, I should have moved her."

Axel rested on Izla's knees and glanced up at her, his amber eyes offering sympathy.

"There has to be a way to fix this. The rain is affecting me for the worse."

She pulled her wand from her pocket and shot a stream of magic up at the clouds. The rain stopped, and the clouds cleared away. A beam of sunlight shone down. Izla got to her feet and waved her wand around Axel and herself. They both dried, and the mud disappeared. Izla couldn't change the weather everywhere, but she could control it for a few miles.

"Come on, Axel. It's time to pull myself together and fix this." She headed back to the cottage, Axel trotting at her side. When they came into the clearing where the cottage lay, her eyes scanned the area. The glass coffin was gone.

"No," she muttered. "No, no, no." She ran to the cottage and pounded on the door. One man opened it. "Where is she?"

He rubbed the back of his neck. "A prince rode past. When he spotted Snow, he felt so sad. He said he'd never seen such a beautiful creature. He asked if he could take her to his kingdom."

Izla put her hands to her head. "And you let him?"

"He can put her in a place of honor."

"Stay here," she commanded Axel. She turned to the man. "Which way did they go?"

He pointed left of the cottage. "They rode through those trees."

Izla lifted her shirts and ran in the direction the man pointed. What had they been thinking? She couldn't have been gone for over ten minutes. Why would they let a stranger take her, especially without Izla's permission? She sighed with relief when she spotted the group ahead. It was Prince Klevin. She shouldn't be surprised. He had ten guards with him, all on horses, and they had Snow White's coffin in the back of a wagon.

"STOP!" she yelled. The men with the prince drew their swords and turned their horses to face her. When they spotted her, they lowered them. She rushed toward them, her red hair slapping against her face. The wind was stronger here.

"Princess Izla," Prince Klevin said. "What are you doing out here?"

"I could ask you the same," she said, placing her hands on her waist. "This is not your kingdom."

"No," he admitted, adjusting his gold crown. She wondered how he kept his black hair so neat after traveling so far. He must take lessons from Thane. She couldn't remember the last time her brother had managed to mess up his hair.

"Why are you here?" she demanded.

"I had heard of Snow White's beauty. After you visited me and mentioned something about her, I wanted to see her for myself. We were turned away at the castle, but a huntsman followed us and told us she might be in these woods."

"You can't take her," Izla said, climbing onto the back of the wagon.

Prince Klevin frowned. "Why not?"

She rolled her eyes. "Why do you want to? You don't know her."

"But her beauty is inspiring."

Izla stood in the wagon bed and bit her tongue to stop herself from telling him how ridiculous she found him. It would be a waste of her breath. She pulled her wand from her pocket.

"No, please!" Prince Klevin begged, unhooking the back of the wagon. The back fell open and slammed against the wooden wheels. The horses startled and ran forward. Izla felt herself fall and made herself disappear and reappear a few feet from the wagon. The glass coffin fell to the ground and rolled.

Izla covered her mouth with her hand, then ran to the coffin and pushed it over. Snow White's eyes were open, and she appeared terrified. Izla unlatched the coffin and pulled the girl out.

Snow spit something from her mouth. Izla looked down at a piece of apple. The fall must have dislodged it from her throat. Why hadn't she thought to try something like that?

"What's happening?" Snow asked, taking a wobbly step.

"I saved you," Prince Klevin said, taking her hand in his.

Izla took a deep breath through her nose and pursed her lips.

"You saved me?" Snow asked, a smile spreading over her face. "Is that true?" she asked, glancing at Izla.

Izla kicked the glass coffin door shut. "If by saved, he means he took your coffin and made it fall off a wagon, then yes."

"Thank you!" Snow said, throwing her arms around Prince Klevin's neck.

He grinned as he hugged her.

"Ridiculous," Izla muttered. She pointed her wand after the runaway horses and made them stop. "Go get the horses," she told the guards. They were all standing around with their mouths hanging open. It was almost as if they had never seen a dead person come back to life.

"You must return to my kingdom and marry me," Prince Klevin said, running his hand over Snow's cheek.

"I would be honored," Snow said. She turned to Izla. "Now you don't have to worry about me anymore. It's good the prince was here to save me."

Snow White and Prince Klevin. That was not what Izla had in mind. "Marriage based on appearance is a bad idea." The two looked at her with confused stares. She sighed. "Never mind. Go. Get married, and live happily ever after."

Snow giggled, and Prince Klevin lifted her and spun in a circle. The guards cheered, and Izla tried not to feel defeated. This was either her biggest victory or her worst failure.

Izla sat on her father's throne, her back straight and her head held high. All she wanted was a nap, but when she arrived home, her father told her he was needed elsewhere, and he wasn't sure where Thane was today. She had no choice but to sit and listen to the problems of the people. It was something she usually enjoyed, but she needed a break after the stress from Snow White.

The man in charge of deciding who really needed to see the royal family, entered the room. Without Levnor, anyone with any complaint would be brought before them, and they would never know peace.

He rushed over to her and dropped to one knee. "Prince James of Glovem is here to see you."

Izla raised her brow. It must be something serious if a prince was here. "Show him in."

Levnor stood and hurried away. A moment later, he led the prince through the doors. Izla had met him once before. At his side was a young woman in a worn brown dress. It was possible she was a servant, but most servants that attended to royalty were well dressed. They both bowed to her, then the prince took the girl's hand.

Ah, that made more sense. Prince James must have fallen for a commoner and wanted Izla to convince his brother, King Danivonalin to allow it. Izla was tired after the disaster that was Snow White, but she couldn't turn down a chance to help two people find happiness.

"Princess Izla, we need your assistance," Prince James said, his eyes locked on her. "We have had some trouble with an imp, and our future happiness may be in danger."

Izla frowned. That wasn't what she expected. "Go on."

He glanced at the girl next to him. "Otelia should probably explain."

Otelia glanced down at her feet and told Izla an almost un-believable tale. Izla hung on her every word. She didn't doubt the girl. King Danivonalin was a fool, and imps were some of the worst creatures. When the girl finished, she looked up, her eyes full of unshed tears.

Prince James took a step forward. "We had hoped you might know the imp's name."

"There are so many imps, and they avoid fairies for the most part," Izla said.

Otelia looked at James, and he nodded at her. "This one didn't. He had a fairy with him."

Izla's eyes narrowed. A fairy with an imp? That was unheard of. Imps were never up to anything good, so if a fairy was choosing to spend time with one, she must be up to something as well. Could it be Nassandra? Izla wouldn't put it past her.

"The fairy was kind," the girl said. "Even the imp didn't seem very bad until he named the last price."

"Did you hear the fairy's name?" she asked. She knew almost every fairy.

"I believe I heard the imp call her Ava one time, but I might be mistaken."

Her forehead wrinkled. What would Ava be doing with an imp? "I may be able to help you. Will you excuse me for a moment?"

Prince James bowed his head. "Of course."

Izla forced herself to walk at a normal speed as she left the throne room and entered the hallway. The heavy door swung closed behind her. She needed to find Ava, and she needed to find her fast. Before she could decide where to look, she saw Ava dash around the corner and rush toward her.

Ava grabbed her arm. "We need your help."

Izla refused to budge when Ava pulled on her. "We who? I need to talk to you. Have you been conversing with an imp?"

"It's Thane."

"What's Thane?"

"The imp."

Izla arched her brow. "The imp is Thane? What are you talking about?"

Ava sighed and dropped Izla's arm. "It's a long story. I turned him into an imp, and we got into a mess, and I can't turn him back."

Izla rolled her eyes. Only one of her friends and her brother could get into this kind of trouble. "Do you know who I have in the throne room right now? Prince James."

Ava's eyes widened. "Oh, dear."

Izla crossed her arms. "He wants to know if I can tell him the imp's name."

"This is alright. We can fix it. You just tell them the name, and they can guess it, and we can be done with the entire mess."

"I can't tell them Thane's name."

"Just make one up. Tell them it's Rumpelstiltskin. I'll go tell Thane." Ava smiled and ran off before Izla could respond.

"Rumpelstiltskin?" Izla muttered. "Why not John?" She went back into the throne room. Prince James and Otelia had their heads together, whispering. They straightened and turned to her when she entered.

Izla forced a smile. "Good news. I can tell you the imp's name."

The couple smiled.

"What is it?" Otelia asked.

"Rumpelstiltskin."

Otelia blinked. "Rumpel..."

"Rumpelstiltskin."

Prince James frowned. "I'm never going to remember that."

Izla nodded. "I'll write it down for you."

<hr>

Thane stood in front of Prince James and Otelia. They were both trying to look serious and failing miserably. He could see the twinkle in both of their eyes. Fine with him. Let them think they were clever.

"Can you guess my name?" he asked. He was ready to be done with this place.

"Is it Peter?" Otelia asked.

Thane shook his head. "No."

"Josh? Andrew? Edward?"

"Nope, no, and no."

Otelia flashed a sly smile. "Is it Rumpelstiltskin?"

Thane wanted to roll his eyes. He thought she would take her time pretending to be ignorant. No one would guess that name after four tries. If he was honest, no one would ever guess it. He doubted it was even a name. Why, of all names, did Ava choose that one? He wouldn't complain. It was over.

"Who told you my name?" he demanded, making a show of being angry. "The devil told you!" He stomped his feet, threw his arms into the air, and yelled up at the ceiling. He wanted to smile when he imagined how ridiculous he must look. He gave them one last glare and disappeared.

Chapter 9

"I don't think the two of you should collaborate on any more projects," Izla said, pacing across her bedroom floor. "It is lucky things ended up working as well as they did."

"Who says you are the boss of what we do?" Thane asked.

Izla glanced at him and frowned. He sat on her bed next to Ava, his imp backside on her pink quilt. Now it would have to be washed. She was surprised Ava could sit next to him while he looked like that. She knew he was her brother, but his appearance had her unsettled.

"I'm just trying to get you to understand that if the two of you want to help me with matchmaking, I don't think you should work together without my guidance."

Thane's beady, imp eyes glared at her. "I don't want to help you with matchmaking. I only got involved in this because I needed to save Otelia from King Dan and her lying father. Ava just happened to be around when I needed someone."

Ava frowned. "I'm sorry I wasn't someone more competent."

Thane sighed. "That's not what I mean. I'm just trying to let Izla know we weren't doing this to help her with any matchmaking."

"It really isn't a bad story," Izla said, tapping her lip. "In fact, I am going to add it to my book." She moved to her nightstand and picked up her diary.

"What do you mean?" Ava asked, leaning forward. "What's in the book?"

Izla smiled. She had wanted to show this book to someone for ages. "It's the place where I write about all of my successes. Every time someone falls in love and I have a hand in it, I write their story here."

Ava's eyes locked on the leather-bound book. "Can I read it?"

Izla's smile slipped. "They aren't written well. I've put the details in here, and I hope to find a talented storyteller someday and ask them to write them into something better. I'll call them fairy tales or something like that."

Ava grinned. "That's a great idea."

"I'll find someone from a different realm. Perhaps one without fairies. That will make the stories even more magical."

"I love that," Ava said with a dramatic sigh. "It's adorable the way some places don't believe we exist."

Izla's stomach was bubbling with excitement. It was about time she got to share her dreams with someone. Saying them out loud made them more real. Perhaps she should tell Ava about her vision for the future.

She sat next to Ava and handed her the book. Ava flipped through some pages, and Izla tried not to be self-conscious. She was confident in most things, but not writing. Handing the book over was the same as exposing her soul. Still, she knew Ava wouldn't judge her.

Thane hopped off the bed and stood to face them. "Hello? Can we do this some other time? I'm still an imp. Can we work on that?"

Izla frowned. Thane should be the priority. If anyone saw him like this, it might cause problems. "Ava has to fix it. She weaved the magic, so she needs to undo it."

Ava dropped the book on her lap, and it slid to the floor. "I already tried and failed."

Izla rolled her eyes and scooped up the diary. "Try again. Try until you get it right."

Ava's lip trembled. "What if I make it worse?"

"What's worse than this?" Thane asked, holding out his arms.

"Very well," she said, getting to her feet. She pulled her wand from her pocket. With a quick flick of her wrist and a green spark... absolutely nothing happened.

Izla didn't know how to guide her. Every fairy used magic in their own way, and expecting two to perform the same was ignorance. She watched different emotions play across her friend's face.

She stood and put a hand on her friend's shoulder. "You can do this."

Ava closed her eyes and muttered something under her breath. She waved her wand and pointed it at Thane. A streak of green flew from the wand and hit Thane square in the chest.

"Ouch!" he exclaimed, taking a step back.

Izla's eyes widened as she watched her brother. "Is he shrinking?"

"I'm shrinking?" Thane asked. "No! I need to grow, not shrink."

Ava covered her mouth with one hand. "Oh no! What should I do?"

Izla opened her mouth, then closed it. She had no ideas.

Thane looked down at his hands. "Why am I turning green?"

Izla glanced down at him. He was less than a foot high and still shrinking. His eyes were bulging and his hands and feet were starting to look webbed.

"He's turning into a frog!" Ava said, dropping to her knees.

"A frog?" Thane asked, his voice sounding more like a croak.

Izla got down on her own knees and watched the rest of her brother's transformation in awe. Ava might do most things by accident, but they were interesting to behold.

"You better not be smiling," Frog Thane said.

"Of course not," Izla said, glancing at Ava. They both burst into laughter.

"I can't believe you are laughing at this," Thane said. It appeared so unnatural when he talked, it caused them to laugh harder.

Ava wiped her eyes. "I'm sorry to laugh, and I'm sorry to be the cause."

Izla grinned. Her friend was trying her best to regain her composure.

"This is worse than being an imp!" Thane protested. "Do something!"

Ava scooped him up and held him in front of her face. "A frog is better than an imp, believe me. Frogs are adorable." She brought Thane closer and kissed the top of his head.

Izla giggled. "Gross, Ava. Put him down."

Ava placed Thane on the pink and blue rug, and a light flashed across the room. Izla closed her eyes to protect them, and she heard Thane yell, and then a crash. When she opened her eyes, Thane was nowhere to be seen.

"Where did he go?" Ava asked.

Izla startled when her pink quilt moved. In a flash, the blanket flew from the bed and disappeared on the other side.

"Don't come over here!" Thane commanded.

Izla grinned. "Why? What did you turn into this time?"

"I'm me, just stay there!"

"Why? Are you naked or something?" Izla giggled, and Ava let out an unladylike snort. The snort sent them both into peels of laughter. Izla hadn't laughed like this in a long time. She felt like a little girl again.

"Could you both just leave? Please?" Thane begged.

"Leave?" Izla asked. "This is my room."

"Fine," he grumbled. He popped up, Izla's pink quilt wrapped around his waist. That was all he was wearing. Izla and Ava burst into another round of laughter.

"You two are impossible," he muttered, hurrying across the room.

Izla smiled. "What are the chances of you making it to your room without anyone seeing you?"

He turned and gave her a dirty look. He snapped his fingers and disappeared.

"Why didn't he just do that in the first place?" Ava asked.

"I don't know, but I'm going to tease him about this for eternity."

Ava laughed and then frowned. "I bet he hates me now. This is all my fault."

"I'm sure he doesn't hate you," Izla smiled. "I would try to stay away from him for a while, though."

Izla's mind was going fast. Thane, changing back into his true form from a kiss, was giving her ideas. It had probably happened because Ava was the one to kiss him and cast the spell. Still, it was possible it was something else.

She smiled. "Love's kiss."

Ava raised her brow. "What?"

"That's what my stories need!" She was excited. That would help so many stories.

"I don't understand."

Izla tossed her book to her bed. "Lily had it right. True love's kiss should be the most powerful thing in the universe! A kiss will wake Princess Rose, and you kissed Thane and broke the spell!"

"Whoa!" Ava exclaimed, throwing her hands into the air. "I am not in love with Thane." She crossed her arms and glared at Izla.

"Oh, I know," Izla said, not completely convinced. "But think of how nice it would make stories. I think I'll write one about a prince that gets turned into a frog, and he can't change back until he gets kissed by a princess. Doesn't that sound fun?"

Ava was still glaring. "I suppose."

Izla was sure she was onto something. Snow White's story would have been a lot better if a prince had kissed her. She would ex out the part in her diary about the apple coming dislodged. A kiss was much more romantic than a regurgitated apple.

Ava looked so irritated. Izla was almost positive it must be because she had feelings for Thane. Now wasn't the time for Thane. He wasn't ready for love. He'd said so more times than she could count, and she didn't want to encourage Ava when she might get hurt.

"Can I tell you a secret?" she asked.

Ava's brow softened. "Of course."

Izla clasped her hands together and smiled. She had been wanting to tell someone about this for so long. "I'm going to make a shadow world."

Ava cocked her head. "A what?"

"A shadow world."

Ava stared blankly at her.

"You don't know what a shadow world is?"

Her friend shook her head. "It sounds creepy."

"Not at all. A shadow world is just a world that mirrors this one, but it isn't real."

"And you can't make one without permission from the king," Thane said from behind them.

Izla spun around to glare at her brother. "Nice of you to join us in something more presentable."

Ava giggled, and Thane's face turned a violent shade of pink. He straightened his blue tunic and frowned.

"So, you can make a world? But it isn't real. What's the point then?" Ava wondered.

Thane didn't take his disapproving glare away from Izla. "It's something that only the royal family is supposed to know about."

Izla didn't agree with keeping things in the family. She hadn't known this was a secret. There was no reason to keep it from Ava now. She would just wonder, and her imagination would turn it into something it wasn't.

"It feels real, even though it isn't. You can live in a shadow world forever. You can also bring people to them. Haven't you ever wondered where all the royal people who aren't the king go?"

"I know your brothers are all ruling parts of this world."

Izla nodded. "Yes, but what about my father's brothers?"

Ava shrugged.

Thane walked to the window and stared out at the ocean. "You are going to get into trouble."

Izla ignored him. "Since the throne is handed down father to son, that leaves a lot of siblings with nothing to do. If nothing unfortunate happens to the king, he will rule forever. My grandfather ruled for over five thousand years before he became tired of it all and passed it to my father."

"Where is he now?" Ava asked.

"He made his own shadow world. It was the same with all our uncles. They made places they want to live in and brought people there. That way, they can rule if they choose, or they can live any way they want. They can even create people that aren't real to live there and be their servants or whatever they want."

Ava's eyes widened. "How has something this big stayed a secret?"

Izla shrugged. She didn't really care. She only cared that it could benefit her.

"Why haven't your brothers made these worlds?"

Thane turned and looked at Ava. "My father doesn't like shadow worlds. He thinks they give the people there a hollow, unfulfilled life. It's like living a lie. That's why he divided up the kingdom to give something to his children. They rule their areas under him."

"Think of this," Izla said. "I make a shadow world where I have control. I bring people to the world, and I get them to fall in love there."

Thane rolled his eyes. "That seems like a waste of time and a world. You get people to fall in love here, so what is the point?"

"Think of how messy some of these things are. If I had taken Snow to a place I controlled, I wouldn't have to worry about things taking unexpected turns. I could have found a more suitable prince and brought him there to fall in love with her. It would be a magical world full of love."

The room was quiet. Izla hated the looks Thane and Ava were giving her. Thane appeared irritated, and Ava looked skeptical. She had been imagining something like this for years, and it was hard to explain it to people now that she was ready.

"You can't force two people to fall in love," Thane finally said.

Izla shook her head at the ceiling. "Of course not. That doesn't mean I can't place people in the right situations to help it along."

"Shadow worlds take a long time to make."

"Oh, I know. I'm planning on it taking a couple hundred years at least." Izla's mind was already ahead of the conversation. She should probably start now. Thinking about it would only get her so far.

"A couple hundred years?" Ava asked. "I would never have the attention span for that."

Thane nodded. "I've never heard of any taking that long. Uncle Uri took fifty years."

Izla's eyes sparkled. "I'm planning on making one a lot bigger than that."

Thane rubbed his temples. "The bigger the shadow world, the more chance of trouble."

She didn't know why Thane was looking stressed. It wasn't like he had to help or ever go there. "It has to be big. I have big plans."

"Why is big worse?" Ava asked.

Thane walked back to the bed and sat down. "If you don't fill the entire area, it fills itself. If you leave a space, a swamp or a mountain might spring up. That stuff can spread and wipe out things people have already created there. If you aren't careful, you end up like our great-great uncle, and you have to burn the entire thing down."

Izla wasn't worried. Most people who made shadow worlds did it to create their own perfect place where they could relax and waste time. Izla was doing this for others. She would be careful and make sure it was perfect. She would be vigilant at keeping an eye on things.

"I'm going to have to leave some space," she admitted. "I need to make sure there are areas to make new things when I come up with them. I'll just be careful about stopping whatever pops up in those spaces."

"Do you need help?" Ava asked.

Izla tilted her head and studied her. "I might. For now, you need to keep watching out for Princess Rose. That needs to be your priority. I'm going to make a better plan soon. I need to show my father it's a good idea."

Thane smiled. "I don't know why I was worried. Father will never agree to this."

Izla pursed her lips. She would not argue with her brother. She would make such thorough plans her father would have no choice but to see the beauty in them.

Chapter 10

The wind blew rain into Thane's face. He closed his eyes and smiled. He loved being at sea during this time of year. The wind and rain might make others turn back, but he loved it. It had been too long since he'd had a chance to come out here, and he had missed it. The ship tossed against the waves, making some of the crew sick, but not him.

"It's been a while, huh?" Thane's friend Sebby said, joining him at the railing.

The rain ran down Sebby's brown skin and soaked into the collar of his white tunic. Nothing fazed Sebby. In the years Thane had known the man, he had seemed nothing but calm. It was probably best. If Sebby were an angry person, he would be frightening to behold. He reached over six foot three and had enough muscle to get second glances from passersby.

"It seems like forever," he said, pushing his bangs from his eyes.

Sebby leaned on the railing and gazed over the ocean. "This might turn into a nasty storm. Are you up for it?"

"Of course. You know I love it."

"You are the only one I know that enjoys sailing in these messes. I wouldn't be out here if I didn't have to be."

Thane nodded. It probably wasn't fair to feel as free as he did on the ocean. Unlike the others, he could disappear and take himself elsewhere if he needed to. He could also take the crew, but he couldn't tell Sebby that. He told his friend almost everything—except two very important things. That he was a fairy, and that his father was King Henan.

Sebby's father owned this ship and had allowed Thane to ride with them for a large fee. Thane had met Sebby ten years ago, and they had quickly become friends. That was just after Izla had told him about her plans to make a shadow world. Had it really been ten years? It didn't feel like it.

These ten years had been less stressful than the ten before. Izla had almost given up on matchmaking while she made plans for her shadow world. King Henan had gone against his regular self and forbidden Izla from making one. She was stubborn, of course, and was making elaborate plans to prove it was a good idea. She figured if she planned it well enough, her father would have to give in.

Sebby ran a hand over his wet, black curls. "You used to come around at least once a week. I haven't seen you in at least three months."

"I had to help my father with some things. It's a busy time of year."

"Are you ever going to tell me what your father does?"

Thane grinned and shook his head. "My family has some… peculiar things about it. If I tell you about them, you won't think of me the same."

Sebby turned and leaned back, resting his elbows on the rail. "Every family has its problems. You already told me you have a crazy matchmaking sister and a bunch of brothers. I envy you there. I wish I had siblings. Maybe you don't want to tell me that your father is the fairy king?"

Thane looked up sharply, and Sebby laughed.

"I'm kidding. It's funny you have the same name as the fairy prince, though. I know there are lots of people named after royal families, but that was mean of your parents to name you after a fairy."

Thane narrowed his eyes. "Yes, well, what kind of name is Sebby?"

Sebby smiled. "You got me there. It's strange you keep your family life mostly secret. I assume your family has money since you let my father overcharge you for coming with us."

"It's worth it. Your father has a clean ship and a respectable crew. That's a rare thing. Believe me, I've been on some disgusting ships. This one is amazing." Thane wasn't exaggerating. Some ship captains had no standards.

"So, you've been helping your father for the last while? What else?" Sebby nudged him playfully with his elbow. "You didn't meet a girl, did you?"

Thane rolled his eyes. "What do you think? You've seen me talk to girls."

Sebby laughed. "Yes, and it is painful to behold."

"The water really is my favorite place. I live right on the ocean. When I get the chance, I walk along the beach. It clears my head."

"I think we were born in the wrong places. Sometimes I wish I could move far away from the ocean. Even to be off this ship for more than a few days at a time would be nice."

Thane looked at his soaked friend. "I thought you enjoyed sailing."

Sebby shrugged. "Not really, but my father needs my help, and what else would I do? I've been doing this my entire life."

"Perhaps your father would let you take a long vacation?"

"I don't know."

A chill ran over Thane, and he glanced around the deck of the ship. He had the feeling someone was watching him, but only the men working and the two of them were crazy enough to be out in this storm.

Sebby narrowed his eyes. "What's wrong?"

"You might think I'm crazy."

He flashed his teeth. "I know you are."

Thane paused and wondered if he should confide in his friend. "Have you ever had the feeling you were being watched?"

Sebby tilted his head. "A time or two."

"It's been happening to me a lot lately. Every time I walk near the ocean, and just now."

"I don't think anyone is paying attention to us," Sebby said, scanning the ship. "It's probably in your head."

He shivered in the rain and crossed his arms for warmth. "I tell myself that, but it makes me nervous."

Sebby grinned mischievously. "Maybe it's a mermaid."

Thane let out a short laugh. "A mermaid? There's no such thing."

"Says you."

"Yes, says me."

Sebby looked out at the dark ocean. "I've seen one."

"I know I can be gullible, but you aren't tricking me this time."

"I'm not teasing you. We were out one day, and I saw her. It was broad daylight, so I knew it wasn't a strange shadow or anything. She was the most beautiful creature I've ever seen. I've seen her a few times since."

Thane watched Sebby's face. He seemed to be telling the truth. Thane knew mermaids existed regardless of what he had said, but most mortals didn't, and that was how the sea king wanted it.

"I don't care if you don't believe me," Sebby said. He was almost yelling to be heard over the rising wind, "I know what I saw." He slipped a bit and caught himself. "We better go beneath. This is getting crazy."

Right when he said it, a large flash of lightning lit up the eastern sky. The deafening boom of thunder followed, and Thane jumped in surprise. They made their way across the deck, and for the first time, Thane was worried. The ship was rocking back and forth, making it hard to keep their footing.

Thane called over the storm, "Why don't you go down, and I'll join you in a minute?" If he could do it unseen, he could try to use magic to calm the storm. He didn't really think he could make a lot of difference, but he could try.

"I'm not leaving you out here on your own!" Sebby called. "You trip enough when there isn't a storm."

Thane's eyes swept across the deck. Sailors were running around now, working to keep the ship safe. Going below might not be best for anyone.

A large cracking noise and a blinding flash caused everyone to fall over. Thane felt a sliver embed itself in his palm as he slid across the wooden floor. He glanced up to see the ship on fire. Lightning must have hit them.

Someone was calling out orders, but Thane wasn't listening. They were far from shore, and with the ship on fire, they wouldn't make it. He was going to have to put out the fire and take them all back to land. Everyone on the ship would know his secret.

The ship was rocking so hard it was impossible to stand. He got on his hands and knees and looked up at the burning mast.

"We aren't going to make it!" Sebby yelled, crawling up to him. "It's too far to shore!"

"I can save us," Thane called.

He closed his mouth and eyes as an enormous wave smashed over the ship. His body flew through the water and was pulled down into the salty ocean. Thane held his breath and swam in the direction he thought was up. He could take himself home, but if he did, everyone else would die. He wouldn't be able to return to this exact place because he didn't know where in the ocean they were.

His head broke the surface, and he took a deep gulp of air. The ship was on its side and still burning. He scanned the water for signs of the crew. With the way the waves were rising and falling, it was hard to make out much of anything. Raising his hands in the air, he tried to calm the sky. It might have worked if he wasn't moving with the tireless waves.

He could see one person holding onto a large plank, so he tried to swim in their direction. It was pointless. He couldn't get where he wanted. He could sprout wings and try to fly, but the water would make them useless. Panic filled him, and he wished Izla was there. She would know what to do. Her magic had always been superior to his.

Something smashed into the back of his head, and colors swam before his eyes. He was going to have to take himself out of here. That was the last thought he had before the world went dark.

~eee~

A pounding on her bedroom door had Izla scurrying to roll up all the scrolls scattered across her bedroom floor. She didn't want to use magic on them because she'd burned one by accident a few days ago. The scrolls were covered in her plans to make a shadow world, and she didn't want anyone to see them until she was ready. She rolled them under her bed and rushed to the door.

King Henan stood at the doorway wearing a large frown. "There was a shipwreck."

"Oh no," Izla said. "What can I do? Were there survivors?"

"Yes," he said, guiding her down the hallway. "The mermaids intervened. They pulled people from the water and dropped them on the beach."

Izla walked fast to keep up with his long strides. "That's odd. I've never known mermaids to save humans."

He nodded. "It's very peculiar. I need you to do a memory spell on the survivors. They cannot be allowed to remember.

That could cause terrible problems for the mermaids who helped. The sea king would punish them for their involvement."

"Yes, of course," Izla agreed. She had only met the sea king once, and he was an intimidating ruler. He hated humans with a passion Izla couldn't understand. He made a rule that any mermaid who dared break the surface of the ocean would be locked up for a year, so they would learn to stay where there was no chance of ever being seen.

King Henan's eyes looked heavy, and small creases rested in the corners. He needed to sleep more. There were so many things going on that demanded his attention. A guard opened the large wooden door to the outside, and Izla followed her father down the steps and into the fresh air. She shaded her eyes from the sun and rushed to keep up. The storm from the night before was only a memory.

"There is something else," he said.

"Oh?" Izla asked, holding up her skirts as they stepped into the sand.

"Thane was on the ship."

Izla stopped, her hands covering her mouth. "Is he alright?"

The king glanced over his shoulder. "Keep walking."

Izla ran a few steps to catch up.

"There are only two people from the ship that haven't been found. Thane and his friend Sebby."

Izla's heart hammered against her chest. It might be alright. It was highly likely Thane had saved his friend and himself. Killing a fairy wasn't easy.

"Sebby's father came to the castle in search of help. He was battered and bruised, but he will be alright. He said the rest of the crew are gathered just down the shore. I sent some medical fairies ahead of us, but I knew you would be best to erase their memories."

Izla nodded and tried not to let the worry consume her. She loved all her brothers, but Thane had always been the closest to her. They were much younger than the other children and had formed an unbreakable bond. If she lost him, she didn't know what she would do.

⁓ eℓℓe ⁓

Thane's head throbbed, and he tried to peel his eyes open. The bright sun made it difficult, so he gave up and kept them shut. He could feel the warm sand underneath him, and he tried not to worry about the crew. If they hadn't survived, there was nothing he could do now.

"Thane?" A hand brushed over his cheek, and he tried to identify the voice. He must be hallucinating. It sounded like Ava. She hadn't come around in years. Princess Rose was turning out to be a handful and took constant supervision.

"Come on, Thane," said a deep voice. "You can do it. Open your eyes." It was Sebby. He was alive.

He pried his eyes open and stared into Ava's face. She was kneeling beside him, running her hand over his cheek again. He was too sore and tired to wonder why she was there. She was just as beautiful as ever. Sebby sat at his other side. His clothing was torn, and his shoulder was covered in blood, but he looked alright.

"What happened?" he asked, forcing himself to sit up. "I thought we were dead for sure."

Sebby glanced from Ava to Thane. "You aren't going to believe me. A mermaid saved us."

Ava frowned. "That's what Izla said."

Thane rubbed a bump on his head. "That's going to cause problems."

Ava stood and held out her hand. "Everyone is looking for the two of you."

He took her hand and let her help him stand. "Where is Izla?"

She glanced at Sebby. "All the sailors saw the mermaids. She's... dealing with that."

Sebby watched them, his forehead creased. He stood, not taking his eyes off Ava.

"We better get back," she said. "Your families are worried about you, and they need to call off the search."

"I don't think I can take myself back," Thane said, not sure what to say around Sebby. It probably didn't matter. Izla would probably make him forget. "My mind is too blurry."

Ava nodded. "We can walk. It isn't far."

"How else would we get there?" Sebby asked.

Thane shrugged, and they started up the beach. Ava hurried ahead, not waiting for the exhausted men.

"You said there wasn't a woman in your life," Sebby said. He was limping slightly, but Thane would not point it out.

Thane glanced at him. "There isn't."

"I saw the way your eyes lit up when you looked at her."

Thane barked out a fake laugh. "Ava? She's my sister's best friend."

Sebby turned to him. "Who is Izla?"

"My sister."

"Hm. Izla and Thane. Your parents named you both after the fairy king's children?"

Thane kept walking, his eyes on Ava. "Maybe." It was pointless to keep it from him. He would find out as soon as they got to the castle. "King Henan is my father."

Sebby let out a low chuckle. "That means you're a fairy."

"I'm a fairy."

"You don't look like a fairy."

"What is a fairy supposed to look like?"

Sebby scratched his head. "I dunno. Whimsical? Definitely smaller. And where are your wings?"

Thane took a deep breath. "It doesn't really matter. I'm sure my father will have Izla erase your memory of today. The sea king doesn't like people to see mermaids. It could cause problems."

Sebby stopped abruptly. "She can't erase my memory."

Thane turned to him and paused. "Why?"

"I don't want to forget. I won't tell anyone."

"You don't want to forget being in a shipwreck?"

Sebby glanced out at the ocean. "I don't want to forget the mermaid."

"What mermaid?"

"When I was in the water, I saw you. I started swimming in your direction, but before I could get to you, a large piece of debris hit you in the head. I swam faster, but before I could get to you, a mermaid grabbed you. She saw me and motioned me forward. I thought she was going to drown me, but she held on to both of us and swam us to shore. I can't believe she could swim so far. It felt like it took hours."

Thane squinted out at the water. "I don't remember any of it."

"She was the same mermaid I told you about. I've seen her before."

"I can ask my father to let you keep your memory. I don't know what he'll say, though." He would probably allow it if he could get Sebby to promise not to talk about it to anyone. Thane trusted Sebby. If he said he wouldn't tell, he believed him.

"Who is that up ahead?" Sebby asked.

Thane gazed over the landscape until his eyes landed on Ava and Izla. "That's my sister." Ava was gesturing at them, and Izla was nodding. Izla disappeared and reappeared in front of them.

"Whoa!" Sebby exclaimed, taking a step back. "That was incredible!"

Izla's mouth formed a tight line, but Thane could see her eyes twinkle. She enjoyed impressing people. "I'm so glad you are alright," she said, giving Thane a hug.

Thane told his sister what had happened, and her eyes swept over the ocean. Her brows came together, and she frowned, and then she smiled. "There she is."

Thane turned and searched the waves. "I don't see anything."

"Neither do I," Sebby said. "I'm hoping you won't erase my memory. I've seen the mermaid before, and I won't tell anyone."

Izla peered at him and then smiled. "We don't have to decide that right now. You both go up to the castle, and I will meet you there."

Thane knew that smile, and there was nothing innocent about it. Izla was up to something. "Come with us."

"I won't be long."

Thane sighed. There was no point in arguing with her. She had decided something, and nothing was going to change her mind.

Chapter 11

Izla walked around a large mound of boulders and sank down behind them. The mermaid probably wasn't paying attention to her. She was most likely watching Thane and his friend. She would wait until they were out of sight and then she would go to the ocean. Transforming into a mermaid would be easy, and then she could talk to the mermaid and see what the sea folk were saying about the crash.

The men were out of sight, which meant the mermaid was probably gone. Izla sprinted from her place in the sand and ran to the ocean. She trudged through the shallow water and then dove in when an enormous wave climbed up in front of her. A shimmering green tail replaced her legs, and she smiled as the murky water became clear to her mermaid eyes. Transforming into a mermaid was a breeze. She'd done it often enough as a child.

Izla swam toward the rock the mermaid had been on. She hoped she wouldn't have to search too long. Her father still needed help with the people from the shipwreck.

"Who are you?" a melodious voice said at her side.

Her heart almost stopped as she swam in a circle and faced a beautiful raven haired mermaid. She resisted the urge to put her hand to her chest. No sense in letting the mermaid know she had startled her.

The mermaid was watching her with a curious expression. "I saw you on the shore. You were human."

Izla frowned. She hadn't thought the girl would recognize her from that distance. Her mind raced. There had to be something she could say that wouldn't sound suspicious.

"Are you magic?" the girl asked. "Can you change anyone?"

Izla nodded. "I can, but it's not something I do often."

Her eyes widened, and she smiled. "Can you change me?"

Izla arched her brow. "Change you into what? Why would you want to change?" The mermaid was beautiful. Her long hair fell to the middle of her back, and her skin was flawless. Mermaids had that in common with fairies.

"Can you change me into a human?"

Izla narrowed her eyes. "Why would you want to be a human? You know humans are mortal, right?"

The girl's head bobbed up and down, and her hair floated around her face. "Being mortal would be better than living down here."

"What's your name?"

"Marina."

Izla tilted her head. "Well, Marina, what is so bad about living down here?"

"Look around," she said, holding her hands out to the sides. "It is so boring down here. Half the time it's too hard to see because of the dirt getting stirred around."

Izla wasn't convinced. Turning a mermaid into a human would probably end up getting her into trouble. Izla looked down at the ocean floor. All she could see were a few plants and shells. She could imagine it getting boring. Her mouth turned down. She was still wearing her green dress. She must look ridiculous with her dress and tail.

"There is something else," Marina said, glancing down at her hands. "There is this man... I've fallen in love with him, and I cannot be with him if I am a mermaid."

Izla smiled. It had been a while since she had helped two people fall in love. "Oh? Is he in love with you as well?"

"Oh no," she said, shaking her head. "He doesn't even know I exist. Literally."

"Then, how can you be in love with him?"

"I know it's silly," she said, ducking her head. "I've been watching him for a while now. He is the most handsome creature I've ever seen."

Izla took a deep breath through her nose and frowned when her nostrils filled with water. Thankfully, it felt natural. Little bubbles filled her nose, and she resisted the urge to rub at it. Izla was all about people falling in love, but she would have to make sure the man was good if she was going to try to help.

"I'll do anything if you just turn me human," Marina pleaded. "I can give you gold or jewels."

"What if he isn't everything you imagine? You can't judge a person by their appearance."

"Yes, I know," Marina admitted. "I am sure he is good. I can tell from watching him. And you must know him. I saw you speaking with him. I believe he is a sailor."

"Oh," Izla said, taken off guard. She didn't know Thane's friend, but Thane only surrounded himself with good people. The man must be safe. But what could she ask for payment? A mermaid wouldn't take something for free. Mermaids were mistrusting and usually mischievous. She would have to make Marina think she was giving something really important, or she might think Izla was up to something.

"Name a price. Anything."

"Your voice."

Marina blinked. "My voice?"

"Yes. You give me your voice, and I will give you legs." Izla regretted her words immediately. How would the girl get someone to fall in love with her if she couldn't speak?

Marina narrowed her eyes. "That's all?"

"All?" Izla asked. What had she been expecting?

The mermaid crossed her arms. "That can't be all there is. What is the catch? I want to be prepared."

Izla wished she could pace and think, but she was having enough trouble staying afloat and talking at the same time. "If the man you love falls in love and marries anyone but you, you will have a broken heart and turn into sea foam."

Marina's mouth turned up in a stunning smile. "That seems fair."

Izla wanted to shake her head. She would have turned her human to help her find love for free, but that wasn't a mermaid's way. She wouldn't have come up with such ridiculous terms if she wasn't confident in her matchmaking abilities. Marina and Thane's friend were as good as married.

Thane took an enormous bite of toast and shrugged at Sebby's questioning glances. He had no idea what Izla was up to. They walked down the beach, following her. After eating a huge dinner the night before, Sebby and Thane had gone to bed early. They both felt better than the day before, but neither one of them wanted to be out here walking down the beach with Izla. She said it was important, or he wouldn't have come.

King Henan had allowed Sebby to keep his memory—so long as he promised to never tell anyone about the mermaids. The other crew members had been made to believe they all washed ashore in the storm, and none of them seemed to suspect that wasn't true. They were all sent home with enough gold to keep them comfortable until they found new jobs. King Henan believed in caring for people.

Sebby's father was in the market for a new ship, so Sebby was going to stay here until his father returned. Thane couldn't wait to take him on a tour of the surrounding villages. This was the first time they would get to spend time together off the ship.

Izla was walking so fast she was going to lose them if she ever turned from a straight course. He wondered what she was getting them into.

"A lot of strange things have happened in the last two days, but the oddest has to be finding out you are a fairy," Sebby said. "Not only that, but a prince."

Thane stumbled over a piece of driftwood and sighed. "You understand why I didn't tell you, right?"

"Yeah, I get it. I probably wouldn't tell, either. If you had, my father would have been nervous about letting you on the ship."

"That's how it goes. When people know who I am, they never stop staring at me. It's uncomfortable."

"Any idea where your sister is taking us?"

Thane shook his head. "None. Once Izla gets something in her head, you might as well go with it, because she will not leave you alone until you do."

Izla stopped and waited for them. They picked up their pace and hurried toward her.

"Sebby?" she said. "I think I heard something over there." She pointed past a pile of rocks twenty feet away. "Do you think you can go check?"

Sebby glanced at him, and Thane just rolled his eyes. Why would she send Sebby to investigate a noise when he was the one without magic? Izla was up to something. Sebby nodded and walked toward the rocks.

Thane crossed his arms and turned to Izla. "What are you doing?"

Izla put a finger to her lip. "Shh!"

"No. He's my friend. What are you doing?"

"Just wait a moment," she whispered. "It will be worth it."

Thane looked up at the clouds and shook his head. He couldn't think of any reason for Izla's behavior.

"Don't be so dramatic. Your friend is fine."

Thane's eyes narrowed as he studied her. "He better be. What's with the necklace?"

Izla touched the orangish pink locket that was hanging around her neck. It sparkled and almost seemed to glow. "It's nothing."

"Is it magic?"

"Don't worry about it."

He opened his mouth to say something, then shut it when Sebby came running back to them.

His eyes were wide, and he was moving fast. "There is a woman over there," he said, glancing over his shoulder. "She must have washed ashore during the storm. I tried to get her to come with me, but she won't."

Thane frowned at his sister. Her eyes were sparkling. She had to be involved.

"Let's go," Izla said, grabbing her blue skirts and rushing toward the rocks. Thane and Sebby rushed behind her.

A young woman with long black hair and wide eyes sat on the sand. Her dress was dirty and wet with a few tears in it. When she saw them, she got to her feet and tipped.

Sebby hurried over and helped her right herself. "Careful. Are you hurt?"

The girl shook her head.

"Can you walk?"

She bit her lip and put one foot in front of the other. Her legs shook, and she fell into Sebby. She grabbed hold of his arms to keep herself up.

"You better carry her to the castle," Izla said, her cheeks red with excitement.

Thane glared at her.

"I'm going to pick you up now," Sebby said softly. "Is that alright?"

The girl looked from Sebby to Thane to Izla. After a small encouraging nod from Izla, the girl shrugged. Sebby lifted her up like it was nothing. The girl peeked at Thane and then looked away.

This was ridiculous. Izla must be up to her matchmaking again and had her eyes set on this poor girl and Sebby. If the girl was really hurt or in danger, Izla would have used magic to take her to the castle. She wanted Sebby to carry her. He would protest, but Sebby didn't seem to mind.

The walk to the castle was slow. Sebby might be strong, but it was still a long way to go while holding someone. When they got to the castle, Izla called for servants to go prepare a room for the girl. She led Sebby to one of the best rooms and had him place the girl on the bed.

The girl's eyes were wide as they took in the room. When she spotted the crystal chandelier, her mouth made the shape of an o.

"What's your name?" Sebby asked her.

She shrugged.

His eyes narrowed. "You don't know?"

She touched her throat and shook her head.

"You can't speak?"

The girl frowned and shook her head again.

Izla grabbed Thane and Sebby by the arms and led them to the door. "I'll get her settled in. Don't go far." She shoved them out and closed the door.

Sebby ran a hand over his black curls. "That was weird."

"Yeah, it was, but that's Izla for you. I know she's plotting something."

"What do you mean?"

Thane rubbed his chin. "It doesn't matter. Just don't let Izla force you into anything."

"Like what?"

"You know I told you she likes to make matches? Well, I think she's got her eye on you and that girl."

Sebby stared at him blankly for a moment. "She's the mermaid."

"Who?"

"That girl in there. She's the one that saved us."

Thane's lips formed a tight line, and he put a hand to his head. He wanted to say that Sebby must be wrong, but something told him it was true. Nothing good could come of this. The sea king would be furious if he found out about it, and his anger wouldn't be good for any port cities or ships.

Sebby put a hand on Thane's shoulder. "You look worried."

Thane glanced at him. "I am worried. The sea king doesn't like his people to interact with land dwellers. It goes against everything he stands for. With any luck, this girl isn't anyone significant enough for him to notice her disappearance."

"What should we do?"

"I doubt there is anything we can do. If Izla cast the spell, she's the only one that can easily undo it."

"Maybe the sea king won't find out. We could take the girl far away from the ocean."

"We might have to. It could be unsafe for anyone who helps her."

"Unless they never go by the ocean. If he's the sea king, can he do anything on land?"

Thane sighed. "Not if they were far enough from the water. He could still get angry and cause a lot of damage to the cities along the ocean."

"Thane!" Ava called, barreling toward them. Her long hair and pink dress flew behind her.

Thane tried to look natural. He didn't want Ava or Sebby to see how his heart sped up when Ava appeared. He wanted to deny it, but she had been on his mind for years. Whenever he dwelled on her for too long, he forced himself to think about something else.

She smiled when she reached them. "You are hard to find."

"Sorry. Izla has been... being Izla."

She nodded in understanding. "I just wanted to say goodbye before I go back to Thurin."

Thane swallowed. "Back already? You haven't been around lately."

Ava peered down at her feet. "Princess Rose is a lot of work. She is the most curious ten-year-old I've ever met. If there is something to get into, she gets into it."

"Lily and Zina can't keep her in line?"

She glanced up. "Not really. No one can. Last week she was climbing the wall of the castle. It will be a miracle if she makes it to her seventeenth birthday to prick her finger."

"Still, you've stayed away for a long time. It only takes a second to pop in and say hello."

She gave him a half smile. "Yes, and none of you have popped in to see us."

"I guess that's true." Thane wanted to keep talking, to keep her there, but he couldn't think of anything to say. "Well, good luck with the princess."

"Thank you. Do you know where I can find Izla?"

He pointed at the door behind them. "She's in there." He moved away from the door as Ava knocked.

The door cracked open, and Izla peeked out. "Ava! Come in." She walked inside, and the door closed again.

Sebby grinned. "Now that I know you're a prince, does that mean I can't tease you anymore?"

They stared down the hall, and Thane shook his head. "I doubt I can stop you."

"Probably not. So, why are you in denial about liking that girl?"

Thane rubbed the back of his neck. "I keep telling myself I don't, but I am to the point that I know I'm lying to myself."

"Are you going to do something about it?"

"No."

"Why not?"

"I've known her forever. She's never going to think of me as anything but her best friend's annoying brother."

Sebby laughed. "Maybe not. She came to say goodbye to you."

"I think she was coming to say goodbye to Izla but ran into us and thought she might as well say something."

"So, you aren't even going to try?"

Thane ran a hand over his face. "No. If I did, she would probably get scared and never come around again. Then, Izla would badger me into telling her why, and I would never have peace."

"Interesting."

Thane stopped walking and turned to him. "What?"

"I always thought princes were brave, not chicken gizzards."

He narrowed his eyes. "I will not deny it when it comes to women. Put me in front of a dragon, and I'll barely break a sweat, but you don't have to charm a dragon."

Sebby nodded. "Maybe as a prince you get used to thinking things always go your way, so that scares you away from things that might go wrong."

Thane chuckled. "You obviously don't know enough about my life if you think things go my way. I'm the one in the family that everyone shakes their head over. Ask Izla. I'm sure she would love to give you a list of my failures."

"You've told me your sister is a matchmaker. Why hasn't she found someone for you?"

"Because she knows better. She would never try to match me with one of her friends, even if the notion came into her head."

Sebby tilted his head. "Perhaps I should talk to her. I could team up with her and help find you a match."

"If I were you, I would avoid Izla," he said with a mischievous smile. "You are the one she is focusing her matchmaking on this time, and whatever Izla wants, she gets."

Chapter 12

Izla stared at Marina as the girl sat at a desk and wrote frantically with a quill. It might have been a mistake to take her voice. It was going to complicate things. She would give it back, but that would make the girl untrusting of her. Mermaids were complex creatures. Marina shoved the paper into Izla's hand.

Izla cleared her throat and read out loud, "There has been a misunderstanding. It is the man with the reddish brown hair that I love." Izla lowered the paper and glared at Marina. "Seriously? Thane?"

The girl nodded.

"That changes everything. Thane is not a human."

The girl's eyes widened.

Izla sighed. "Thane is a fairy, and my brother. What to do... This is unexpected, to say the least." She began pacing across the blue carpet, her hands clasped behind her back. Who would look at Thane and Sebby and choose Thane? That wasn't fair. Her brother was attractive, she supposed. He was a fairy, and Sebby wasn't, so it made sense he would catch her eye.

Marina watched her pace. Izla ignored the girl's look of distress. She had every reason to be upset. There was no way Izla was going to help Marina win Thane. She might feel comfortable manipulating some people, but not her brother. At least, not to this extent.

"Any chance of you changing your mind?" she finally asked. Marina shook her head.

"What spell did I use when I turned you human?" she muttered. "I can't remember if I tied it to Sebby or to the person you were in love with." She really needed to take better notes, and probably not act in the moment. "Stay here. I'll be back." It was a silly command. Marina wasn't going anywhere. She hadn't figured out how to walk yet.

Izla tore through the castle in search of Thane.

"Izla!" King Henan called from behind her. She turned and waited for him to catch up to her. He adjusted his golden crown and smiled. "I need a favor."

"Oh?" she asked, trying not to look impatient.

"King Evard of Brenun has finally lost patience with his son."

"I'm not surprised," Izla said, suddenly interested. She had been meaning to interfere with King Evard's son for some time, but she'd been so busy with other things. Thane rounded the corner and joined them.

King Henan smiled. "I think some of us kings are having the same problems," he said, glancing at Thane.

Thane folded his arms. "What do you mean?"

"King Evard has given Prince Alveen a time limit on finding a woman to marry."

"He sounds like a tyrant," Thane said.

Izla smiled. Her brother and father argued about Thane getting married at least once a year.

"Izla, that is what I need from you."

Thane snorted. "You want Izla to marry Prince Alveen?"

Izla tilted her head. "Ha ha."

King Henan just shook his head. "I want Izla to go make sure Prince Alveen ends up with a suitable bride. We can't have him choosing an unsuitable match out of pressure from his father. That would be detrimental to the kingdom. I've seen the harm that comes when mortals choose poor partners and ruin kingdoms more often than I would like."

"I would love to help," Izla said. "I can start next month?"

"Today. Now. I told the king you were coming to help council him."

Izla's mouth hung open for a moment. "But, Father, I'm in the middle of something."

"I have heard about the girl you all rescued. Thane can deal with her. I need you to go now to make sure the prince doesn't end up married before you can act."

"That won't happen," she protested. "Prince Alveen has put it off this long. He isn't going to rush into something."

King Henan rubbed his chin. "Perhaps, but I won't risk it. I want you to go now."

Izla sighed. She could tell her father would not be swayed. "Fine. Thane, the girl's name is Marina."

"How do you know?"

She rolled her eyes. "I gave her a piece of paper and had her write things down. It's not that difficult of a thing to do. You need to go help her. She's sitting at a desk, and she can't walk."

King Henan frowned. "That's unfortunate. I'm sure Thane and his friend can devote their time to her."

Izla wished her father would leave so she could tell Thane more.

"I'll go see how she's doing," Thane said, walking away.

Her father opened his arms, and she stepped into his hug. "You better go now. We will miss you until you return."

"I'll miss you as well. I need to give Thane a hug."

His eyebrow rose. "I haven't seen that in a while."

Izla ran to her brother and wrapped her arms around him. His eyes widened in surprise. She leaned in and whispered as fast as she could, "Marina is a mermaid. I gave her legs because I thought she was in love with Sebby, but it turns out she's in love with you. Try to get her to fall in love with Sebby and him with her, or she could end up turning into sea foam."

Thane pushed her away and opened his mouth to speak and then shut it.

Izla patted him on the cheek. "You will do fine."

Thane gritted his teeth. "I can't even think of a bad enough curse word for you."

Izla smiled. She hadn't thought he would take it well.

"I don't know what you said to make your brother turn pale, and I don't want to," King Henan said from a distance. "Hurry along, Izla. King Evard is waiting."

Sebby sat on a large blue chair in the corner of Thane's room and stared at Thane, his eyes as wide as plates.

"I know," Thane said, pacing across the floor. "Izla can be crazy sometimes."

Sebby leaned forward. "So... I... she... I mean..."

"Yeah, that's about what I thought." Thane hated to fling his friend into something like this.

"I don't get it. Why would she turn into sea foam? And why would the two of us need to fall in love to prevent it?"

"No idea. I'm guessing Izla had a plan that didn't go the way she wanted. She does a lot of spontaneous things without thinking them through. She didn't have time to tell me everything."

"Why would she think the mermaid was in love with anyone? We don't know her."

"I don't know."

"If she's in love with you, how am I supposed to compete? You are a fairy prince, for goodness's sake."

"She's not in love with me," Thane said, rubbing the back of his neck. "She doesn't know me. It's just some weird fancy she must have. I wonder if she is the reason I've felt like I was being watched when I'm near the water."

"What about the sea foam?"

"When mermaids die, they turn into sea foam or something like that."

"So, she'll die if she doesn't fall in love with me?" Sebby asked, pointing at himself. "No pressure."

"I doubt Izla would really let it go that far."

"I'm not against trying," Sebby admitted. "I told you, I've seen her before. Still, I don't know what she's like. I'm not daft enough to think that a beautiful woman has a beautiful personality. Where is she?"

"Izla said she's sitting at a desk in the room we took her to. She doesn't know how to walk."

Sebby jumped up. "I'll go help her."

Before Thane could speak, Sebby was out the door. Thane thought about following, but if Marina thought she was in love with him, he should probably try to stay out of the way. If the girl was smart, she would fall in love with Sebby. Sebby had a lot going for him. He was strong and kind, which was what Thane assumed a woman wanted. Those were two qualities that didn't always go together.

This would be fine. Thane wiped the sweat from his brow. All he wanted was to avoid the mermaid. Talking to women was hard, and it would be even more difficult knowing she had a thing for him. What type of person decided they were in love from only seeing someone? He sighed. This would be a long week.

Izla watched the king and prince stare at each other from across a large oak table. Both men had sandy brown hair and green eyes. If it wasn't for the thirty-year age difference and thirty extra pounds on the king, they could be twins. She sat at the middle of the table and tried to think. She had been here listening to the two of them argue for over an hour, and nothing good was coming from it.

"You have gone too long without getting married!" King Evard roared. "If you don't settle down, the people of the kingdom will see you as irresponsible."

Prince Alveen gripped the table's edge with his hands and glared at his father. "So, you would have me married to appease the people? You and Mother loved each other. Don't you want that for me?"

King Evard leaned back in his chair and placed his thumb and middle finger over the bridge of his nose, rubbing it. "You know I want that for you, but you are not trying."

"I am. I just cannot imagine happiness with any of the snooty women you keep introducing me to."

The king stood and pointed his finger into the air. "They have been from the best families!"

The prince's mouth turned down. "By whose standards?"

"Alveen, I swear—"

"If I may?" Izla interrupted.

The king sank into his chair and motioned for her to go on.

"I believe that this can be easily solved."

Prince Alveen sniffed. "I don't see how."

"If you both agree to have a respectful attitude and compromise, I believe I can give you a solution."

The king crossed his arms. "I can compromise."

Alveen shrugged apologetically. "I can try, but I'm not promising anything."

"Alright," Izla said, standing. "The prince might do well with a match to a woman that is not noble."

"I don't like the sound of this," the king huffed.

"But you want your son to marry and be happy."

"Yes."

"What if you hold a ball?" Izla said, her eyes lighting up. "Invite every woman in the kingdom. Old, young, noble, and common. Have the prince dance with all of them. At the end of the ball, the prince may choose the woman that is the best suited to him."

The king jiggled his knee and put a finger to his chin. The prince blinked a few times, and his frown softened. She gave them a moment to process what she had said.

The prince cocked his head. "I can't fall in love in one night."

"No, but at least you might meet someone you could come to fall in love with."

"I suppose."

The king cleared his throat. "But what if he chooses a commoner?"

"Then, at least he will have chosen someone."

The king glanced at the prince. "I can agree with that. Son?"

Alveen nodded. "Let's try it."

"Not try," the king said. "You will choose a woman, and you will court her."

The prince gritted his teeth. "Fine."

"Wonderful," Izla said, bringing her hands together. "Now let's start planning!"

Thane and Sebby led Marina through the busy market street. Vendors of every kind were selling anything a person could want. Marina's eyes were wide with every new discovery. It had been six days since Izla had brought Marina here, and she was still getting used to walking. Sebby stayed close in case she slipped.

Thane was doing his best to ignore her, and Sebby was devoting every moment to her. It wasn't surprising. Mermaids were fascinating creatures, and it was said they could make the hardest mortal fall desperately in love. Many a sailor had been trapped and killed because of their devotion to a mermaid.

That wasn't fair. Those stories had never been validated. Stories like that were told by mortals to entertain themselves the same way they talked about fairies. Besides, Marina was not trying to get Sebby's attention. She kept trying to get his. It was annoying, but Thane didn't know what to do about it. She kept stumbling in front of him, causing him to catch her. He wondered what would happen if he let her fall on her face.

He sighed. He didn't know why he was having unkind thoughts. The girl seemed nice enough. Of course, she couldn't talk, so that could be the reason. It would be nice if Izla could pop in and tell them why she couldn't talk.

They stopped in front of a plump, smiling woman selling pastries. They smelled heavenly, but Thane would not act pleasantly. It was his plan to let Marina think he was dull and then she would have to switch her attention to Sebby.

"Should we get something?" Sebby asked.

Thane shrugged. "If you want to, go ahead." Sebby talked to the woman, and Thane studied the crowd. This was one of the best markets of the year. It brought people from all over, and it was the first time Thane had seen it. He had been missing out.

He glanced down when someone took hold of his arm and saw Marina smiling up at him. He gave her a bored smile, then yawned. Her mouth turned down for a moment and then back up into a smile.

"Here you are," Sebby said, handing her a pastry. She released Thane and took a bite. Her smile grew. It must be good. "Hey, isn't that your friend?" Sebby asked, pointing ahead.

Thane squinted through the sun and smiled. Ava was bartering with a woman selling cloth. She was wearing a tan peasant dress and a ridiculously large floppy hat. She must not want anyone to know she was a fairy. He didn't blame her. He was also wearing the clothing of a commoner to avoid notice.

A man with a large brown mustache and thick sideburns tapped Ava on the shoulder. She turned, and he began talking to her. Thane frowned. It looked like he was attempting to sell her a necklace. Ava shook her head and turned back to the woman with the cloth. The man tapped on her again. She said something over her shoulder, then turned away.

Thane took a step forward, and Sebby put a hand on his shoulder. "Don't. You don't need to cause a scene."

Thane nodded. The man grabbed Ava's arm and turned her to face him. She tried to pull her arm free, but he wasn't letting go. Thane sprinted in their direction, and just as he was about to reach them, Ava shoved her palm into the man's face. The man stumbled back and put a hand over his bleeding nose. He muttered some obscenities and disappeared into the crowd.

"That was glorious," Thane said, staring at Ava.

She rubbed her hand and smiled. "Thanks. I thought about turning him into a toad, but that was much more fulfilling."

"Have you been to this market before?"

"Yes, I come every year. Lily and Zina hate it, so I come alone to get quality material for Princess Rose. I love being in the middle of the crowd. There is something exciting about so many people gathered together."

"How often do you have to bloody someone's nose?"

Ava giggled. "That's only the second time. It hurt worse than the last time I did it."

Thane took her hand and studied it. "It looks fine."

She smiled. "Thanks, Mr. Compassionate."

He smiled back. "Sorry."

"Should I go say hello to your friends? They are looking at us."

"Are they?" he asked, not turning to see.

"Yes. The woman who was with Izla the other day looks irritated."

Thane straightened his back and smiled. An idea was forming. It was a stupid idea, but it could work. "Will you do me a favor? I'll owe you one."

"Sure. What?"

"Will you let me kiss you?" Thane's heart pounded in his chest. This really was a bad idea. He could end up regretting it for eternity.

Ava's eyebrows almost raised off her head. "What?"

"That girl over there, she's part of Izla's silly matchmaking scheme. My friend Sebby was the intended target, but she seems to have something for me."

Ava tilted her head. "I see. So, you want to make her jealous?"

"No, no, nothing like that. I just want her to realize nothing is going to happen between her and me." He knew it sounded pathetic, and he also knew he wanted to kiss Ava way more than he should.

Ava looked troubled. She glanced from him to Marina, then back to him.

"Never mind," he laughed nervously. "It's a stupid idea. Probably wouldn't work."

"But it might," she said, taking a step toward him. She locked her hands around his neck and gazed into his eyes. "How long are we talking? Five seconds?"

Thane just nodded. His stomach tumbled, and he worried he might throw up or pass out. He placed his arms around her waist.

"I'll count," she whispered. She went up onto her toes and pressed her lips to his. All the tension of the last few days faded as he held Ava in his arms. The roaring sound of the market disappeared, and all he could think about was Ava. She was all he wanted to think about. He had tried to push it away for years, but he loved her. This kiss was going on for much longer than five seconds. This was the worst idea he'd ever had. Now he would never get her out of his head.

Ava pulled away, and he gave her a half smile. "You are terrible at counting."

She nodded. "I really am." She turned, and he watched her disappear into the crowd. He ran his hand through his hair. Being immortal meant he could spend eternity with a hole in his heart.

Chapter 13

The man who owned the bakery was going to wonder about Izla. She had been coming in at least twice a day for the last week. The bakery was the only place in the village with a place to sit and eat something, so here she was again. She sat at a small table with a cup of cider and a large piece of bread covered in jam.

It would probably be alright if she went home, but she wouldn't feel like her job was finished until she saw Prince Alveen fall in love with a suitable woman. The happiness of a kingdom depended on it. She had been lurking around the kingdom hoping to find a woman that would be acceptable. So far, no one stood out as being better than another.

The door to the bakery opened, and three finely dressed women entered, followed by a young servant woman. Izla's heart sped up. Perhaps one of these women would be suitable. One was older and must be the mother, and two were the perfect age for the prince. Neither one was stunningly pretty like their servant, but they were both passable.

The man behind the counter smiled when they entered. "Ah, hello, Lady Anna. What can I get you on this fine day?"

"Three cups of hot cider and a loaf of bread," the woman snapped. "Make it fast. We are exhausted."

"Yes, of course," the man said, scurrying to serve them.

Izla frowned. The mother wasn't pleasant.

"It is so cramped in here," one daughter said. "And it's almost as hot as outside."

The mother pulled out a fan and began waving in front of herself. "Yes, you would think the owner would try to make this place more comfortable for their customers."

The baker frowned as he wrapped a loaf of bread in some brown paper. Izla sighed. She was going to have to keep looking. These women were already full of themselves. Give them a crown and they would be unbearable. They sat at a table on the opposite side of the small room and waited for their cider.

The servant girl stood in the corner, holding a pile of packages, and she stared out at nothing. Izla imagined her life wasn't great, working for these people.

The baker brought them steaming cups of cider, and no one at the table acknowledged him. He turned to the servant. "Ella, you are welcome to put your packages on one of the empty tables."

Lady Anna glared at the baker. "She's fine. Do not speak to her." Her daughters giggled, and Ella's mouth turned down ever so slightly.

Now Izla was irritated. Who did this woman think she was?

"Ew, this cider is too bitter," one girl said, shoving her cup across the table. "And it's too hot. Who serves hot cider at this time of year?"

"I'm not paying for that," Lady Anna said, sipping her own cider.

The baker pursed his lips and nodded. He returned to his place behind the counter and stared out the window.

"Let's go," the youngest of the women said, tossing her brown hair over her shoulder. "It smells funny in here, and I want to try on my new hat."

The three of them stood and shuffled out of the bakery, not bothering to pay. Lady Anna turned to the baker and paused in the doorway. "We will be lenient today and not tell the rest of the town what poor service we experienced here. Ella, grab the bread and come." She slammed the door behind her.

The baker's face turned red, and Ella rushed to the counter to grab the bread. She shifted the packages to free one hand. The baker picked up the loaf and placed it on top of her pile.

"Thank you, sir," she said. "Sorry about my stepmother. I have a few coins saved at home. I'll bring them to pay for the bread."

Izla went from mad to furious. That woman was her stepmother? What a horrid woman.

"No, Ella," the baker said. "I'm doing just fine. You keep your money." He walked around the counter and put something in Ella's apron pocket. He winked. "Some sweets for later. Don't tell your stepsisters."

Ella smiled, thanked the man, and left.

Izla tapped her lip as she thought. She stood and walked to the counter. "Who was that atrocious woman?"

The baker rolled his eyes. "That is Lady Anna. She married a rich man some years ago and has been the bane of my existence ever since. Her husband was a decent fellow. She didn't show her real colors until he passed. I could ignore her if it wasn't for poor Ella. Her husband wasn't in the ground for two days when the woman made Ella her servant."

"That's awful," Izla muttered.

He rubbed his smooth chin. "It is. She's the sweetest girl you will ever meet. I've never seen her say or do anything that wasn't kind and thoughtful."

"Interesting," Izla said, watching the family from the window as they crossed the street.

"I would hire Ella to come work for me, but I couldn't pay her enough to be free of those people. I always hope something good will come to her."

Izla smiled. "I think something very good is about to come to her."

"Oh?" the man asked.

Izla clasped her hands together and rested her elbows on the counter. Not very princessly, but she wasn't concerned with that at the moment.

"I have a feeling I can trust you. Can I?"

He leaned forward. "Yes, of course."

Izla pulled on Prince Alveen's arm. "You need to hurry!"

"Why won't you tell me where we are going?" he asked, as they rushed through the thick trees. "How is tromping

150

through the forest going to help anything? And why did I have to dress like a commoner?"

"Most people don't argue with fairies. Especially with the daughter of King Henan, who controls everything." It was a lie. Plenty of people argued with her, but she didn't have time.

"Very well," the prince said, matching her pacing. If Tom the baker had done his part, they would run into Tom and Ella any moment.

Alveen stopped, causing her to halt. "I hear voices."

Izla made a show of listening. "I think you are right. It sounds like it's just through the trees. Shall we check?"

He frowned. "I'm not sure. What if it's bandits? I have heard of some in these parts."

"We can walk softly and peek," Izla said, forcing herself to go forward cautiously. She could see Tom in the distance. He stood with his hands on his hips, staring up into a tree. "Oh, look," she whispered to the prince. "Isn't that the baker from the nearby village?"

Prince Alveen shrugged. "I've never been to the bakery. My father is a bit bossy about what I'm allowed to do."

Izla nodded. She was glad her father was more lenient with his children than most rulers. "I'm sure it's him. Let's see what he's doing way out here."

"I would like to know what *we* are doing out here," the prince said, following her.

"Tom! Is that you?" Izla asked, walking into a small clearing.

Tom turned and acted surprised. "Nice to see you!" he said. "We seem to have a bit of a situation."

"Anything we can help with?" Alveen asked. Izla smiled. She liked Alveen more than most royals. He might complain on occasion, but he was helpful when called on.

"My cat got stuck up in this tree. A kind young woman offered to help, but now she is stuck, and the cat climbed down. I would go up there, but I'm not as young as I used to be."

Alveen and Izla peered up into the tree. Izla hid a smile. Ella's face was red from embarrassment. She held her dress in a way to keep it modest. Izla should have thought of that. Climbing trees in a dress wasn't the best idea. Still, this was perfect. She had made sure the cat was positioned just right so Ella would step between two branches and get her foot stuck. She put a spell on the tree so that there was no way Ella would get down on her own.

"I'll be right up," Alveen said. He climbed up the tree in a snap. Maybe King Evard wasn't as bossy as Izla had supposed. The prince definitely knew how to climb a tree.

Izla waved her wand and pointed at Ella's foot, allowing it to come free when the prince tugged on it.

"Come," Izla whispered, touching Tom's elbow. They took a few steps back, and Izla made them both disappear and reappear in Tom's bakery.

"Wow," Tom said, putting a hand to his head. "I knew fairies could do that, but still, it's amazing."

Izla grinned. "The obvious place for them to come will be here. I'm going to go follow them to make sure."

"You get them here, and I will be ready," Tom said.

Izla took herself back into the woods but made herself invisible. Alveen was helping Ella climb down the last part of the tree.

"Thank you," Ella said, pushing a stray blonde lock of her hair behind her ear.

Alveen smiled, making him look even more handsome. "You're welcome."

Izla smiled. The two of them really would make a delightful couple.

Ella's head moved from side to side, and she looked panicked. "Where is Tom?"

Alveen frowned and scanned the area. "That's odd. I was with someone as well. Where could they have gone?"

Ella placed her hands on her cheeks. "I am going to be in so much trouble."

"Why is that?"

"I shouldn't have come here. My stepmother is going to be angry."

Alveen gestured toward the trees. "Let's hurry and get you back then."

They began walking in the wrong direction. Izla rolled her eyes. She pulled out her wand and gently pushed them toward the village. She walked behind them and waited for them to talk. Neither one of them seemed to have anything to say.

After a few minutes, Alveen turned to her. "I'm Al. What's your name?"

"Ella."

"That's a nice name."

Ella gave him a half smile, and they kept walking.

Izla walked impatiently behind them. She could understand being shy. She assumed Ella was, but she knew Alveen wasn't. Perhaps he felt like he was better than her because she was a commoner.

Five minutes of silence passed, and Izla was ready to act. Before she could grab her wand, she stumbled over a tree root. She caught herself before she could fall, but she must have made a noise because Alveen and Ella spun around and looked around.

She held her breath and stood still.

Alveen drew his sword and gently pushed Ella behind him. Ella's eyes were wide as she scanned the trees. Izla covered her mouth and resisted the urge to giggle. She felt ridiculous standing right in front of them, trying not to breathe too loud.

"I see nothing," he said, replacing his sword. "Let's hurry, just in case." He grabbed Ella's hand, and they scurried away.

If Izla ran after them, they would hear her. She decided it would be better to go back and wait with Tom. She would stay invisible. Appearing in the bakery was faster than walking anyway. When she got there, Tom was in the back, whistling.

"Tom, I'm here," she called back. "They are on their way. I'm going to stay invisible in the corner."

"Alright," he called back. "I'm almost ready."

The middle table was covered in a white tablecloth with a candle in the middle. It wasn't overly fancy, but this was a bakery after all. Tom came out carrying two fancy silver cups and placed them on the table, then he peeked out the back window.

"Here they come."

Izla clasped her hands together. "Make sure they stop here."

Tom opened the back door. "Come in!" he called.

A moment later, Alveen and Ella entered the bakery. Alveen was telling Ella something, and she laughed. Izla smiled.

"Where did you go?" Ella asked Tom.

Tom scratched his head. "Oh... well, uh... the cat ran this way, so I followed him."

"I need to hurry home," Ella said.

"Oh, I forgot," Tom said. "Lady Anna came by and said one of your sisters tried to make a cake and the entire house was filled with smoke. They are going to stay at her sister's house until tomorrow. She told me to tell you to air out the house if you came by." He sounded rehearsed, but it would do. Izla smiled. She'd enjoyed causing the cake to catch fire.

"Oh," Ella said, looking thoughtful. "I guess I don't have to hurry."

"Wonderful," Tom said. "I had some people make a reservation for dessert here, and they canceled. I can't let the food go to waste. Why don't the two of you sit down, and I'll bring it out?"

Ella looked at the table. "I better not."

"Why not?" Alveen asked.

Ella swallowed nervously and rubbed her arm. "Well, I suppose I could stay for a few minutes."

"Great," Tom said. "Sit there, and I'll bring the food."

Alveen pulled a chair out for Ella, and she sat down. Izla felt a little guilty spying on them, but not enough to leave.

Tom brought out two plates. Both had a large cinnamon pastry covered in icing. He poured them both a cup of something and went to the backroom.

Izla sighed. The dessert looked messy. This could go poorly. Tom came back and gave them knives and forks. That was better.

"Do you live nearby?" Alveen asked.

Ella nodded. "Less than a mile. And you?"

"Further. Come to think of it, I don't really know where I live."

Izla rolled her eyes. That didn't sound impressive. Alveen didn't know where he was because Izla had brought them from the castle to the forest, but the way he said it would make Ella think he was a bit thick.

She scrunched her forehead. "I can try to help you find your way."

Izla shrugged. Ella was sweet. She didn't seem to be judging him.

"I'm sure I'll figure it out. I came here with... a friend, and she seems to have run off."

"Are you new to the village?"

Alveen nodded. "You might say that. It's my first time in this area."

They started talking, and Izla quickly became bored. It was hard to find mortals interesting for long. It was probably a good time to go see how Thane was doing.

Chapter 14

The rolling sound of the creek had Thane in a tired stupor. He stared at the rushing water without really seeing it. He should return to the castle, but he didn't know what would be waiting for him there. When he had turned to find Sebby and Marina at the market, they were nowhere to be seen. He didn't know how to take that. It could mean so many things. Like a coward, he had slunk over to the water to sit and think.

Kissing Ava had been the most amazing experience of his life, and he'd asked her to do it as a favor. Who knew what she was thinking now? Would it be awkward next time he saw her? Probably. She must think he was a fool. He sure did.

"Hey," Sebby said, sitting on the ground next to him.

Thane threw a rock into the water. "You disappeared."

A low chuckle came from Sebby. "Yes, well, someone had to chase after Marina when she went running off. You are not her favorite person at the moment."

"That was my goal. It worked?"

"It made her mad. I don't know about anything else. She locked herself in her room, and she won't come out."

Thane threw another rock. "And I'm supposed to feel bad? She has no claim on me. She doesn't even know me. I can't believe Izla left me in this mess. What am I supposed to do?"

Sebby shook his head. "I don't know. I feel bad for her. She's young, and infatuations can be painful. I wish I could talk with her. I can tell she's smart. While you've been trying to avoid her, I've been playing games with her, and she has won all except the first time she plays, and she only just learned them. I'm not even letting her win."

"Why can't she fall for you?" he groaned.

Sebby threw his own rock. "I wish she would."

"Really?"

"Why not? She's smart and pretty." He grinned. "She has poor taste, but I'll forgive that."

Thane laughed. "Yeah, she does."

"So does Ava."

"I wish."

Sebby shoved him playfully on the shoulder. "I saw that kiss."

"Yeah, but you didn't hear me ask her to do it as a favor."

"A favor? She bought that?"

Thane let out a long sigh. "I don't really want to talk about it."

"Well, what are we going to do?"

"About Ava?"

Sebby shifted his weight. "About Marina."

"No idea. I wish Izla was here. She might be annoying with all of her matchmaking, but she usually does what she sets out to do. It's too bad messing with people's memories isn't ethical in these situations. We could just make her think she fell in love with you."

Sebby shook his head. "I wouldn't want that. If she falls for me, I want it to be for real."

"Just keep her away from me. Take her around the kingdom, but do it without me. Eventually, she'll see that nothing is going to happen between us, and she might give it up."

"I can do that."

"How did you find me out here?"

"Your father said you come out here sometimes."

Thane stiffened. "You talked to my father?"

"Yeah. He wanted to know why Marina came storming through the castle."

"What did you tell him?"

"I didn't tell him anything. One guard had been at the market, and when he saw Marina run off, he followed us. He told your father what happened."

Thane covered his face with his hands. "Oh no."

"Your father asked me to find you and tell you he wants to see you."

He stood. No use putting off the inevitable. "He's going to be mad."

"Why?"

Thane offered his hand, and Sebby grabbed it. He helped pull him to his feet. "As a prince, there are certain things a person should not do in public."

Sebby grinned. "Like kissing women?"

"Exactly."

"Your father doesn't seem like the angry type."

"He isn't. Not usually. Still, he knows how to let his children know when they have disappointed him. He's good at making me feel guilty without even saying anything."

They hurried to the castle, and Sebby left him in front of the throne room. Thane entered to find his father pacing across the floor.

King Henan turned and smiled. "Thane. There you are."

"What did you need?" Thane pursed his lips and waited for the lecture.

"You were kissing a girl in the middle of the market."

"Yes, sir."

His father clapped him on the back. "It's about time! Who is she?"

Thane arched his brow and frowned. "About time? Aren't you going to lecture me about inappropriate public behavior?"

The king laughed. "If you were one of your brothers, I would. I've been waiting for you to fall in love and take your place for a long time. Do you know how much relief I will have when you take over your part of the kingdom?"

"Whoa, whoa, whoa. You are getting ahead of yourself. Who says I've fallen in love?"

King Henan's smile fell. "What?" He straightened to his full height, and Thane had to force himself not to cower. When his father wanted to be intimidating, he was a master. "You don't mean to tell me you were kissing a girl you weren't in love with?"

"Can we talk about this later?"

"No. You better start explaining. Now."

Thane ran a hand over his eyes and held in a growl. "If you are going to get angry at anyone, it should be Izla."

"You can't blame your sister for your behavior."

"I agree," Izla said, popping in beside them.

His eyes narrowed. "For this, I can."

"Did Izla force you to kiss the girl?"

Izla's eyes widened. "You kissed Marina?"

"No! It was Ava, and it wasn't a genuine kiss."

The king's eyes lit up. "You kissed Ava?"

"It was just... I needed... I needed Marina to see it so she would move on and leave me alone."

Izla glared at him. "You used Ava?"

"No... Yes. No. It doesn't count as using because I explained it to her first."

King Henan shook his head. "This is not a good way to deal with a situation."

"I shouldn't be in this situation. Izla shouldn't have brought Marina here to begin with."

"How can you say that?" his father said. "You all saved her from a shipwreck. It would have been uncharitable to leave her there."

"Marina is a mermaid!" Thane said, a little too loud.

Izla shot him a dirty look.

King Henan's head slowly turned toward her. "Izla?"

Izla glared at Thane. "It's not as bad as it sounds. Thane is supposed to be helping her fall in love with Sebby."

The king ran a hand over his face. "Mermaids should not be falling in love with humans. That's how wars start."

Thane moved over to stand by the wall. With luck, his father would forget he was there. It wasn't likely. Izla would have it turned around and back on him, like usual.

Izla rolled her eyes. "Love has no boundaries."

"The sea king despises humans. He tolerates fairies, but only a little more than mortals."

She shrugged. "I don't see why he would suspect any of his mermaids to be here. If anyone is searching, it would be in the ocean."

"Even if you are right, her family is probably upset," the king said. He put his hand on Izla's shoulder. "I would be devastated if I couldn't find you."

"I'll send an anonymous message letting them know she is safe. Perhaps I should have her write it so they know it was her own choice."

Thane snorted. "That will fix it."

King Henan shot him a look. "Not now, Thane."

Of course.

"There is no time for this," Izla said. "I need to get back to helping Prince Alveen. I just wanted to check in."

"No," King Henana said, crossing his arms. "This isn't something we can ignore. Turn the girl back into a mermaid and send her home."

Izla looked down at her feet. "I... can't."

"Can't?" her father growled.

Thane wanted to smile. It wasn't often Izla looked ashamed, or that she was on the other side of their father's wrath.

She threw her hands into the air. "Alright, I admit it. I messed up this time. I thought Marina was in love with Sebby, and I wanted to help her. I turned her human, but I made her give me her voice. To weave the spell, I made it so she has to get Sebby to fall in love with her, or she will turn into sea foam. I thought it would be easy, but it turns out she was in love with Thane."

The king's eyebrows knit together. "Why would you do that? Why take her voice, and why sea foam?"

Izla kicked at the floor. "I wanted it to be a good story, and I thought it would be simple."

The king let out the longest sigh Thane had ever heard. Now was the part where Izla would get punished. Not that he wanted his sister to be unhappy, but it always seemed unfair the way she got away with everything.

"I suppose you did what you thought was best," the king said, wrapping Izla in a hug.

Thane's mouth hung open. "Are you serious?"

"I'm sure we can figure this out," his father said. "You go make sure things go smoothly with Prince Alveen, and Thane will fix this mess."

Thane wasn't a stomper, and he wasn't one to overreact, but this was beyond unfair.

"Thanks, Daddy," Izla said, kissing him on the cheek.

Thane glared at his sister. "So, I have to fix Izla's mess? Why don't I go help Alveen and Izla fixes this? It would probably go better if I weren't here since Marina seems to be focused on me."

"I've already got things in motion with Alveen."

"Wonderful," King Henan said. "I want a report from both of you by the end of the week." He strode from the room without looking back.

"I'm sorry," Izla said, focusing on Thane. "I know I've messed this up a bit, but I have faith in you."

"At least give Marina her voice. Then, we can have a conversation and straighten things out."

Izla rubbed the locket around her neck and frowned. "Mermaids aren't trusting of gifts. If we give it back, she might think we are up to something."

"I'll chance it."

Izla scrunched her eyes and studied him.

"Come on, Izla. If it's up to me to fix it, I should get to make the terms."

"Fine," she said, unclasping the necklace. She handed it to him.

He studied the pink and orange locket. "What am I supposed to do with this?"

"It's her voice. If you break it, she should get it back."

Thane shook his head. "I swear, you come up with the strangest things."

She grinned. "I know. That's why all of this will make a great story someday." She disappeared in a puff of pink smoke.

Thane shook his head as he waved the smoke with his hand. Izla could do nothing the simple way.

The door opened, and Sebby poked his head around the corner. "Can I come in?"

"Yes," he said, holding up the locket. "I've got something for you."

Sebby's brow arched as he walked forward and took the locket. "It's not really my style."

Thane chuckled. "It's Marina's voice. If you break it, she should be able to speak again."

"Whoa," he said, giving it a closer look. "Should I break it now?"

"If I were you, I would warn her first. I thought about talking to her and trying to get her to understand that nothing is going to happen between us, but it might be better if I just stay out of the way and see if anything comes of that."

Sebby placed the necklace in his pants pocket. "She's still pretty upset about that kiss. How was it, by the way?"

"How was what?"

"The kiss."

Thane rolled his eyes. "I'm not talking about that."

"That bad, eh?"

Thane sighed. "No. It wasn't bad at all."

Chapter 15

The smell of freshly baked bread filled Izla's nose as soon as she entered the gate of Lady Anna's manor. She should probably shrink down, but there was something exciting about trying not to be seen. She crept around the side of the house and ducked under an open window when she heard voices inside.

"Cinderella!" a shrill voice called. "I told you I needed my blue dress today! It's soaking wet!"

"I'm sorry," Ella's voice answered. "You didn't tell me until it was late last night, so it didn't have time to dry."

"How dare you speak to me in that manner! Mother! Cinderella is being impertinent!"

Izla gritted her teeth. If she ever needed to practice turning someone into a cockroach, she knew who she was coming to visit.

"Ella!" Lady Anna's voice boomed through the window. "If you cannot speak respectfully, do not speak."

"Yes, Lady Anna," Ella said meekly.

Izla turned to see the royal carriage bouncing down the road. She smiled. Everything was about to begin. She waited until the horses stopped in front of the house and then moved forward. Peeking around the corner she saw the royal messenger pound on the door. She couldn't take this view. She made herself invisible and hurried over next to the messenger.

The door opened, and Ella stood there. "May I help you?" she asked.

"Please give this to the lady of the house," the messenger said, handing Ella an envelope.

Izla shrunk down and flew through the door before it could close. She landed on a chair next to a window and watched Lady Anna come down the hallway.

"This just came," Ella said, holding it out. "It's from the castle."

Lady Anna snatched the envelope from her hand, and her two daughters came rushing down the hall.

"Did you say the castle?" one asked, trying to take the envelope.

Lady Anna held it out of reach. "I will open it." She slowly peeled the envelope apart and pulled out an official-looking invitation. Izla couldn't see it well, but she couldn't miss the neatly scripted writing.

"Well, what does it say?" the eldest sister asked.

Lady Anna's mouth curved up in the most wicked smile Izla had seen in a while. "The prince is hosting a ball."

Ella's two stepsisters squealed. One jumped up and down and clapped her hands.

Lady Anna held up a hand. "Not only that, but every unmarried woman in the kingdom may dance with the prince."

"Oh, I may die," the younger girl said, fanning herself with one hand.

"You realize what this means, of course," Lady Anna said. "The prince is in search of a wife. If it wasn't so, they would not have him dance with every unmarried woman. The king is finally tired of waiting for an heir."

Izla frowned. There were a lot of unmarried women in the kingdom. It might take a while to dance with everyone. She hadn't been thinking clearly on that point.

"May I go?" Ella asked.

Lady Anna's eyes flashed with fire. "How dare you even ask?"

Ella glanced down at the floor. "It said every unmarried woman."

The two sisters laughed, and Lady Anna rolled her eyes. "They didn't mean serving girls."

Ella took a deep breath. "My father—"

"We aren't speaking of your father," Lady Anna growled, crushing the invitation in her hand. "Go about your work."

Ella nodded and slipped away.

"This is so exciting," one sister said, smiling. "I'm going to wear my brown dress. It brings out my eyes."

Lady Anna rolled her eyes. "You will not wear brown to a ball. We will all get new dresses."

The girls squealed again.

Lady Anna put a hand to her head. "We will go as soon as I find my bag. Go tell Ella to get ready."

Izla sat on a bench in the corner at the dressmaker's shop and watched Ella's *family* touch every bolt of material they could get their hands on. Ella stood next to Lady Anna, holding a bolt of yellow material. Her gaze kept wandering to the pink fabric against the wall. Izla smiled. Pink must be Ella's favorite color. The only color she had seen her in was brown, probably the same dress every day.

"I can't make any new dresses before the ball," the dressmaker said. "I have too many orders already."

Lady Anna stepped up to the short, balding man and gazed down at him. "Excuse me? Do you know who I am?"

The man cowered. "Yes, of course, Lady Anna, but it takes time to make dresses, and I've had people coming in making orders all week."

Lady Anna sneered. "All week? The invitations only came today."

The man cleared his throat. "Some people received theirs earlier. It takes a lot of time to take invitations all over the kingdom."

She glared at the man, and he cleared his throat again. Izla was growing bored. They had been to three different dress shops trying to find the best one.

"Fine," Lady Anna said coldly. "We will go to the dress shop down the street. We don't need your help."

The man gulped and nodded. Lady Anna smacked the cloth in Ella's hands, causing it to fall to the floor. When Ella bent to grab it, Lady Anna grabbed her arm and pulled her through the door. The two sisters followed. Izla stood and quietly slipped out with them.

"That man has no idea who he is dealing with," Lady Anna muttered.

Izla glanced at the dirt road in front of them and smiled as she spotted a fresh pile of horse manure. She pulled out her wand, intending to fling the manure at Lady Anna, but she settled on making it disappear and reappear in front of the woman. They were walking so fast that Lady Anna and her eldest daughter stepped in it before they could stop.

Izla held in a giggle as the girl screamed and tried to wipe her shoe against the ground.

"Oh, gross!" she exclaimed. "Why do things like this have to happen?"

Lady Anna looked just as upset, but she reacted with more decorum. She tried to discreetly wipe her boot on the grass at the side of the walkway. The younger sister was holding back a smile, and Ella looked horrified.

"Ella," Lady Anna said through gritted teeth. "Take our boots and clean them." She kicked off her boots and her daughter did the same.

Ella picked up the boots, and Izla frowned. She hadn't thought about it affecting Ella. Lady Anna and her daughters walked down the street, heads held high, like they hadn't just stepped in manure. Izla swished her wand and pointed at the three. She smiled. Now they would smell like they had been rolling around in a cow pasture.

She swished her wand again and pointed it at the boots in Ella's hand. Ella glanced down at the boots, and her eyes widened as they cleaned themselves. She turned and hurried after the others. They disappeared into a small shop, and Izla zapped herself inside.

The dressmaker was a happy, plump woman with a dazzling smile. The smile slid from her face when she saw Lady Anna enter. "Oh, you again."

"Yes," Lady Anna said to the grandmotherly woman. "We have decided to use your services as there is not a decent dressmaker in this village."

The woman arched an eyebrow and put her hands on her hips. "I can't make any more dresses this week. I'm booked until after the ball."

Lady Anna frowned. "I will pay double."

The woman looked thoughtful. "If I do three more dresses, I will have to stay up every day this week. Pay triple, and I'll do it. That is my final and only offer."

Lady Anna's cheeks reddened, and Izla worried the woman would crack her teeth. She was grinding them so hard. "Fine."

The woman sniffed the air. "Do you smell something?"

Lady Anna took a sniff and frowned. "No."

Izla grinned. There was no mistaking the smell of cow that was hanging onto the three of them. They all shifted uncomfortably. Ella took a sniff and wrinkled her nose.

"Pick out the material you want, and I'll have them ready before the ball," the woman said. She rubbed her nose. "You can wash your hands at the pump before you touch the material."

Sebby and Marina sat at a fancy table in the castle's ballroom. Thane figured it was as good as any place to have a romantic dinner, but now that the small round table was set and they were sitting there, the room seemed enormous. There was a lacy white tablecloth and three candles in the middle of the table, and Thane had found their best dishes.

Now that he looked at it, he probably should have asked a maid to help him. It wasn't bad, but it could be better. Thane stood invisible, far enough away to give Sebby a sense of privacy, but close enough to hear what was being said. He didn't want to be here, but Sebby had asked him to stay.

The door opened, and a servant entered, carrying a tray of food. Once they began eating, Thane tried to ignore his growling stomach. He should have eaten first. It smelled like seasoned potatoes, his favorite.

Sebby talked, and Marina nodded or shook her head. After a few minutes, Sebby put his fork down and sighed. "Marina, I have this." He held out the locket. Marina dropped her fork and touched her throat with one hand. "Do you want it?"

Marina's eyebrows came together. She shook her head.

He put the necklace on the table and leaned forward. "I can break it."

Marina shook her head again and looked down at the table. "Why?"

She shrugged.

"Is it because of Thane?"

She shrugged again.

"You know it isn't going to work, right?"

Marina grabbed her fork and started eating.

He leaned against his chair and watched her. "You aren't in love with Thane. You don't know him. I can't believe a person can look at someone and fall in love with them."

She kept her focus on her plate and ignored him.

"We can break the locket. It won't affect anything with Thane, and you will be able to communicate. You know I've seen you before? More than once. You used to follow my father's ship. Most sailors don't believe in mermaids."

Her eyes widened.

Sebby smiled. "Yes, I know you are a mermaid. I recognized you when I saw you on the beach. I'm surprised you wanted to be a human. It would be exciting to live in the ocean and be able to see all the majestic sea creatures. Maybe Izla can make me into a merman, and I can go see it all someday."

Marina placed her fork on her plate and dabbed at her mouth. She glanced up at Sebby and shook her head. She made some motions with her hands. Thane wanted to laugh. She would be terrible at charades.

Sebby tilted his head. "You hated the ocean?"

She nodded, then made some more motions.

"It's dangerous?"

Marina's head bobbed up and down.

Thane chuckled quietly. How Sebby got that from what Marina was doing was beyond him.

Marina pointed at the locket and made a breaking motion with her hand. That Thane understood.

Sebby picked up the locket and held it up. "Are you sure?"

She paused for a moment and then nodded vigorously. Sebby stood and threw the locket at the floor and pressed his boot into it. A small plume of purple smoke rose from beneath his boot and traveled over to Marina. She sucked in a breath as the smoke bumped into her throat and disappeared.

"Did it work?" Sebby asked.

"Um... it would seem it did," she said.

Sebby grinned and sat back down. "Wonderful. Now, will you tell me about the ocean?"

She smiled. It was the first genuine smile Thane had seen from her. "I don't mind talking about the ocean, but I don't want to go back. The ocean has its beauties, but it's also very dangerous. I feel like I spent every day of my life wondering if something was going to eat me."

Sebby rested his elbows on the table. "There are dangers on land as well."

"I know. It just seems... different somehow. Everything here is so clear. If anything happens on the ocean floor, the water becomes murky and it's hard to feel happy. I've tried and tried, but I could never stop dreaming about land."

"Is that why you follow ships?"

"Partially. I have always been fascinated by humans. I love to watch people. They react differently than my people."

Sebby leaned forward again. "In what way?"

Marina stared up at the ceiling as she thought. "Mermaids are very superstitious. They are also vindictive and don't trust easily."

"Some people are like that."

She pushed a lock of black hair over her shoulder. "I don't have a lot of experience, but I think we are worse. I love my family, but they are some of the worst. My father has caused a lot of shipwrecks just because he was angry. When he's angry, the ocean rages, and he doesn't care who pays for his temper."

Sebby frowned. "That's awful."

"It really is. I want to get away from the water. You are right about Thane. I saw him, and he seemed so carefree. Something about him called out to me, but as you said, I don't know him."

"Did you ever see me? When I was on the ship? I could have sworn we made eye contact once."

Marina looked down at her plate, then back up. "I did. You scared me a little."

His mouth curved down. "Why?"

"You look really strong. My father always warned us about humans, and you made me nervous, the way you stared at me. I stayed away from the ship for a while after that. My father told us all humans would kill us on sight. I knew he was wrong, but it still gave me a chill."

"I'm sorry I made you feel that way."

"It's not your fault. It's the way I was raised."

It didn't seem Thane was of any use here. He might as well leave and let them have some privacy. Of course, Marina didn't know he was there, and Sebby wouldn't know he left.

Chapter 16

The ballroom wasn't as colorful as Izla would have liked, but that was mortals. The neutral colors of the walls and floors were worthy of a yawn, if not two. Even the refreshment tables were covered in dull brown, and all the candles and sconces were white. She supposed the dullness of the room would really make all the women's dresses stand out. Perhaps that was what they were hoping for.

Prince Alveen paced across the floor of the ballroom. Izla couldn't understand why he appeared nervous instead of excited. He looked fabulous in his white doublet and black fitted breeches. His black boots had been meticulously polished, and a crimson cape flowed behind him. Any woman would be impressed, even if he wasn't the prince. In Izla's opinion, he had nothing to worry about.

Izla strode over to the prince, her green dress rustling with each step. She had purchased a new dress for the occasion. There were several dresses in her closet, but once she found the color that worked for her, she didn't see any reason to not use the knowledge. Green was her color, and she was going to use it.

"Don't worry a path into the floor," she said, handing him his golden crown.

He took the crown and unceremoniously plopped it on his head. "I don't think this was a good idea."

Izla placed her hands on her hips. "Why would you say that?"

"It's just... I don't know. I met a girl the other day." He pushed his crown into place. "It wasn't a big deal or anything, but I felt like we connected. Now I wonder if I'd just had more time if I could have found someone on my own."

Izla smiled. "Perhaps the girl will come to the ball. Who is she?"

He sighed. "I don't really know who she is. All I know is that her name is Ella. I doubt she will be here. She's not... someone that would probably come to something like this."

"I see. Well, don't fret. That never does any good. Have a good time tonight, and try to relax."

He laughed bitterly. "Relax. Right. It's only the day my happiness is determined. I can't believe I let you convince me to make that deal with my father."

Izla turned and glanced at one of the large glass windows to hide the sparkling of her eyes. "It may go better than you suppose."

"It doesn't matter. Good or bad, I made an agreement."

Izla nodded. "You certainly did."

❧

If a heart could burst from a person from excitement, Izla would have lost hers. She hid in Ella's broom closet and waited for Lady Anna and her daughters to leave. It would have been preferable to be invisible, but Izla had a lot to do tonight, and she didn't want to get magic fatigue. The broom closet wasn't large, and it smelled like lye, but she could handle anything for a short amount of time.

"See that the house is in perfect shape when we return," Lady Anna demanded from the other side of the door.

"Yes, ma'am," Ella's meek voice answered.

"Don't wait up for us. I am sure we will be quite tired tomorrow and will need you in tiptop shape."

Izla rolled her eyes. It's not like they did anything when they weren't tired. She didn't know how Ella managed to live with these people. Of course, a person could handle a lot if they didn't have a choice. Jobs for women were difficult to come by, so the girl had little choice.

After the front door slammed, Izla waited. She didn't want to come out too early in case Lady Anna forgot something and came back. The closet felt like it was getting smaller, and the smell was irritating her nose.

A sniffing sound caused Izla to frown. Was Ella crying? Probably. Who wouldn't with that family? Still, a few more minutes would be enough. Izla shifted her weight from one leg to the other. If she didn't move a little, her leg might cramp up.

She took a step back and hit her head on a shelf. "Ouch!" she said, louder than she should have. She stepped forward and tripped on a metal mop bucket and slammed into the wall. She covered her mouth and froze. There was no way Ella could have avoided hearing the bucket. Izla listened hard, but it was silent on the other side of the door.

The door burst open, and light flooded the small closet. Ella stood at the doorway holding a potato masher over her head, ready to attack. Her wide, tear-filled eyes took in Izla, and she frowned in what Izla could only assume was confusion. Izla was dressed well for a burglar.

"Who are you?" Ella demanded, not lowering the masher.

Izla smiled and walked out of the closet like it was the most natural thing in the world. "Hello, Ella. I'm your godmother."

Ella tilted her head. "My godmother died years ago."

Of course she did.

Izla pulled her wand from her pocket. "Yes, but I am your fairy godmother."

Ella didn't ease up on the death grip she had on the masher. "Why were you in the closet?"

"Magic can be funny sometimes. It doesn't always take me to the exact place I want to go."

Ella let her arms drop to her sides, and she took a step back, allowing Izla to step out into the kitchen.

"Sorry about the rude welcome," Ella said. "You scared me."

"That's alright," Izla said, brushing off her dress. She hoped she didn't smell like lye all night.

"You don't look like a godmother."

Izla grinned. "Perhaps not, but I look exactly like a fairy godmother."

Ella didn't look convinced, but she placed the potato masher on the counter. Izla sighed. Maybe she really should consider appearing as an old woman. People seemed to be more trusting of people who had seen more than a few years.

"Why are you here?" Ella asked.

"To help you, of course. I've come to make your dreams come true."

"Which dreams?"

"Your dreams of going to the ball and meeting the prince."

Ella's mouth turned down. "That isn't my dream."

Izla placed her hands on her hips. "Isn't your dream? That is every young girl's dream."

"Is it yours?"

She rolled her eyes. "Of course not. Fairy godmothers don't have those types of dreams."

"What types of dreams do you have?"

Izla wanted to snap at the girl, but she looked genuinely curious, not indignant. She thought for a moment. "My dream is to help people like you find happiness, and by happiness, I mean love."

Ella leaned against the counter. "But what about you? Don't you want happiness?"

"When I help others find happiness, it completes my own."

"I can understand that would be fulfilling. Don't you want to find love yourself?"

Why was this girl so full of questions? Of course Izla wanted to find love someday, but she had hundreds of years before she would need to worry about it. Helping others find love was a lot less awkward than finding it for herself.

"Don't worry about me," she said. "I'm here to help you."

"Look at me," Ella said, standing tall. "I am not the type of person anyone wants to see at a ball." Izla studied Ella. Her brown dress was faded and smudged. The apron she wore had seen better days, and her shoes were worn on the toes. Her blonde hair was pulled back in a ponytail, and she had a streak of soot across one cheek.

"Nothing I can't work with," Izla said, excitement bubbling through her. "By the time I'm finished with you, you will be the belle of the ball."

Ella looked at the floor. "I don't care about the ball."

"Then, why were you crying?"

Ella sighed. "I'm just tired, I guess. I would like to go places and do things, but I never get the chance. The other day, I... met someone. A man. He was nice. I could tell he came from some money, so he would never give me a second thought, but it made me feel hollow inside. I know I miss out on so many things, and I try to be content, but sometimes it's hard."

"Let me help you. Please."

Ella glanced at her. "I don't see how you can."

"Let me help you have an unforgettable evening. It's a start, if nothing else."

"I can't go to the ball. My stepmother will see me, and she will be angry," she said, fiddling with her hands.

Izla smiled and held up her wand. "I will make sure she doesn't. Now first things first, we need a coach. Most people won't pay attention to how you arrive, but in case anyone does, we want to make sure you arrive with an elegant flair." Izla glanced around the kitchen, looking for anything that resembled a coach. She couldn't make something from nothing after all.

Three pumpkins sat on the table. Izla picked one up and peered in a hole at the top. This might do.

"I was just cleaning them out to make pie," Ella said. "If you stop by tomorrow, I can give you a piece. Pumpkin pie is my specialty. I always make it when Lady Anna has a grumpy week. It lightens her mood."

"That sounds lovely," Izla said. "Do you need all three pumpkins? Can I use one?"

"Of course," Ella said. "We have plenty in the garden, so I can get what I need."

Izla opened the back door. "Let's take it outside. If I change it here, it won't fit out the door."

"Change it?" she asked, following her out.

"It won't be helpful if we don't."

A large yard spread out before them. It was clear for a way and then turned into a forested area. Izla made sure they were far enough from the house, placed the pumpkin on the ground, and waved her wand. A stream of gold flowed from the wand and into the pumpkin. The golden stream was all for show, but Izla loved the look of awe people got when she did it.

The pumpkin began expanding. Ella's eyes were as wide as dinner plates, and Izla made sure she kept her smug grin to herself. The pumpkin continued growing until it was the size of a coach. Swirls of gold ran around the outside and intricate decorations formed around the sides. Sparkling gold wheels were probably overdoing it, but Izla did nothing small.

Ella put a hand to her chest. "Oh my. I've seen nothing like that in my life."

"If you liked that, just wait." Izla pulled four mice from her pocket and placed them in the dirt. She swished her wand, and they watched the mice transform into beautiful white horses. "Drat. I forgot to bring something for the coachmen. Are there any animals around here?"

Ella closed her gaping mouth. "There are always lizards on the trees. Would that work?"

Izla tapped her wand against her lip. "Lizards should work. See if you can find two."

She nodded and hurried over to the trees. She was back within a couple of minutes, carrying two spotted brown lizards in her hands. Izla wasn't scared of animals, but a shiver went down her spine at the thought of how many lizards must be on the trees for her to find them that fast.

"Just place them there," she commanded, pointing to the horses. Ella put them down, and Izla aimed her wand at the two creatures. Within seconds, they were two coachmen. They wore matching blue clothing, and their hair was pulled into neat ponytails. Their eyes were a little vacant, but no one was expecting much from them. They grabbed the horses and led them to the front of the coach.

Ella placed her hands on her cheeks. "I've heard of fairies and magic, but I never would have believed all of this if I hadn't seen it for myself."

Izla grinned. "Now for you."

"Me?"

"You can't go to the ball in that dress."

Ella glanced down. "It is pretty old."

"Spin in a slow circle." The spinning wasn't any more necessary than the golden streams she liked to make, but it felt more magical, in her opinion.

Ella turned slowly, and Izla waved her wand. Ella's brown dress faded away as a long pink dress replaced it. Izla smiled as she examined her work. The silk dress came down to the ground, which might make dancing difficult, but it was the style. The sleeves were puffed up enough to be fashionable, but not enough to get in the way. Her blonde hair wrapped around itself in an attractive bun with small ringlets falling at the sides.

"Lovely," Izla smiled. "I wish I could wear pink."

Ella twirled around, watching the dress spin. "Why can't you?"

Izla held out a long red curl. "It clashes with my hair."

"Your hair is a beautiful color, and that green dress brings out your eyes."

"Now for shoes," Izla said, ignoring the compliment. Tonight wasn't about her. Izla swirled the wand again and pointed at Ella's feet.

"Wow," Ella said, holding her dress away from her feet. "Are they made of glass?"

"Yes, so try to walk carefully. I reinforced them, so they should be alright." This was something she had practiced before. Glass slippers were a sure way to stand out. No one else would be foolish enough to try it. Magic had its advantages.

Ella took a step and grimaced.

Izla smiled sympathetically. "I know they aren't comfortable. I'm still working on that."

"It's alright. They are beautiful."

Izla opened the door of the coach. "You better get going. The magic only lasts until midnight. On the stroke of midnight, all the magic vanishes and you will be as you were before. Be mindful of the time. You don't want to change back in front of the entire kingdom."

"I'll leave before that. Thank you," she said, climbing into the coach. Izla shut the door and nodded to the coachman. Tonight was going to be a night to remember.

Izla loved a good ball. She enjoyed watching people dance across the floor, and she enjoyed all the fancy dresses and hair-styles. The music kept her toe tapping and a smile on her face. There were so many people packed into the ballroom. It made her wonder if it was really possible for Prince Alveen to dance with every unmarried woman. One of his men was bringing the women to him, and he would dance with them for a few steps and then change partners. That was no way to get to know anyone.

Izla had turned down more men than was polite when they asked her to dance. If she danced, she might miss something. Prince Alveen had already danced with Ella's stepsisters, and they didn't seem to interest him more than anyone else. Now they were both pouting. Lady Anna was desperately trying to send any wealthy looking men her daughters' way, and Izla would have found it comical if she had time to focus on it.

A tapping on her shoulder startled her, and she spun around. One of Alveen's men stood before her. "Would you care to dance with the prince?" he asked. "He requested a dance with you specifically."

"Of course," she said, following him across the dance floor. When they reached Alveen, he released his current partner and took Izla's hand.

They danced, and Alveen sighed. "This is miserable."

"I'm sure it is. Being the center of attention can be difficult," she said with a small laugh.

"I've been the center of attention my entire life. It isn't something I enjoy."

Izla had a hard time understanding that. She enjoyed the attention she received as the fairy princess. "I'm sure the night will get better."

"My toes have been stepped on at least five times," he muttered. "Make that six," he said as Izla stepped on his boot.

"It's your own fault. Your dancing is clumsy tonight."

"I suppose it is. I am trying, but I wish I was anywhere but here."

Izla tilted her head. "There are a lot of places worse than here. I can take you to some of them if you prefer."

"I know. I'm being dramatic."

The prince looked at something over Izla's shoulder as he stopped dancing. Izla turned and smiled when she saw Ella at the top of the enormous staircase. All eyes were on her, and Izla could almost see the tension in the girl.

Ella slowly began descending the stairs. She was probably moving slowly because she was nervous, and her shoes were probably giving her blisters. Izla would have to work on perfecting them.

"It's her," Alveen whispered. "It's Ella."

"Well, go get her," Izla said, pushing him gently in the right direction.

Alveen hurried across the floor, and Izla decided now was the time to be invisible. She was too excited about tonight to leave anything to chance. She shrunk down and flew to Alveen's side.

He reached Ella as soon as she stepped off the last step. "Ella. I didn't expect to see you here."

Ella's perfect pink lips turned down in a frown. She looked up at his crown. "You are the prince?"

"Yes."

Her eyes went down to the floor. "Oh."

"Would you like to dance?"

Ella blinked a few times. She looked like she might weep. What was wrong with her? Izla was giving her everything she could want. She nodded reluctantly, and Alveen whisked her across the dance floor. Izla tried to stay near them, but they were moving in such an odd pattern that she couldn't keep up. It was probably just as well. If Thane were here, he would tell her to give them some privacy.

Izla kept herself small and invisible. If no one could see her, no one could ask her to dance. One song ended, and another began. Alveen continued to dance with Ella. Izla felt warm and happy. They were going to be a wonderful couple.

Chapter 17

Thane wondered where Izla had gone. The ball was in full swing, and he had seen his sister disappear. She was probably buzzing around the prince's ear, trying not to miss any moments. When King Henan had learned of the ball, he had convinced Thane to go. Thane had convinced Sebby and Marina to come, and Sebby had convinced him to invite Ava. He felt funny about the kiss, but she didn't mention it, so he pretended it hadn't happened.

"I've never been to this kingdom," Ava said. "There are a lot more people here than at any other ball I've been to."

Thane nodded. He was trying not to stare at her. She looked beautiful in her blue ball gown. Most of the women were wearing their hair up, but Ava's long black hair hung down to her waist. She was, without a doubt, the prettiest woman in the room.

"Thanks for coming with me. I owe you. I didn't want to look like a loser coming here on my own."

Ava nodded. "You are starting to owe me quite a bit. What are you going to do when I call in all these favors?"

He chuckled. "I just hope you don't call them all in at once."

Sebby and Marina were dancing on the other side of the room. That was a relief. Ever since Marina had begun talking, she seemed to enjoy Sebby's company a lot more.

"Are we going to dance?" Ava asked.

"Oh. We don't need to. Just having you here is enough. People won't expect me to dance with anyone else."

Ava narrowed her eyes and crossed her arms. "I love dancing. If you don't want to dance, that's fine, but I'm going to find someone who does."

Thane swallowed hard. Not that he didn't want to dance with Ava. He just knew he would probably make an idiot of himself. He knew how to dance, but now that he knew he had feelings for Ava, he felt nervous.

"I'll dance," he said. Acting like an idiot was better than having her dance with someone else. He took her hand and put his other hand on her waist. She put her hand on his shoulder, and they began dancing. There wasn't enough room for any large movements, so he didn't have to worry about being fancy.

Ava was a superb dancer. If her magic was as good as her dancing, she would be unstoppable. His hands were sweating, but she was too polite to say anything. He opened his mouth to make conversation, but someone pushed past him, causing him to turn.

The girl who had been dancing with the prince was running full speed toward the steps. She gathered her pink skirts and ran up the stairs. The prince came tearing after her. Izla would not like this. If her plans for Prince Alveen didn't work, she would be a mess.

"That's not a good sign," Ava said, watching the door the two had run through.

"Probably not."

The prince came back in. He was holding something in his hands. He looked rejected. Poor guy. Thane could imagine how he must feel. The prince walked across the ballroom and disappeared behind a large wooden door.

Thane turned to Ava. "Should I follow him?"

She shook her head. "What would you do? I'm sure Izla will talk to him and figure it all out. If we do anything, it might mess with her plan."

"This is a weird way to find a wife. Izla comes up with some strange notions. How well can anyone really get to know a person after a few dances?"

Ava placed both of her hands around his neck, and they started dancing again. It was good his father wasn't here to see this. He still remembered dancing lessons from his younger days, and he was sure this was not a proper way to dance, but it was nice to hold her close.

"You better hope your father never gets any ideas like this."

Thane blinked, confused for a minute. The ball. That's what she was talking about. "I've been worried about it," he admitted. "My father will not be patient forever."

"Are you against getting married?"

"I'm not against it. I'm against my father trying to force me into it before I find the right person."

"Do you even try to find that person?"

In his head he said, "I already found her." Out loud he said, "No, not really." Ava may go along with his antics, but he doubted she would ever really fall for him. Still, there was that kiss that went on much longer than agreed... but Ava had never given him any sign she might think of him as anything other than her friend's brother, or a friend at the most.

"Are you sure you aren't running from responsibility?"

Thane's feet stopped moving. "What do you mean?"

She looked up at him. "If you get married, you have to start ruling part of your father's kingdom. Maybe you don't feel ready for that."

"It's not that," Thane said. "I'm more than ready for that."

"Then, what is it?"

"Like I said. I want to find the right person."

"But if you don't try, you'll never find her."

This conversation would be easier if they didn't have their hands around each other. It would only take a little leaning, and Thane could kiss her. Then, she might slap him, and everyone at the ball would be focused on them.

"I've never been great at talking to women. You know that."

"You talk just fine to me and to Lily and Zina."

"That's different. I was forced to talk to the three of you so many times I got used to it."

She stiffened. "Forced?"

"You know what I mean. You all came around enough that I was comfortable with the three of you."

"That's what it takes sometimes. You have to force yourself to talk to women so you get used to them."

"I talk to women all the time. It's part of being a prince."

"Yes, but not about personal matters."

Ava didn't like him. If she did, she wouldn't be encouraging him to talk to other women. Although, she was running her hand through the back of his hair. She must not realize she was doing it. He cleared his throat, and she dropped her hands and stepped away.

"I'm going to go get some air," she said, rushing toward a balcony. If there was one thing to be said about this castle, there were lots of balconies. She pushed open the glass door, and he watched it close behind her.

"Don't mess it up," Izla said, appearing beside him.

Thane jumped, then glared at his sister. "Don't scare people like that."

She rolled her eyes. "Just go, Thane. Don't be scared, or you will never win her. She's going to move on eventually if you never act."

"What do you mean, move on? She's never felt that way about me."

"Please," she laughed. "I'm an expert about these things, and I can see it as clear as day."

Thane swallowed and tried to calm his pounding heart. "What if you're wrong?"

"Then, you will know, and you can get over it. Come on. You are going to rule a kingdom one day. You can't let yourself ignore things that matter."

He took a deep breath and nodded. Izla was a meddling pain in the side sometimes, but she was right. He walked away from her and made a steady line to the balcony. He pulled open the door and made his boots carry him through.

Ava turned when she heard the door. Her arms were folded to ward off the cool night air. The rounded balcony was covered in rose bushes, and the moonlight shining on Ava's hair created a picture he wouldn't soon forget.

"It's cold out here," he said, moving near her.

She rubbed her arms. "A little."

He stood facing her, feeling like an idiot. He didn't know what to say or how to go back to their previous conversation.

Ava took a step back. "What?"

Thane's eyes widened. Had he said something out loud? "What do you mean what?"

She tilted her head and frowned. "You were looking at me like you were about to give me a lecture."

Thane laughed. It was a horrid, nervous laugh. He should probably leave before he made a bigger fool of himself than he already had.

Ava raised her eyebrows.

He took a deep breath and let it out slowly. "I don't know how to say what I want to say."

"You've said ridiculous things around me plenty of times," she said with a half smile. "My friends aren't here, so I won't even make fun of you behind your back."

He smiled. "Gee, thanks."

"Can we go back to the conversation we were having before?"

She grinned. "About you fearing girls?"

His mouth turned down. "I'm not scared of girls."

"But you won't talk to them, unless it's about things concerning the kingdom."

He took a deep breath. If he didn't say it now, he would never say it. "The truth is, there is a woman I'm interested in." If he wasn't seeing things, she twitched a little when he said it.

"Oh? Well, that's good then. Your father will be so happy."

"There's no reason to tell him. I said she captured my interest. I didn't say she felt the same."

"Have you asked her?" Ava asked, her expression blank.

"Of course not."

"You'll never know unless you ask her."

Thane leaned forward against the balcony and gazed up at the half moon. "I'm really busy. I don't have time for a broken heart."

She copied him, resting her elbows on the balcony and leaning forward. "If you find out now, you will know before your heart gets involved."

He turned his head and studied her. She was frowning and staring up at the moon. "My heart is already involved."

"I don't see how if you never talk to anyone. Izla told me all about the mermaid. You aren't acting like Marina and falling in love with someone you don't know, are you?"

"No. It's someone I talk to. Someone I've known for a long time."

She glanced at him, and her brows came together. "Who?"

Izla burst through the door, and her eyes landed on Thane. She shot him an apologetic look. "Father needs you. It's an emergency, and I can't go because I need to check on Ella and Alveen."

Thane nodded and sighed. It was probably just as well. He wasn't doing so well out here.

Izla frowned. "Father said to have you come immediately." She disappeared.

Thane turned to Ava. "Sorry. I guess I have to go. Do you think you can bring Sebby and Marina back to the castle?"

She nodded. He gave her a small smile. Whatever the problem was back home, he hoped it wasn't as bad as the mess he was making here.

Chapter 18

Lady Anna's manor was dark when Izla arrived. She let herself into the kitchen and started a fire. The night air was icy, and Ella would be cold when she returned. Izla had tried to find her, but she must be off the main road because she couldn't locate her.

A door opened and slammed from somewhere in the front of the house. Footsteps rushed toward the kitchen, and Ella burst into the room. Her hair hung loose around her face and her beautiful pink dress had turned back into the brown rags she had worn before.

Izla might need to rethink her plans. If she hadn't made everything change at midnight, Ella could have spent a lot more time with the prince, and she could have ridden home in the coach. Telling her everything changed at midnight had a nice ring to it, though, and it would make a wonderful story someday.

"I'm sorry," Ella panted. "I waited too long, and everything changed back except my shoe." She pulled the glass slipper from her pocket and placed it on the table. "The other one broke when I ran down the steps of the castle. I would have picked it up, but I didn't want the prince to see me change back into myself."

Izla ran her hand over the slipper. "I should have given you more time. You may keep the slipper as a reminder of this evening. Did you have fun?"

Ella picked up the glass shoe and smiled. "It was the best night of my life. I've met the prince before."

"Oh?" Izla asked, feigning ignorance.

Her smile fell. "The man I told you about earlier was actually Prince Alveen. I didn't know he was the prince."

"Well, that's a good thing, isn't it?"

She turned the shoe in her hands and stared down at it. "Not really."

Izla put her hands on her hips. "Why not?"

"He was so kind tonight. And funny. It's almost worse that I went because now I'll never see him again."

"Perhaps he will come looking for you."

"I don't think so. A prince will not spend his time with a commoner, and a servant at that."

"You might be surprised."

Ella sighed. "No. It's best if I think of it as a beautiful dream and leave it at that."

⸺ ella ⸺

Prince Alveen paced across the floor. His father sat on his crimson and gold throne and tapped the arms with his hands. Izla watched both of them in silence. From the sound of it, she had missed a nasty fight between the two and now they were waiting each other out. If one of them didn't talk soon, Izla was going to burst.

Izla couldn't take it anymore. "I don't think last night was the mess you both seem to think it was."

"Not a mess?" the king asked, gripping the throne. "He finally finds a girl he can handle spending time with, and he lets her run away? And did he ask her where she lives? No. Did he ask about her family? No."

"I didn't know she was going to run off," Alveen muttered. "It happened so fast."

"And all you have to give you any clue to her identity is a broken shoe."

"I know her name is Ella."

The king looked at the ceiling and shook his head. "That barely narrows it down. Ella is a common name. Every other girl is named Ella."

Izla rolled her eyes at the exaggeration. "Where is the shoe?"

Prince Alveen pulled two pieces of the broken glass slipper from his pocket and handed them to her. Izla frowned. The shoe had broken right in half. She took the heel in one hand and the toe in the other. Glass was a bad idea, but it looked so elegant. She held the pieces together and used a bit of magic to mend the break.

She handed it back to the prince. "There. It's as good as new."

"What good is that to us?" the king asked.

"Take the shoe and try it on all the girls in the kingdom. Whichever one it fits, the prince marries."

"That will take far too long," the king complained.

"Well, try it on all the women in the surrounding area."

Prince Alveen narrowed his eyes. "That sounds like a waste of time."

"Yes," the king agreed. "Why not just try it on every woman named Ella?"

"I know what she looks like. I don't need to try it on her. I just need to find her. Did you see her at the ball?" he asked Izla. "She's the same girl that we found stuck in the tree. I should be able to search around that area."

"Stuck in a tree?" the king bellowed. "What respectable woman climbs a tree? She seems to lack judgment. Climbing trees and wearing glass slippers?"

"She is the woman I want to marry," the prince said. "I'm going to find her."

Izla pointed at the slipper. "With the shoe."

"I don't need the shoe."

Izla fixed Alveen with a hard stare. "You need to try the shoe on as many women as you logically can. You let the kingdom know you are doing this and that you will marry the woman it fits. It will cause excitement throughout the land. People need excitement. People will speculate and tell your story."

The king smiled. "Yes, yes. It will raise morale, and all the people will celebrate with you when you find her. Cheerful people lead to a happy kingdom."

Alveen shook his head. "You've forgotten something. The shoe could fit hundreds of women."

"Not this shoe," Izla said with a smile. "This shoe will only fit the woman it belongs to."

Thane stood on a large group of rocks in the ocean. The storm raged, blowing his hair back from his forehead. Waves crashed around him, and it took more power than he was used to wielding to keep them from smashing him into the water. The sea king was not happy.

Earlier in the day, the sea king had sent a message to King Henan asking him if he knew where his daughter Marina was. King Henan believed in being honest and told the sea king that his daughter was somewhere on land. He had been able to honestly say that he didn't know where she was, and now the sea king was causing massive waves and lightning to rain down on all the port cities.

This was all Izla's fault, and Thane was growing tired of helping fix her problems. She was the one who should be here. If someone didn't soften up the sea king, who knew what kind of damages he would cause?

If there was one type of creature Thane never wanted to be, it was a merman. Something about being part fish didn't sit right with him, but now he was going to have to become one. He pulled off his elaborate white tunic and threw it on the rock. He shivered as the cold sea wind slapped against his skin. How was he supposed to find the king? The ocean was vast, and he'd never gone very far out before.

Ava appeared on the rock beside him. "I don't think this is a good idea," she called over the storm.

Thane shook his head. "You should tell my father that."

Her dress whipped around her legs, and she pulled a blue cloak around her arms. "The sea king is known for deception and a lack of compassion. Why would your father make you do this?"

"Someone has to. This storm is going to cause all types of damage. People might get hurt."

"Do you want me to go with you?"

Thane hesitated. He wanted her to go with him, but he couldn't have her getting hurt. "No. You stay where it's safe."

"I don't think you should go alone."

"And I think we should throw Marina back in the ocean, but my father won't allow it. He thinks she might be in danger if she goes back."

Ava bit her lip. "Be careful."

"I will." He hoped the king would be easy to deal with, but Thane had heard the stories. What if he didn't come back? "Ava?"

"Yes?"

"I would never ask someone I didn't care about to kiss me as a favor." He didn't look at her. He just turned, took a deep breath, and dove into the ocean.

Thane's body was growing tired from the unfamiliar strain of swimming for so long. He didn't want to admit it, but having a tail had been fun in the beginning. The distance covered with a tail versus legs was astounding. It was amazing how much he could see and how many colorful fish were all around. He had been out here long enough that the novelty was wearing off, though, and he was exhausted.

Something caught onto his tail and brought him to an abrupt stop. He turned to see a thin green plant wrapped around him. He bent and tried to pull the plant off, but it wouldn't budge. Another plant struck out and wrapped around his wrist, and a moment later, another one had his other arm.

He panicked and pulled against his bonds. If he couldn't break free, he was going to have to try magic, and he was wary of doing that. His father taught him that magic performed by fairies underwater was unreliable and often brought undesirable results.

"Resisting is time wasted," said a voice behind him.

He twisted around, his bonds tightening. Three mermaids were watching him with amused expressions. Two of them had long black hair and resembled Marina, and one had short brown hair that appeared to wave at him. She grinned when he gave it a second look.

"I am Prince Thane, son of King Henan. I've come to speak with the sea king."

The mermaid with the lively hair swam up and looked into his face. "A prince? Are we supposed to be impressed?"

"Fairies are almost as bad as mortals," one other said. "They might be worse, using their magic to appear any way they choose. It's disgraceful for you to appear like that in front of us."

The third mermaid nudged the other. "Don't be so harsh, Prizzy. He is attractive, if nothing else."

Prizzy crossed her arms and studied Thane. "Hm. I suppose he is, but what are we to do with a pretty fairy?"

Thane wanted to growl. He didn't have time or patience for this. "I appeared this way because I need to speak to the sea king, and he can't come on land to talk to me."

"What shall we do with him?" Prizzy asked again.

The mermaid that came to his defense smiled. "I'll keep him."

"Don't be ridiculous, Cora. What do you think, Meegen?"

Meegen ran her hand over her short hair. "Let me think. We could turn him into a sea sponge."

Thane rolled his eyes. "Mermaids don't have that type of magic."

She narrowed her eyes. "What makes you a mermaid expert?"

"Just let me go. Do you really want a war between our people?"

Prizzy frowned. "We might have one anyway if we don't get our sister back."

"Marina is your sister?"

Meegen poked a long fingernail into his chest. "You know Marina?"

"I've met her."

"Where is she?" Prizzy asked. "Why didn't you bring her back with you?"

"I'm not her keeper."

Meegen poked him again.

Thane sighed. "Look, take me to the sea king, and we can deal with the situation."

Cora's mouth turned down. "You really think the sea king can be dealt with? He can't. Not by you."

"So, you are prepared to go to war?"

The three of them all shared nervous glances.

"No, we aren't," Meegen said, "but that doesn't change our father. He is not one to deal gently. He is angry with our sister's disappearance, and he won't be happy until she is found."

"What if she left on purpose?"

They shared another look. Cora's mouth formed a tight line, and Prizzy rubbed her arm and gazed into the distance.

Meegen's frown deepened. "We are sure she did. Marina has never been content with her life."

Thane raised one brow. "So, why do we get the blame?"

"Because if you don't, she will."

Thane didn't respond. He just watched the three sisters shift nervously. Meegen snapped, and Thane's bonds were loosened. He rubbed his wrist and tried to come up with a plan. If it came down to a fight, mermaids wouldn't be able to overpower him. Not even three to one.

"Is there any chance of no one getting the blame?" he asked.

"With Father, there will always be blame," Meegen said. "The only solution I can see is to have Marina disappear forever. If she never came back, and Father knew it was of her own doing, he would be angry at her and perhaps turn his wrath away from anyone else."

Cora shuddered. "He will be awful to live with for a time."

Meegen nodded. "But do you see any other solutions?"

Cora shook her head. "We are lucky he never found out we helped those humans when their ship was on fire. Marina is always getting us to do things that will anger him."

A fish swam in front of Thane's face, and he jumped. Either the mermaids didn't notice or didn't care enough to mock him. He crossed his arms. "How do we convince your father she left of her own will?"

Prizzy tapped her lip. "Father isn't stupid. I'm sure he already knows it, but he doesn't want to think Marina would betray him. She is his favorite, after all. He's looking for someone to punish so he doesn't have to punish her. He knows someone else is involved. We can't change our forms like you can."

This might be tricky. Thane couldn't do or say anything that would point a finger at Izla. It was probably a good thing she hadn't come. She would have said something to incriminate herself and would have been proud of saying it.

"She was changed by a witch," he lied. "Marina made a deal with her. She can never come back to the ocean or she will turn to sea foam."

Cora covered her mouth with both hands, and her eyes widened. "Marina is too young to be turned into sea foam."

"Too young?" he asked.

Prizzy nodded. "After mermaids have lived for a few hundred years, they turn to sea foam."

Thane frowned. "It must be terrifying to know that is in your future."

Meegen shrugged. "It's not so bad. Sea foam lives on in a way a fairy couldn't understand. If Marina has made this deal, then there is no coming back. I think it would be best if we told Father that Marina has already turned to sea foam because of a deal with a witch. That will give him no reason to seek war, and he will have closure regarding our sister."

Thane's insides flooded with relief. Could it be that easy? If so, he could avoid speaking with the sea king, and they wouldn't have to worry about any retaliation.

"Make a promise to us, though," Meegen said.

He should have known there would be something. Mermaids always wanted something, and if someone broke a promise to a mermaid, they would spend the rest of their life cursed. That was a long time for someone who was immortal.

He tried to mimic his father's intimidating eyebrow raise and hoped he didn't look ridiculous. "What promise?"

"When you return to land, find Marina, and tell her to never come back. If Father finds out we lied to him... it will benefit none of us. Tell her she must move away from the ocean and never come near it."

Thane nodded. That was easy enough. He didn't look forward to talking to her, but he wouldn't mind telling her she had to leave the kingdom. "I promise."

Thane shook hands with the mermaids and swam away. He broke the surface of the water so he could use magic instead of trying to find his way back through the water. The storm was still in full rage when his head came from the water, and as quick as he could, he took himself to the shore.

It was darker than a normal night because the sky was full of black clouds. The waves whipped the shore with the vengeance of the sea king. With hope, his daughters could calm him soon. Thane shivered and waved his hand, causing his warmest black pajamas to appear. They were going to get wet, but he didn't care. He quickly put them on and stood silently, watching the storm. There was something terrifying, yet exciting, about it.

Thane's bare feet were slowly sinking beneath the wet sand. He closed his eyes and let the rain hit his face. He loved the smell of rain, and it had been a long time since he stood out in it.

Someone pushed him from behind, and he stumbled a few steps forward. Thane spun around, ready for a fight. "Ava?" He frowned. What was Ava still doing out in this storm? Her long black hair was straight from the rain, and she crossed her arms and glared at him.

"How dare you?" she asked.

Thane wiped the water from his face. "What do you mean?"

"How dare you say something to me like you did and then just jump into the ocean?"

"I—"

"No! Not only that, but you jumped in the water and took whatever spell you were doing to keep the waves away with you! As soon as you dove beneath the surface, I got smacked by a wave the size of your castle! I was upside down in the water and getting blown all over the place!"

Heat rushed to Thane's face. He'd thought his declaration and dive must have appeared heroic, and he had been an idiot. "I'm so sorry. I forgot I was holding the waves off."

"You know my magic isn't what it should be. It's amazing I got out at all! You should have seen me. I looked like a drowned cat."

Thane didn't want to tell her she still did. Not with that fire burning in her eyes. "I'm sorry."

Ava took a deep breath. "Alright."

"We're good?"

"Yes, but you owe me."

"Anything."

She looked down at the spot her feet would be if they weren't covered in wet sand. "Pull me out of here before I disappear beneath the sand and take us to your castle. It's hard to talk with all the noise."

Thane pried his feet from their sandy prison and took three slow, deliberate steps toward her. She attempted to pull her foot from the sand and fell forward, her arms flailing. He caught her, and she locked her arms around his neck. He put his around her waist. Ava looked up at him with her beautiful brown eyes, and he willed himself to stay focused.

He cleared his throat and shook his head. "I'm going to pull you up. Are you ready?"

Her eyes didn't leave his. "Did you mean what you said?"

"When?" he asked, knowing exactly when she meant.

"You know when."

He paused, his heart trying to beat out of his chest. It was time. If she rejected him, then he needed to know and move on. "I more than meant it."

"Really? You aren't just teasing me?"

"You know how bad I am at things like this. I would never tease you about something like this."

Ava smiled and shifted awkwardly in the sand. "I've been in love with you for so long."

Thane's eyes widened. That was hard to comprehend. He thought about questioning her, but now wasn't the time. Before he could say anything, Ava pulled his head down and pressed her lips to his. This kiss was ten times superior to the first one—because this one was real.

Ava pulled back slightly and gazed into his eyes. "Thane? Why are you standing on the beach in your pajamas?"

Chapter 19

Getting the prince to try the glass slipper on so many women's feet had seemed like such a good idea until Izla traveled around with the prince and watched him do it. She had to promise to stay invisible or Alveen wouldn't let her come, and being invisible meant she couldn't join in the conversations.

The first day was entertaining. It was amazing to see how many women were trying to pretend they were Ella. Because of the magic Izla had placed upon the slipper, it wouldn't fit anyone but Ella. It changed sizes over and over, dashing the dreams of so many would be prince catchers.

It was strange to think of the number of women who wanted to marry a prince without even knowing him. Izla knew her fair share of princes, and she didn't see the appeal. Her brothers were alright, but not better than anyone else. If Izla ever got around to falling in love, she was more likely to look among commoners. Her father might not approve, but they appealed to her more.

By day three of the glass slipper escapades, Izla was worn down. It was worse for poor Alveen. He had to touch all the smelly feet of every woman. By the fourth day, Izla stayed in the carriage, and by the fifth day, she directed them to Ella's house. Enough was enough. Alveen had proved his willingness to work hard to find Ella.

Alveen sat on the red velvet seat in the royal carriage and sank down. "I'm beginning to smell stockings in my dreams, which have turned them into nightmares. I worry my hands will permanently smell of feet."

Izla laughed. "If that happens, I'll send you some of my rose lotion. I only wear it when I need to overpower other people's smells at parties."

He wrinkled his nose. "Roses mixed with feet would not be much of an improvement."

Izla grinned. "I have a feeling we are getting close."

"I hope so."

An hour later, they pulled in front of Ella's home and Izla had to resist the urge to clap her hands and giggle. She made herself invisible and hurried from the carriage.

Alveen glanced around as if he might see her. "You are coming again?"

"Yes."

Alveen smirked and started toward the door, the slipper in his hand. She'd probably given it away by wanting to come, although Alveen didn't know that she knew where Ella lived. The door opened, and Ella's stepsisters peeked out. Alveen stopped in his tracks and groaned.

"What is it?" Izla whispered.

"Those two women were the worst two I had to dance with at the ball. The taller one kept breathing in my face, and I assume her food of choice is rotten salmon. They both told me how wealthy they were at least twice in the minute we danced. Can't we skip this one?"

Izla gave him a slight push toward the home. "No. Keep walking."

Lady Anna pulled her daughters inside and smiled at the prince. "Welcome to our home, Your Highness. Please come in."

Izla followed close behind him so she could get in without the door smacking her. Lady Anna led the prince into a fine sitting room. It wasn't large, but it was neat with blue padded furnishings and a large, beautiful fireplace against one wall. There were three vases full of pink roses, which made Izla smile. Maybe they would smell feet and roses today after all.

Lady Anna pointed her oldest daughter toward a blue chair. The girl sat down and held out her foot. There was no way the slipper would fit, with or without Izla's magic. Alveen had a memorized speech he gave at each house, but he looked defeated. He didn't say a word, he just kneeled on one knee and tried to put the slipper on her foot. It didn't fit.

"Push harder, darling," Lady Anna encouraged.

Alveen shook his head. "It doesn't fit. Next."

The eldest sister jumped to her feet and stomped over to her mother. She crossed her arms and glared at Alveen. The younger sister sat down, and the slipper was too large.

"It fits!" Lady Anna exclaimed.

"No," Alveen said. "It's much too large."

Lady Anna whispered something into the oldest's ear.

The girl's brows came together, and she yelled, "I will not cut off my big toe!"

The prince stood. "We are done here." He hurried and stormed from the room, muttering something about gold diggers.

Izla hurried to stop him, bumping into Lady Anna on her way. Lady Anna let out a small yelp, then quickly composed herself. Her eyes darted around the room suspiciously. Izla smiled. She grabbed the back of Alveen's tunic, stopping him mid-step. Izla was surprised he hadn't heard the frantic doorknob sounds going on upstairs. It had to be Ella. It figured Lady Anna would lock her away for this event.

"Upstairs," Izla whispered in his ear.

Alveen paused and tilted his head to the side. The doorknob turning had turned into pounding. "What's going on upstairs?"

"Cat," Lady Anna said.

Alveen rolled his eyes and took the stairs two at a time. Izla had to hurry to keep up with him. He stopped in front of the banging sound and called through the door. "Ella? Are you in there?"

"Prince Alveen?" Ella answered.

"Stand back. I'm going to break the door."

Izla smiled and leaned against the wall. This should be entertaining. Alveen stood back and then charged the door. To Izla's surprise, the door busted open. Ella stood off to the side. Her cheeks were stained with tears, but she was smiling. Alveen held out his hand, and she came forward and took it. He led Ella from the room and down the stairs.

The sound of glass smashing met their ears. Izla rolled her eyes. Lady Anna was unique in so many ways.

"I hope that wasn't the slipper breaking," Alveen said in a stern voice.

Lady Anna appeared before them. "I am so sorry, Your Highness. It seems my daughter has accidentally broken the slipper."

"Don't cut your fingers when you clean it up," Alveen said, putting a hand to Ella's arm and leading her from the house.

Izla smiled. Alveen was a prince that she could get behind. Izla summoned a new glass slipper and stuck it in Alveen's free hand. He held the shoe up to Ella. He bent down and placed the shoe on her foot.

"It fits," he said.

"Yes, and after today, I never want to wear it again. It's so uncomfortable."

"I would imagine." He got to his feet and took Ella in his arms. "Will you marry me, lovely Ella?"

She smiled. "Yes."

Izla's heart was full as she watched them kiss.

Lady Anna came running from the house. "Ella! Wait!"

Ella turned and frowned. Prince Alveen took Ella's hand and led her to the carriage. Izla pointed her wand at Lady Anna. Izla wasn't cruel, but that woman needed an itchy, week-long rash.

Thane sat in Izla's room at her desk, staring out the window. The rain fell gently, and he couldn't help wishing he was back on the beach. He could see the ocean from the window. It wasn't nearly as bad as it had been earlier in the week. He thought about Ava, and the corner of his mouth turned up.

"Are you even listening to me?" Izla asked.

He turned to see his sister standing there with her hands on her hips. "Sorry. What did you say?"

"Have you been ignoring me this entire time?"

Thane scanned his memory. He was sure he had heard her start talking, but he had quickly blocked her out when he started thinking about Ava.

"Why are you grinning like a fool?"

He shrugged. "It's natural, I guess."

Izla narrowed her eyes. "No, it really isn't. You smile, but not like that. Have you heard anything I said about Ella and Prince Alveen?"

"Um... they are in love?" he guessed.

She smiled and clasped her hands together. "Yes, and it is so cute! I am really proud of this. I've made Ella's life so much better."

"That's nice."

"Nice? It's fantastic!"

"Great."

She frowned. "I don't feel you're with me in this, Thane."

"Sorry. I have a lot on my mind, which reminds me. I fixed the mess you made with Marina."

"Mess? How can you say that? Marina was a prisoner in her own life. Now she has the chance to live her dreams... at least the ones that don't involve you."

"She's decided I'm a cad. Sebby is the best guy a person could meet. I think she's falling for him."

Izla nodded. "And that is what I'd intended from the beginning. So, how did you placate the sea king?"

"I didn't talk to him at all. I spoke with Marina's sisters. I need to have a conversation with Marina as soon as she gets back to the castle. Every time I go look for her, she's out somewhere with Sebby. I almost wonder if they are avoiding me."

"What did her sisters say?"

"They want their father to believe Marina turned into sea foam. They said that would stop any war. I need to tell Marina she needs to stay away from any port cities to keep the peace."

"That's a good idea. If the sea king finds out he was lied to, he won't be happy. I should probably talk to her, though. I don't think she likes you."

"That would be great." He picked up a sketch from the desk. It looked like a toddler had drawn it. "What's this?"

Izla beamed. "That is my plan for the Cinderella part of the world I'm going to make. Isn't it great?"

He held the picture up and studied it. "You drew this?"

"Yes. I didn't even get anyone to help. It's all mine."

He nodded. He hoped the actual world was going to look better than Izla's art.

"I have scrolls and scrolls of these pictures. When I'm finished, Father will have no choice but to let me make my shadow world. I've already put so much time and effort into it. I'm going to make one of the biggest anyone has ever seen."

"That might be dangerous. You know shadow worlds need a lot of attention. If you make it too big, it could go bad fast."

"Oh pish," she said, waving her hand in dismissal. "I'm up for it."

Thane just shook his head.

"I'll show you my plans if you promise not to tell Father. I want to show him when it's ready."

"He already knows you want to do it. It's not a secret or anything."

"Yes, but I want to surprise him with how detailed my plans are." She got down on her hands and knees and pulled her comforter back to glance under the bed. She started pulling out scrolls, and Thane's eyes widened. She had a lot. She began unrolling them. Each one was at least ten feet long and two feet wide. She pushed them together, so they formed one long plan.

"It looks complicated," he said, getting up. He walked around the scrolls and tried to make sense of them.

"Oh, it is. It's going to take years to get it all figured out."

"You're being oddly patient. You usually jump in pretty fast."

"Yes, well, this is my dream. It has to be perfect, and that requires time."

"So, how will it all work?"

Izla smiled. "First, I need to get my stories out. I'm planning on finding a talented storyteller and having them write about my experiences. The stories will spread, and everyone will know them. Of course, I'll do it in some other world. Perhaps Earth."

Thane nodded. Earth was the place their father's sister Kyra had gone to live. It was a simple place to get to and not too different from where they were.

"I'll find people who have given up on love, and I'll bring them to my shadow world. I'll make a bunch of shadow people so I don't have to worry about anything. If I can control everything, it will go smoothly."

Thane cocked his head. "I don't understand. So, there will only be one real person there?"

"Only one real person in each story. So, I might place one woman in Cinderella. I will base the story on Ella's experiences and have the woman play Ella's part. Once she falls in love, or learns to love, I will send her back home."

Thane crossed his arms and thought for a moment. "I don't think it will work."

"Why?"

"What good does getting people to fall in love with shadows do?"

"It makes them realize love is possible."

"What if they don't want to follow your stories? You can't force people to cooperate."

She grinned. "If they don't follow the story, their day will start over. Once they do it right, they move on."

"That sounds horrid."

Izla's lip turned down in a pout. "It's not horrid. It's romantic. Once they kiss, they will fade into a new story. When I'm convinced they believe in love, I'll send them home, making their world a better place."

"I don't think it's going to work."

"That's because you aren't a romantic. I'm going to be careful and not hurry my work. Once Father gives me permission, it will probably take me a few hundred years to get the world working."

Thane opened his mouth to respond, but there was a knock on the door.

"Come in," Izla called.

Ava, Lily, and Zina all filed in. Thane stood straight and tried not to grin like an idiot when Ava looked at him.

Izla began rolling up her scrolls. "What are you three about today?"

Zina tossed her blonde curls over her shoulder and sighed. "We are having a bit of a spat."

"A friendly one," Lily said when Izla raised her brows.

Ava glanced at Thane and then at the floor.

"What is the problem?" Izla asked, shoving the scrolls under her bed and standing.

Zina peered over at Ava. "Ava keeps leaving Thurin and coming here. Princess Rose is a real handful, and no one tries to control her except the three of us. It isn't fair that she leaves so much."

Thane held in an eye roll.

Izla tapped her lip. "None of you need to be there all the time. Why don't you take turns?"

Lily frowned. "It stresses King Fredrick when we aren't all there. He wants to be able to call on us at any moment."

Izla let out a breath. "That's ridiculous. There are lots of kings and queens with fairy counselors, but none have three. He should be happy you're there at all."

Zina's head bobbed up and down in agreement. "We told him that, but he is insistent. The king and queen both worry a lot."

Lily shifted from one foot to the other. She never liked confrontation. "It is only seven short years until Nassandra's curse will be fulfilled. That isn't so long. Ava should really stay with us."

"I'll do better," Ava said, rubbing her arm with one hand. "I'll stay in Thurin until everything with Rose is finished."

Thane frowned. "That could take forever. It isn't just pricking her finger. Who knows how long it will take to wake her? What if it takes the entire hundred years?"

Ava looked back at her slippers. "Then, I guess I will stay for a hundred years. Princess Rose is the priority in all this."

Thane ground his teeth together. A hundred years might not seem like a long time in the grand scheme of things, but at the moment, it felt like an eternity. Ava continued to study her slippers as if they were the most interesting thing she had ever seen. He narrowed his eyes. Fine. He wasn't a priority.

"Stop grinding your teeth," Izla ordered. "You don't want to break them."

He glared at his sister, then headed for the door.

"Wait," Ava said. "Where are you going?"

He glanced over his shoulder. "Who cares?"

Ava hurried over and caught his arm. "I do."

"Do you?"

Her eyes filled with tears. "Please don't do this."

"Do what?"

"You know I have to take care of Rose. I hate it, but I promised. Can't you understand that?"

Lily laughed. "Why would Thane care if we take care of Rose or not?"

Zina tilted her head. "I don't think he cares if *we* take care of her. He wants Ava to keep sneaking over here."

"But why?" Lily asked.

Thane blocked them out. He looked down at Ava. "A hundred years is a long time."

"We might defeat Nassandra before Rose pricks her finger."

"And you might not."

Her eyes pleaded with his. "Please understand. And please wait for me."

The anger left him, and he just felt tired. He threaded his fingers through hers. "I'll wait."

"What is going on?" Lily asked. "Thane and Ava? I never saw this coming."

Izla rolled her eyes. "Shhhh."

Ava smiled up at him, and his insides melted. He leaned forward and pressed his lips to hers. He would wait for two hundred years if he had to.

Chapter 20

King Henan walked around Izla's scrolls with a deep frown. She had spread them across the throne room to show the depth of her plan. The last ten years had flown by, and she desperately needed her father's approval. After spending all of her spare time on this project, she would be devastated if he refused to let her proceed. The plans were much neater than when she first started because she had figured out a way to use magic to enhance the maps.

She waited patiently and tried not to fidget. Her father squatted down, and his brows came together as he studied the area that would tell Snow White's story. She held her breath as he scanned it. It was one of her best areas. If he didn't like this one, he wouldn't like any of it.

"It is definitely well thought out," he muttered.

She smiled. "It is. I've been working on it for years."

He glanced at her. "I should have known you were up to something. You haven't been around as much as you used to be."

"Can't you see how wonderful it could be?"

He let out a long sigh. "I understand what you want to do, and I think your intentions are good."

"But?"

"But I am not sure it is a good idea. Something like this could really mess with mortals."

"I would be careful. I'll make sure it's safe, and I'll watch out for everyone I bring here. Please, Father? I've worked so hard on this."

He closed his eyes and rubbed his temples. "I can't say yes yet."

Izla's heart fell into her stomach. "Oh?"

"You should make a small version of this as a test and see if it works."

She frowned. "Even a small version will take a lot of time."

He pursed his lips together. "What if you only make one story and leave the rest blank? You try it and see if it works. If it doesn't, you destroy it immediately. If it does, I will let you continue."

A smile spread across her face. She had won. Her father wouldn't say that, but she knew. "Thank you."

He raised his brows and pointed at her. "Be careful. Leaving open space in a shadow world breeds all sorts of trouble."

"I know, I know. Swamps and strange creatures can creep in."

"Exactly. Remember Uncle Horth?"

She smiled. "I'll never forget." Her uncle Horth had built a shadow world. He filled it with people, but he wanted to leave the edges blank for expansion. It didn't take long for strange frog creatures to take over. Uncle Horth was unreasonably scared of frogs. He had burned down the entire thing and had to start over. All the people had to relocate, and he made a new world where frogs did not exist.

"I want to inspect it once a month to make sure you aren't neglecting anything."

She hugged her father. "Thank you." She started rolling up scrolls. This was it. She finally got to begin.

The door opened, and Thane entered. Izla smiled up at him, and he frowned. "No! You didn't tell her she could do it, did you?"

King Henan sighed and put his hand on Thane's shoulder. "Your sister needs a project. This could be good for her."

"For her, but not for the people she's interfering with."

Izla picked up a scroll. "They will be happy. You'll see."

"You let her do whatever she wants."

Izla glared at her brother, and King Henan ran a hand over his face. She would excuse Thane this time. She knew the last ten years had been hard for him. He'd only seen Ava twice in all that time, and both times were at crowded parties. He should understand the power that love had over people.

"What would you prefer she did?" the king asked.

"She could go help her friends. Princess Rosamond pricked her finger three years ago. How long are we going to let that go on? That seems like something Izla should want to fix."

Izla tilted her head. It was something she wanted to help with. It would also make a delightful story for her shadow world. "I'll wait to get started and help them."

Thane's eyebrows rose. "Really?"

"Of course. All you had to do was ask. I know you want your life to move on, and you can't do that without Ava. What has happened so far? I admit, I've been focused on my own things. I know she pricked her finger and fell asleep, and I know princes from all over have failed to wake her."

Thane shrugged. "I've stayed out of it."

King Henan glanced out the window. "Once the princess pricked her finger, King Fredrick demanded your friends do something. Lily panicked."

Izla put a hand to her mouth. "Oh dear. What did she do?"

"She put a spell on the entire kingdom. A spell that makes them all sleep until Princess Rosamond awakens."

"That's not too bad. In fact, it's rather clever. What are they doing to wake her?"

The king rubbed his goatee. "They have put out several proclamations asking every unmarried prince to come and try to wake her. After a year, they changed it to any of noble birth. I'm not sure what has gone on, but none has been successful."

Izla sighed. How had she gotten so wrapped up in her own things to miss all of this? It wasn't long ago she would have jumped right in and tried to help. Well, three years wasn't too bad for a kingdom to sleep. Her friends weren't failures yet, and she would help them. In the process, she would free Ava, and she and Thane could finally make a life together.

That thought made her frown. She would love to see Thane and Ava marry, but that would mean Thane would take over his piece of the kingdom and she would rarely see him. That was what happened with her other brothers. They were all too busy to bother with their younger siblings.

"Are you going to help me?" she asked Thane.

"I have nothing better to do."

"I've neglected those three for too long. I don't know where to find them if they aren't in the castle anymore."

Thane grinned. "Then, I guess we make it a game. Do you want to wager on how easy it will be to find them? My guess is five minutes. I don't believe Lily can do anything discreetly. She's probably started a fire by accident somewhere."

Izla rolled her eyes. "They aren't that bad."

"Lily is. Zina's not much better."

Izla's eyes sparkled. "What about Ava?"

Thane just smiled and refused to respond.

King Henan ignored the ribbing. "Now that it's decided, I can't believe I've let it go on this long without assistance. You should work on this immediately."

"I'm ready," Izla said. "Just let me put my scrolls away."

Thane bent down and helped scoop some of them up. Izla smiled. She might fight with her brother from time to time, but Thane really was a good brother. Her heart felt lighter than it had in a while. She'd been focused so long on her scrolls that she had done nothing fun.

Thane looked at Izla and smirked. They had just appeared on the outskirts of Thurin, and the first thing he smelled was fire.

She scowled. "It might not be them."

He pointed toward the castle. "So, what do you have to say about that?" Large thorny briers grew up so high they couldn't see the castle. The thorns were as big as daggers, and the branches were thick. It would be almost impossible to get through.

"Oh my," Izla said, walking up and touching a large thorn. "That could impale a person as good as any weapon I've ever seen. The question is, who made it grow?"

"My guess is Lily."

"You try to blame everything on her."

"And I'm usually right."

"It could have been Nassandra. She might try to keep the kingdom asleep. I'm sure she wasn't happy about Lily changing her curse."

Thane looked up at the large plant. "That could be true. I have heard nothing about Nassandra since she cursed the princess."

"I hope it's because she realized she did something rash and was ashamed of herself."

"That would be nice, but I doubt it."

Izla's mouth turned down. "So do I."

"So, why does it smell like fire?"

She sniffed the air. "I'm not sure. I don't see any smoke."

"IZ!" Lily yelled. She came running from the forest behind them, her messy brown hair trailing behind her. She grabbed Izla and wrapped her in a hug. "I knew you would come! I wish you'd come a few years ago, but you're here!"

Izla hugged her friend. "If you needed me, why didn't you come for me?"

She kicked at the ground. "Ava and Zina said we could figure it out without you." She lowered her voice. "Between you and me, I think they are wrong."

"Where are they?"

"In the woods. We've been staying in a tent."

"For three years?"

"Yes."

Izla pulled a small twig from Lily's hair. "Who made this bramble grow up?"

"That was me," Zina said, as she and Ava came out of the trees.

Thane's heart sped up as they walked forward. Ava looked just as beautiful as ever. He wasn't sure how to react. It had been so long since that last kiss.

"Why?" Izla asked.

Thane wasn't sure if he cared about the why. Sometimes he wished he was more like his brother, Verit. If Verit had been away from the girl he loved for almost ten years, he would already be kissing her. Ava was watching Izla too closely. She was going out of her way to not glance in his direction. That could mean so many things. Had she changed her mind about him?

Zina motioned at the thick hedge in front of them. "Once Rose pricked her finger, men from all over kept coming to kiss her. We couldn't just let everyone on the planet kiss her, so I grew this to keep people out."

Izla narrowed her eyes. "How is anyone supposed to break the spell if they can't get to her?"

"I figured that anyone who was willing to take the time and effort to get to her would be more worthy."

Izla put a hand to her head, and Thane tried not to smile.

Zina frowned. "I can tell you think it was a bad idea, but put yourself in Rose's shoes. If you were unconscious, would you want a bunch of disgusting men kissing you?"

Izla looked thoughtful. "No, I supposed I wouldn't. Still, if no one can get to her, how do we break the spell?"

"Someone will make it," Zina said.

"We thought Prince Jerim would make it," Lily said. "He got about halfway before..."

Thane raised his eyebrow. "Before what?"

"The dragon."

"A dragon?" Izla exclaimed. "Why would you put a dragon in there?"

Zina shrugged. "The dragon wasn't us. He showed up one day and wouldn't leave. We can't prove it, but we think Nassandra is behind it."

Everyone was quiet while Izla thought. Thane wasn't sure if his eyes had left Ava, and she was still avoiding his gaze. Her hands were fisted, and she looked nervous. It would have been better if he had walked up and kissed her. Then, this would be over and he would know if she was over him.

"We have a prince staying in a tent near us," Lily finally said.

"What?" Izla asked.

Thane shook his head. Izla's friends had always amused him. He wasn't sure they had been ready for this task.

"When a person comes who wants to brave the thistles, we have them stay nearby for a few days. It gives them a chance to rest and prepare. We don't like the one staying here now. We hope he changes his mind and leaves."

"I've tried to get Zina to take down the briers," Ava said, breaking her silence. "It's too dangerous. It always ends in injury or worse."

Thane turned his attention to Zina. "It will not look good if all the princes disappear."

"Only one actually died," Lily said. "And that was the dragon's fault."

Izla turned and looked down the road to the village. "I hear a horse."

They all watched the overgrown road until a horse rounded the bend. A man on a black horse galloped toward them. He had on a fine tunic and shiny black boots. Thane was always impressed when a person could keep their boots clean on a horse ride. His clothing was nice enough to be royal, but he wasn't wearing a crown. Not that it mattered. Thane rarely wore his.

When the rider reached them, he dismounted. His short black hair was wet with sweat, and he looked tired. He was younger than Thane would have expected. No more than nineteen, from the looks of him.

He placed a hand on the sword at his waist. "My name is Prince Lewyn. Who might you all be?"

Izla stepped forward. "We don't have time for pleasantries. Are you here to try to break Princess Rosamond's curse?"

"Yes."

Lily looked him over. "You realize many have tried and failed?"

"I won't fail."

Izla arched her brow. "What makes you so sure?"

"Because the curse said it could be someone who might love her, and I already do."

Zina narrowed her eyes and placed her hands on her hips. "I recognize you. You're the little scoundrel that used to come around in the summers." She turned to Izla. "His mother used to send him for visits. He was into everything."

"And you are the annoying fairies that don't let Rose out of your sight, although it appears you failed to protect her."

Zina frowned. "You say you love her, and it took you three years to get around to coming here?"

He sighed. "That wasn't my choice. My mother worries about things like this. She doesn't know I'm here. I finally was able to sneak out." He walked over to the briers and touched one of the massive thorns.

Thane jumped when a hand touched his arm. He turned to see Ava looking up at him. She leaned toward him and whispered, "Prince Lewyn isn't very competent with things like sword fighting and not... falling on his face when he's walking. I don't think he will make it. He's a bit annoying but has a good heart. Rose favored him."

He placed his arm around Ava's back and took it as a good sign when she didn't move away. "Then, let's help him."

"How?"

"I'm not sure."

Prince Lewyn pulled his sword from its scabbard and glanced at them. "So, I just chop my way through?"

Zina poked the prince in the shoulder with her finger. "If it was as easy as that, someone would have succeeded by now."

He nodded. "I suppose that's true. How many have failed before me?"

"We lost count."

He swallowed. "How many died?"

Lily frowned. "Only one, but some others needed serious medical help when they were found."

Lewyn took a deep breath. "I guess I should get started. At least if I die, it will be because of love."

A smile the size of Thurin broke out across Izla's face. "Beautiful. And we will help you."

"Thank you," he said, bowing his head to her. "I don't believe I've met you before."

"I am Princess Izla."

"The fairy princess? I should have known. Everyone speaks of your beauty."

Izla waved her hand in dismissal, but Thane could tell she was pleased. "First things first. You need a rest and a good meal. It is better to be prepared than to run into this like a scared chicken." She turned to Ava. "What is there to eat around here?"

"We have a fire going with some stew," Lily answered. "It's just through the trees." Prince Lewyn and Izla followed her into the forest.

Thane hoped to have a few minutes with Ava, but Zina was still there, her red lips pursed as she glared at the briers.

"Do you think you can move them?" Thane asked. "Prince Lewyn might be the one, and he might have a hard time getting through."

Zina ran her fingers through her blonde curls and sighed. "I can't. I tied the briers into the curse. They won't go away until the spell is lifted."

232

Thane wanted to ask why, but that wouldn't get them anywhere. If it was done, it was done.

"I guess you should go eat," Ava said when Zina didn't seem to have anywhere better to be.

Zina's eyes went from Thane to Ava, and she rolled her eyes. "You could just say you wanted to be alone." She turned and stomped into the trees.

Ava turned to Thane. "It's been a long ten years."

He ran his hand over her cheek. "It really has. I thought you would sneak away and come see me sometime."

She arched her brow. "I promised I wouldn't. There was nothing stopping you from visiting me."

"I asked King Fredrick if I could come. He wanted to know why... and he wouldn't let me come without telling him."

"And that stopped you? Won't you rule over his kingdom someday?"

He shifted. "I will, but there has to be some respect between the other rulers and me. If I force myself into things, they will see me as a tyrant. I don't want that."

She nodded. "I suppose that makes sense. Still, I've been living in these woods for three years now."

"I'm sorry. The longer I didn't see you, the more insecure I felt."

She smiled. "When have you ever been insecure?"

"Every day of my life."

"You hide it well."

"I try."

"Now what?"

"Now we need to make sure Prince Lewyn makes it through this thing alive, and then nothing will keep us apart."

She tilted her head. "Promise?"
He wrapped her in his arms. "Promise."

Chapter 21

Izla squinted against the bright morning sun. If they were going to get Lewyn to Princess Rose, then the earlier the better. They didn't want to end up in the briers in the dark. She kept expecting someone to suggest flying, but no one had, and she was glad. The story would be so much better if they had to fight their way through. Flying would be complicated anyway. The prince couldn't fly, and flying while carrying someone wasn't easy. If they made him appear in the castle, that would feel like cheating.

The other prince who had been camped with them had decided not to risk it after Izla told him the horror stories that awaited him in the briers. She felt guilty, but she didn't have the patience to deal with two princes.

"The briers are thick," Lewyn noted. "I'm not sure we can get through without chopping them."

"I hope your sword is sharp," Thane said, motioning to the prince's sword.

Lewyn drew his sword, and his face turned red. "It's not as sharp as it could be."

Thane grabbed the prince's sword and felt the blade. "Why would you even carry a sword that is as dull as this? It's not going to cut anything."

Lewyn rubbed the back of his neck. "My mother doesn't want me to have anything sharper. It makes her nervous."

Thane tossed the sword back, and Lewyn caught it. "It should make her more nervous that you are running around with a sword that can't protect you."

Izla shook her head. They were going to need another weapon. She looked over to where Lily and Zina were whispering with excitement. There was nothing exciting about a dull sword.

Lily ran back toward camp, and Zina stepped forward. "We have a sword and a shield. We might allow you to use them. They are magic. They help whoever is using them."

Lewyn's eyes widened. "Really? That would be welcome."

Izla was sure Zina was lying. She hoped she wasn't talking about the beat up shield and rusted sword she had seen by the tent last night.

"We might let you use them if you promise to be careful," Zina told him.

"I will. I promise," he said eagerly.

A loud clanging sound echoed in their ears. Izla cringed as the banging continued. She was almost positive Lily was out in the trees trying to beat the bent up shield back into shape.

Lewyn stepped toward the trees. "What is that sound?"

Zina grabbed his arm to stop him. "Don't worry about that. Right now you need to focus on how you are going to get through the briers and what you will do if you encounter the dragon."

His eyes widened even more. "Dragon?"

Zina nodded. "What is the danger of a dragon when you have the magic sword and shield?"

"So, I'll be invincible?"

"Not invincible," Izla cut in. She didn't want the prince getting overconfident and possibly killed. "It will serve you well, but you must still take care."

The pounding continued, and Izla tried to ignore the pulse in her head. A few minutes later, Lily came running back. In her hands was the dented shield. Izla wasn't sure if it looked any better than it had before Lily gave it a beating. Lily pushed a stray strand of hair behind her ear and grinned as she handed the shield to the prince. She was breathing hard, and small beads of sweat covered her forehead.

Lewyn examined the shield with a frown. "It looks a bit... used."

"Of course it's used," Ava said. "No one would know how marvelous it was if it hadn't been used. Just think of all the warriors that have used it before you. Each dent marks their bravery. Now you go to add your own dents."

"Wow," Lewyn whispered in awe.

Izla rolled her eyes, and Thane turned away to hide a smile.

"Where is the sword?" he asked.

"Right, the sword." Lily turned and ran off again. Izla was curious to see what they could do for the rusty old sword. In her opinion, it wasn't any better than the one the prince had now. She supposed the rusty one might cause someone an infection and kill them slowly.

A flash of light, followed by a loud boom, blasted from the forest. Izla grabbed her shirts and ran toward the sound. She shouldn't have left so much up to her friends. She would never forgive herself if Lily was hurt.

Lily met her before she entered the trees. The edges of her hair were singed and so was one of her sleeves. In her hand, Lily held the brightest sword Izla had ever seen. "I'm fine," she muttered so only Izla could hear. "I knew that spell would come in handy someday."

"Are you alright?" Ava asked.

"Yes, of course." She handed the sword to Lewyn. "Be careful. If you touch anything with that sword, it will cut it. When you hack at the briers, make sure you don't hit anything else. I would hate to see you lose your arm, or worse."

Lewyn held the sword reverently. "Shall we begin?" He swung the sword in front of him.

Izla watched the prince's confidence grow with each swish of the sword. Confidence was a good thing, but she hoped it didn't go to his head.

"I'm not sure we should all go," Thane said. "What if something goes wrong?"

"I'm going," Izla said. There was no way she was missing out on any of this story. It was going to be a favorite, she could already tell. She felt something touch her hand and looked down to see Axel. He licked her hand, and she patted his head.

"How does he always find you?" Ava asked.

"I'm not sure, but he always does."

"Who stays back?" Lily asked. "I wouldn't mind waiting. I've never liked dragons."

"I'll wait with you," Zina said. "If any of us are likely to fail, it's Lily and I."

Izla glanced from one friend to the next. "That isn't true."

Ava smiled. "Liar. And I'm only a little better, but I want to come."

"Then, I'm coming," Thane said, drawing a sword Izla didn't know he had. He must have popped back home in the night and grabbed it. Izla thought about grabbing one for herself, but two swords in the group were probably enough to protect them from one dragon. He hacked at the briers, cutting part way through the branch. "This is going to take a while."

Lewyn swung his sword and took out a branch with one swing. He turned to Thane and grinned. Thane didn't look amused. The two of them began chopping, and before long, they had a good rhythm going. Every branch Lewyn hit fell immediately. Thane's sword needed two or three cuts on each branch. Ava and Izla walked slowly behind them. This was going to take forever.

Ava leaned in close to Izla and spoke quietly. "You don't suppose we can blast some of the briers, do you? At this rate, we will have grandchildren by the time we get through."

Izla shook her head. "This is Lewyn's quest. He needs to put forth the effort to have the full satisfaction of saving Rose." She stepped over a fallen branch.

Thane was breathing hard. Lewyn was still chopping like it was no effort. Izla wondered what Lily had done to make the sword work like that. It was impressive. Lewyn kept turning and grinning at Thane. The more he smiled, the angrier her brother looked.

Izla muttered a spell and pointed at Thane's sword. Within a minute, he was keeping up with Lewyn.

Ava smiled as they ambled behind. "I saw that."

"We can't let the prince know we are helping, but you are right. At that rate, we would never get to the castle."

Thane was smiling now that he was keeping pace with Lewyn. They were both trying to outdo each other, which was fine by Izla. The faster they went, the closer they were to the castle.

Thane's arms were tired, but he couldn't rest until Lewyn did. He would not let a mortal prince make him look weak. Izla or Ava must have placed a spell on his sword because it was cutting a lot better than it had in the beginning. He hacked at a large branch and moved out of the way as it fell. Behind it was a small clearing about thirty feet wide.

"This is odd," Lewyn said, lowering his sword. "Perhaps it's time for a break?"

"Only if you want one," Thane said.

Lewyn shrugged. "I'm good either way."

Thane wanted to yell. His shoulder burned, but he would not admit it.

Izla pulled her wand from her pocket and pointed at the ground. Sparks flew from the instrument, and a small fire sprung up in front of them. "We will take a break," she said.

"Do we need a fire?" Thane asked, wiping sweat from his brow. "It's boiling out here."

"I was going to make a warm drink," she said. "Would you rather I didn't?"

Lewyn wiped his own sweat covered brow. "How about water?"

Izla shrugged. "If you say so." She waved her wand, and the flames went out. She held out her hand and a glass of water appeared. The prince accepted it eagerly.

Thane summoned his own water and took a deep drink. He wanted to sit, but he wouldn't unless Lewyn did first. He almost smiled when the prince sat with his legs crossed. Thane sat back on his legs and resisted rubbing his shoulder. If this was how he felt after a few hours, how would he feel by the time they reached the castle?

Ava kneeled behind him and began rubbing her hands over his shoulders. He closed his eyes and relaxed as the pain became more bearable. Ava leaned in and wrapped her arms around him. She pressed her cheek to his. He opened his eyes and ignored Izla's smirk. Lewyn was working on chewing a tough piece of jerky. Thane wished they would disappear so he could kiss Ava.

"You can kiss her," Izla said, as if she could read his mind. "I won't look."

Lewyn chuckled, and Thane resisted punching him. Thane had never gotten along with other princes. Something about being around them made him feel the need to prove himself.

Ava kissed his cheek and stood. "We probably should be on our way. Resting only puts off the inevitable." She held out her hand, and Thane let her pull him to his feet.

"I thought fairies were more powerful," Lewyn said. "Like, I thought you could just blow down something like this. Or fly. Can't you fly?"

Izla stood. "Of course we can. What we can't do is fly and carry you. Besides, this is your quest, not ours. We are going with you as a service and nothing more. We could take ourselves inside the castle easier than snapping our fingers, but that would be pointless as we cannot wake the princess."

He looked thoughtful. "I am glad you are with me. I've done nothing like this before." He drew his sword and began hacking at the thorns.

Thane sighed. His father always told them to do as much as they could without magic. He said they would regret it someday if they didn't. He made them chop wood and carry it into the castle with the servants. Thane had always resented it, but he was glad for it now.

"Can I try?" Izla asked him, motioning to his sword. He handed it over. With luck, Izla knew some type of spell that would help her go faster. She walked over and smacked a branch, almost missing it. She shot him a glare when he smiled and tried again.

Ava took his arm and leaned her head against his shoulder. "Stories like this always seem more exciting when you aren't in them."

"We can make it more exciting," Thane said with a mischievous smile.

Ava turned and grinned at him. "Oh?"

He took Ava's face in his hands and leaned down, kissing her. A moment later, he released her.

A sparkle jumped into her eye. "You call that exciting?" She wrapped her arms around his neck and went on her toes to press her lips to his. If he hadn't been kissing her, he would have smiled.

This was ridiculous. Izla had been chopping at branches for ten minutes and wasn't making a lot of progress. Izla knew how to fence, and it wasn't helping her at all. Even with the spell she had placed on Thane's sword, she was struggling. Lewyn was going a lot faster than she was. She might have to change her opinion of him. Even with the sharp sword, he must be feeling some fatigue, and he wasn't giving up.

She could give the sword back to her brother, but when she looked back, it was to see Thane and Ava still in the clearing, kissing passionately. That was something she didn't want to see, but she also didn't want to interrupt. She knew Thane had been aching to be with Ava for a long time, and she would let them have the moment.

Lewyn stopped and turned to her. "Did you hear that?"

Izla paused and listened. Something was coming toward them. She squinted into the briers and tried to see what it was. Thane yelled something, and Izla turned to see her brother pointing into the sky in front of them. She looked up to see a black and gray dragon flying above them.

"What do we do?" Lewyn asked, his eyes not leaving the dragon.

"Back up slowly," she said, taking steps back. He followed her lead, and they made it back to the clearing.

"I haven't seen a dragon that size in a long time," Thane said, admiring the dragon.

It swooped down and landed in front of them.

Ava grabbed Thane's arm. Izla didn't want to fight a dragon, and most dragons weren't out to get people. This one had obviously been put here for a reason, so she wasn't sure how it would react to them.

The large beast took a step toward them, and Lewyn held out his sword. If the shaking was anything to judge by, the prince was terrified. Still, she would give him credit for not running away.

The dragon came closer, and Lewyn took a step back. It was good Axel had stayed back with Zina and Lily. He was a wonderful wolf, but he probably would have attacked. It wouldn't be hard for Izla, Thane, or Ava to get rid of the dragon, but Lewyn needed to do this.

"Should I freeze it?" Thane asked, leaning over to Izla.

"No," she whispered. "Let Lewyn try."

The dragon breathed fire, and they all dropped to the ground. Izla frowned and pulled herself back up. Dragons rarely attacked without cause. Someone was controlling this one.

Lewyn got to his feet and yelled, rushing toward the dragon with his sword in the air. The dragon spun around, knocking him to the ground with his large tail. Lewyn rolled and didn't move. Izla frowned. The fall didn't look bad enough to render him unconscious. The dragon turned to the hedge, and fire poured out of its mouth. Briers caught fire, and it spread fast.

Izla didn't have time to think. She grabbed her wand and pointed it at the hedge. The dragon's tail knocked into her hand, causing her wand to fall. She rolled her eyes. A wand wasn't necessary for any of her magic. She just liked to use it. Fire was surrounding them now, and she tried to make a plan. If worse came to worst, they would have to grab Lewyn and get out.

The dragon moved closer to Lewyn and rolled him over with its snout. Lewyn jumped to his feet and backed away from the dragon without getting too close to the flames. He grabbed his sword and shield but didn't make any moves toward the creature. Izla crossed her arms and glared at the dragon. There was something off about it. She was almost certain it was Nassandra's doing.

"NASSANDRA!" she yelled.

"Where?" Thane asked, looking around.

"I don't see her, but I know she is here," she said. She grabbed her wand and swished it at the fire. It sputtered and died. All that was left was the smell of smoke and several feet of burned branches.

"Why would she be here?" Ava asked.

"To stop anyone from waking Rose."

Ava frowned. "I don't know why she cares so much. She's going through a lot of effort for one little slight."

The dragon threw its head back and laughed. It was a horrifying sight to behold. Lewyn took a step back, and Thane took his sword from Izla. A light flashed around the dragon, and it disappeared. In its place stood Nassandra. Her black dress trailed past her feet, and her long blonde hair was curled in perfect ringlets.

"Hello, friends," she said with a smile. "I didn't expect to see you here."

"You need to leave," Izla commanded.

"Oh? And why is that?"

Thane's eyes narrowed. "You know exactly why."

"Do I? I never heard of a rule stating that I couldn't be here."

"What is the point?" Thane asked. "There is no reason for you to be here."

"Of course there is. Lily messed up my curse, and so I must stay here and make sure no silly prince breaks the spell."

"And you have nothing better to do with your time?"

"Nothing."

Thane shook his head. "That's pathetic."

Nassandra pursed her unnaturally red lips and glared at him. "What's pathetic is the people you choose to spend your time with," she said, motioning toward Ava, who was still clinging to his arm.

"You realize that if you keep this up, my father will eventually get involved."

Izla raised her brow. It wasn't like Thane to take the lead when Izla was there.

Nassandra laughed. "King Henan doesn't want to cause any problems with anyone. He stays out of as much as he can to keep the peace."

Thane glared at her. "Perhaps, but what you are doing isn't keeping the peace. An entire kingdom is in a hundred year's sleep because of you."

"It isn't because of me. That was Izla's little friends."

Ava stepped forward. "You are the reason we are all here. Don't put it on anyone else."

Nassandra sauntered over to Ava with a wide smirk on her face. "Poor Ava. It must be hard to have a friend as powerful as

Izla. I know you make your other two friends look like novices, but that isn't saying much. I suppose that is why you are after Thane. He is going to rule, after all. It will make you more respected in people's eyes."

Thane took a step toward her, and Ava stopped him with her hand. "You know I don't care about that. You were always the one who wanted all the attention on you."

Nassandra ran her hand over Thane's arm, and he flinched. "So true. I do like attention. That is why the slight at Princesses Rosamond's christening couldn't go unpunished. People must realize that they can't forget about me." She ran her eyes over Ava. "I see Thane is trying, but I won't allow it. Not after all we have been through together."

Thane ground his teeth together and narrowed his eyes. Izla frowned as she watched the anger pass over her brother's face. What was Nassandra talking about? As far as she knew, Thane had never said two sentences to the woman before today.

Nassandra turned and glanced at Izla, then back to Thane. "Your sister looks confused. I'm hurt. You never told her about us?"

Ava crossed her arms and looked at Thane, then at the ground.

"There never was an *us*," he said.

Nassandra put a hand to her heart and let out a dramatic sigh. "Breaking my heart again."

There was no point in this conversation that Izla could see. Nassandra didn't need more time to upset them and throw them off their plans, but what to do? Nassandra was about as strong as she was, but not as strong as all of them. Lewyn was cowering behind them all, so he wouldn't be of much use.

Thane's eyes shot daggers at the woman, but she didn't seem to care. "I am warning you. Thurin is in my kingdom. I will protect it, even if that means harm coming to you. You are disrupting so many lives right now."

"It sounds like a threat, but I don't see you taking any action. Besides, Thurin isn't under your rule until you marry, and as far as I know, you are not married. Now that I know where your interests lie, I will thwart that as well. You will not marry unless it is to me."

"I will never marry you."

"You will. I can be very convincing."

Izla reached for her wand and then paused when she spotted Lewyn creeping behind Nassandra. What was he doing? Now she couldn't attack without risking the prince. She racked her brain for a spell she could use to freeze Lewyn, but she couldn't think of anything she could do fast enough. If she threw out a spell, it would alert Nassandra, and she might hurt Lewyn. She could throw something at Nassandra, but she was probably expecting that.

Thane gripped his sword tight, and Izla would bet he had also seen Lewyn.

Nassandra grinned. "The funny thing about your quest is that you think having your princess sleep for a hundred years will save her. What's stopping me from killing her when she awakes? What's stopping me from killing her now while she sleeps?"

"ME!" Lewyn yelled, sword held over his head. He swung his sword down, and Nassandra disappeared, causing the prince to fall over.

Izla rolled her eyes and helped him to her feet. "That was idiotic. You thought you could kill one of the most dangerous fairies in the realm by yourself?"

He brushed off his knees. "I wasn't going to kill her. I was only going to stab her through the heart so you could all get away."

Ava let out a small chuckle, and Thane shook his head.

Izla took a deep breath. "When you stab someone through the heart, they usually die."

Lewyn's brows came together. "But fairies are immortal."

"*Immortal* is a strange word. A fairy is immortal—so long as they aren't killed."

"I don't understand."

Izla glanced at Thane, who was grinning slightly. She frowned and looked back at Lewyn. "We don't die of old age or illness. We can go on living forever, but we can be killed. A sword through the heart would definitely do it."

"Would it have been so bad if I had succeeded?"

"Perhaps not. Nassandra has done some horrible things. She even started a war between two kingdoms once. The problem here is that you won't succeed. She is skilled. I'm not even sure if I could defeat her on my own. We don't want you getting killed on your quest to become a hero."

"I didn't want to be a hero. I just wanted to give you all the chance to get away."

"Well, don't do it again. We are fairies. If it came down to it, we could disappear. You are the one in the most danger from Nassandra."

He nodded. "I'm surprised she hasn't killed Rose already, from what she said."

"She can't," Ava said. "We put a protection over her."

Izla was impressed. Her friends had done a better job than anyone had expected. She also knew Nassandra was like her in some ways. She wanted to see how the story would go, and she wanted to be a part of it. The reason they were different was that Izla wanted to be remembered as the reason everyone ended up happy. Nassandra wanted to be the villain.

"Now what?" Thane asked.

"We stop messing around. We've chopped enough hedges." She waved her hands, and a large ball of light flew into the briers, crushing them into nothing.

Prince Lewyn's mouth hung open. "Wow. Why didn't you do that to begin with?"

"You needed to prove yourself."

"And I have?"

Izla shrugged. He had accomplished nothing fantastic, but he had proved he had a good heart. If his kiss woke Rose, she was almost sure he deserved her. Of course, she didn't know Rose, so she was making assumptions.

Izla looked forward. The briers were all destroyed in the front. Now the only thing to do was walk to the castle. Even without the briers, it was going to be a long walk.

Chapter 22

The castle was getting closer. It seemed a little more dreary than Thane had remembered it, but that might be from the spell that put everything to sleep. The trees around the castle drooped, and even the grass looked tired. They passed a sleeping cat and two sleeping dogs.

Everyone appeared to be focused on their walk to the castle, but Thane was almost positive Izla and Ava were wondering what Nassandra had been talking about back in the clearing. He should probably get it all out instead of letting them guess, but he didn't want to have the conversation in front of Prince Lewyn.

Lewyn turned to him. "What was that fairy talking about? Did you court her?"

So much for his plan to wait. Ava looked up at the approaching castle. She was probably trying to look indifferent.

"No, I didn't."

"Then, what was she talking about?"

Thane sighed. "Nassandra wants power. Every fairy knows it. She's never tried to hide it. One summer, she stayed at the castle."

"I had almost forgotten about that," Izla said. "There were a lot of fairies around that year. I took little notice of her. It was before I knew what she was like."

"Yes, well, she took notice of me. She followed me around and talked my ear off. I didn't even have to respond. She just talked."

Ava had a small frown, but she didn't look at him.

"One day, she asked me to go on a walk. We went down to the beach, and she started talking about what a great queen she would be. It was odd, but I let her talk. After a minute, I realized she was trying to tell me she would be a good queen for me. I've never been good at talking about things like that..."

Lewyn nodded. "I've met girls like that. They only want to spend time with me because I'm a prince. I imagine it would be worse for you. You have a lot more power than a prince like me."

"So, what happened?" Ava asked quietly.

"I told her I wasn't looking to get married anytime soon."

Izla grinned. "I'm sure she took that well."

Thane scratched his head. "I don't know what she said, but there was a lot of yelling. I didn't respond because I didn't know what to say. Eventually, she stomped away."

Ava tilted her head and studied him. "And that was the end of it?"

He shook his head. He wished that was the end. "She cornered me the next day in the castle and apologized. I told her it was fine and then she, uh, kissed me."

Ava frowned, and Izla snickered.

"I pushed her away, and if I thought she was mad the day before, I was wrong. She told me I wasn't fit to rule anything, and without her, I would be a failure. Then, she punched me in the eye and stormed off. For being so small, she has a good punch. I had a black eye for over two weeks."

Izla side eyed him and smiled. "I remember the black eye. I'm pretty sure you didn't tell us that's how you got it."

"Probably not."

"I can sympathize," Prince Lewyn said. "I've had very similar things happen. Not from fairies, of course, but I even have a younger sister that teases me when they happen."

"Did she ever contact you again?" Ava asked.

"I haven't spoken to her again until today, but she sends me a letter now and then telling me to think about her. It's really annoying because I do my best to forget about her. It ruins my sleep every time she crosses my mind."

Ava peered over at him. "So, you never felt anything for her?"

He grabbed her hand. "Never."

She squeezed his hand and smiled. "Good."

They all stopped as they came up to the castle. The drawbridge was up, and everything was closed tight.

"Rose is in that tower," Ava said, pointing at the south tower.

"I can raise Prince Lewyn up to that balcony," Thane said. "Then, we can meet him up there."

Izla tapped her lip. "He needs to climb the tower."

Thane scrunched his forehead. "Why? That will take forever, and he has nothing with him that will help."

"Yes, but someday, when people tell the story of Rose and Lewyn, it will sound a lot better if he climbed up the tower to rescue his love."

Lewyn looked confused but didn't protest. They made their way to the tower, and Thane ran his hands over the smooth stone wall. "He can't climb this. No one can climb this. There aren't any good places to put his hands. Even if he gets part way up, he'll eventually fall."

Izla pulled her wand from her pocket and pointed it at the wall. The sound of rock shifting filled their ears, and the enormous stone wall was now covered in hand and foot holds. They were big enough that even an inexperienced climber would make it.

"How is that different from lifting him up?" he asked.

Izla waved a dismissing hand. "Shush. Go ahead, Prince Lewyn."

The prince dropped his shield and sword to the ground and began climbing. The handholds were easy to use, and he was making good time.

Izla grinned as they watched him. "Do you know what would be fabulous? If Rose had exceptionally long hair. Then, her hair could trail over the balcony, and Lewyn could have used it to help him climb."

Ava and Thane both looked at her like she was crazy. Thane shook his head. "That sounds ridiculous. Think of how painful that would be."

Ava put a hand to her hair. "Really painful. I'm glad you didn't think of it until he was already climbing."

Izla tapped her lip. "If it was magic hair, maybe it wouldn't hurt. It would have to be magic to be that long."

"Please don't," Thane begged.

"Oh, don't worry. This story has gone on just about long enough. Still, it sounds like a great idea. The next time I give a gift to a princess, I'm going to give her long, magical hair."

Thane ran a hand over his face. Why didn't Izla ever tire of meddling? "Why would anyone want long, magical hair?"

Izla shrugged. "You never know. If Rose had it, it could have benefitted Lewyn in his climb."

"But how often is a princess going to be in a tower and need someone to climb their hair?"

Ava pointed up. "It looks like he made it. Should we join him? He can't kiss her until I remove the protection."

They disappeared and reappeared on the balcony. Prince Lewyn had his hands on his knees and was catching his breath. A large wooden door blocked the entrance to the tower. Thane muttered a quick spell and pointed at the door, and it swung open. He would not ask and risk Izla deciding Lewyn should bust down the door by himself.

Lewyn peeked in the door and squinted. "It's dark in here."

Thane followed him inside, Izla and Ava tailing him. It wasn't terribly dark, but after being out in the bright sun, it took a moment for their eyes to adjust. Inside the tower was a small, round room. The only thing in it was a large bed. It had an ornately decorated wooden head and footboard.

On the bed was Princess Rosamond. At least, Thane assumed it was her. He'd never met her before. Her long blonde hair was arranged neatly around her face, and she was covered with a silky blue blanket. Her hands rested on her stomach. As far as mortals went, she was pretty.

Lewyn stepped toward her and fell to his knees. He leaned forward and took Rose's hands in his. "Rose?"

Ava placed a hand on his shoulder. "You cannot wake her by speaking to her, and I must lift the protection that is over her. Once I do, you must hurry. We don't know where Nassandra is or what she is doing. You need to kiss her, and we need to get out. Do you understand?"

"I do," he said, standing.

Ava waved her hands over Rose, and sparkling dust fell from her hands onto the princess. "There. Now hurry."

Lewyn leaned over Rose and kissed her softly on the lips. Thane held his breath, hoping it worked. Rose's eyes fluttered, then opened. Her gaze scanned over Thane, Izla, and Ava, and then rested on the prince.

"Lewyn? What happened?"

He held out a hand and helped her sit up. "We don't have time to speak of it. Come, there may be danger."

Rose stood on wobbly feet and brushed her hands over her blue satin dress. "I feel like I've been in bed for a week."

"Three years," Lewyn told her. "Now come."

"Three years?" Rose exclaimed, as he rushed her to a spiral staircase.

"Better than the hundred it was supposed to be," Ava said, as they followed behind.

"Are we really in danger, Ava?" Rose asked. "Can you help?"

They all rushed down the stairs, and Thane wished Izla would let them do this in an easier way. It seemed ridiculous to be running from something when they could take themselves anywhere they wanted.

"There is danger," Ava told her. "Remember the story we told you of the evil fairy? She caused you to fall into a deep sleep. The rest of the kingdom has also been asleep. We don't know if the fairy is going to come after you to harm you, but we will protect you."

They reached the bottom of the stairs and entered a large stone hall. Rose turned to Ava. "I thought that was just a story you told me to scare me into behaving."

"No, it's true."

"We need to keep going," Izla said. "Everyone will wake up soon, and Nassandra won't hesitate to act just because there is a crowd. She may prefer it."

"Of course I prefer it," Nassandra said, appearing before them. Rose squealed and took a step back. "I prefer it, but it isn't necessary."

"Please let us go," Rose begged.

Nassandra laughed. "Let you go? I'm not keeping you here. Still, if I don't kill you, people won't take me seriously anymore."

Izla took a step forward. "Don't do this, Nassandra. If you kill her, you will never know peace, and neither will I, because I will have to kill you."

Nassandra laughed again and put her hands on her hips. "What makes you think you can kill me? It would be me against you. Thane and Ava don't have it in them to fight."

A gust of wind blew through the hallway, and Thane shivered as it passed over him. He knew that wind. He grabbed Ava and pulled her against the wall. Izla had already pulled Lewyn and Rose to the other side. Nassandra screamed as the wind pushed her to the floor and held her there.

King Henan stood before them. He walked over and glared down at Nassandra. "I've neglected you long enough."

Nassandra bared her teeth. "Let me up!"

"No. Never again. I sentence you to the dungeons for eternity."

"You can't do that!"

"I can, and I will. You will not start any more wars. You should thank me. Some think you deserve something a lot worse."

"I will not stay in the dungeons. You know I will get out."

"If you do, you will be the first."

She grinned from the ground. "I love a challenge." Her eyes moved over to Rose. "And when I get out, I will come for you. Both of you."

She didn't look so threatening on the floor.

"My wife also loves a challenge," King Henan said, "and she is in charge of the prison."

He snapped his fingers, and Nassandra disappeared.

Lewyn put his arm around Rose. "You all have so much power. Why do anything the hard way?"

Izla smiled. "Life is dull if you use magic for everything."

Ava's forehead was scrunched, and she glanced up at the king. "You have a wife?"

Thane smiled. "Of course he does. Didn't you think Izla and I must have a mother?"

"Talla doesn't like royal life," King Henan explained. "She has a few tasks she enjoys doing, but she keeps from the people. She isn't content with all the bowing and protocol."

Ava shook her head. "It's just strange. I've known you all my entire life. I always assumed the queen died."

Thane smiled. "She likes it that way. I will introduce you, though."

"What do we do now?" Lewyn asked.

King Henan motioned toward a door at the end of the hall. "I think you will find the people of the kingdom are waking up. The two of you should go meet them."

"And when you tell the story of what happened, leave us out of it," Thane said. "Once people start talking about how we helped them, we have no peace." He knew Izla enjoyed it, but she wasn't the one who usually sat in for their father when requests came around.

"Of course," Lewyn said. "And thank you."

Rose smiled at Lewyn. "I always knew you were the one for me. I'm glad you finally realized it."

He smiled back. "I knew before you did."

Rose looked down at the floor and smiled. Thane tilted his head and watched them. Even he knew it was time for a kiss.

King Henan disappeared, and Ava, Izla, and Thane stood watching the couple, not kissing.

Izla crossed her arms and tapped her foot on the floor. "Either go out and greet your people, or kiss. We don't have all day."

"Oh," Lewyn said, his eyes wide. "I suppose we should tell your family you are alright."

Rose sighed. "I suppose."

Izla rolled her eyes. She opened her mouth to speak, but Rose beat her to it.

"I don't think a kiss before we go out there would hurt."

Lewyn rubbed the back of his neck and glanced at Thane. Thane nodded at him. "You already kissed her once. It probably goes better when she isn't asleep."

"Right, I... uh... Well..."

Rose shook her head and grinned. "Don't fret yourself into a faint," she said, grabbing the front of his tunic. She pulled on the garment and kissed him. Ava clapped her hands, and Thane grinned.

Izla smiled. "And they lived happily ever after. I love it."

Chapter 23

Queen Maylene sat on her throne, wiping her nose on a lace handkerchief. Izla stood in front of her and waited for the woman to stop sniffling. She had met the queen before and didn't have much of an opinion about her. She had been surprised that the queen had requested an audience with her and wondered if it had something to do with her son, Prince Lewyn.

The queen appeared distressed but had said nothing past an initial greeting. Her eyes were red and puffy, but aside from that, she looked like she was put together. Her tight brown bun was surrounded by a gold crown, and her light blue dress was clean and pressed.

"How may I help you?" Izla asked when it became clear the queen wasn't going to speak.

"It is about my son," she said, wiping at the corners of her eyes. "I know he was with you recently, and I am quite upset that you allowed him to go into danger without my permission."

Izla raised her brow. "I am not sure how to respond to that. Lewyn is of age, and he left of his own accord. I do not see how that is my doing."

"You should have sent him home. He had no business fighting dragons and evil fairies. He told me the entire story and expected me to be excited by it all! And now, to make matters even worse, he wants to get married. Of course, I've told him he is much too young. He used to be obedient, but now he thinks he can defy me."

"I'm not sure what you want from me."

The queen pointed her finger at Izla and frowned. "I want you to fix it. You are known for getting involved with these types of things. I want you to talk to my son and make him see reason. He is too young to get married, and that girl he thinks he loves is not royal enough for him."

Izla frowned in confusion. "Not royal enough? Princess Rosamond is from one of the best royal families." If anything, Lewyn wasn't *royal* enough for Rose. Her father's kingdom was larger and more affluent than the one Queen Maylene ruled.

"I'm not so sure. The blame is on me for sending him there in the summers. I thought it would be good to get him out in the world, but in a safe place. King Fredrick allowed him to come, and we were on good terms. Of course, we wouldn't have been if I had known he would allow my son to get to know his daughter."

Izla just stared at the queen. She really didn't know the right response to her. "You sent him away to stay at King Fredrick's castle, and you wanted him to hide his daughter away?"

"It would have been the appropriate thing to do. You need to make him see reason. I don't believe a prince should get married until he is at least thirty-five. That sounds reasonable."

Izla blinked twice. "You are trying to control your son more than is healthy. When we met him, he had a dull sword. That could have ended badly for him when he met the dragon."

"He should have been nowhere near a dragon."

"I try to help people live happily ever after, not break their hearts."

The queen narrowed her eyes and gripped the arm of the throne. "It wouldn't be so bad if I thought she was worthy. There has to be a way to prove to my Lewyn that she isn't as wonderful as he thinks."

"Have you spoken to Lewyn about your concerns?"

"Of course I have. He's being stubborn, which must be her influence on him. He was always quite obedient before."

"You need to understand that your son has grown up. You shouldn't be dictating his choices anymore."

Queen Maylene slumped against her chair and put a hand to her head. "I should have known better than to ask you for help. Your father obviously allows you too much freedom, so you don't understand."

Izla just smiled. An idea was forming in her mind. "Perhaps you should test the girl to see if she is good enough for your son."

The queen sat up tall, and a smile broke across her face. "That is exactly the type of advice I was hoping for. The question is how?"

"What qualities make a princess *royal* enough in your mind?"

The queen scrunched her forehead and tapped her lip. "Well, she must be of good birth, which I suppose she is, but there is more to it than that. She must be kind and moldable. I can't have a stubborn woman marrying my son. I need to have a certain amount of control over her."

Izla shook her head. That didn't sound like Rose. From what her friends said, the girl was spirited and probably wouldn't let this woman tell her what to do.

"As soon as my Lewyn marries, he will become king, and I need to know I won't lose all power."

Izla frowned. "That I cannot get behind. Once Lewyn is king, you need to take your place as his mother and support him, not control him or the people of this land." She wondered if that was the real reason the queen didn't want her son to get married. She didn't want to lose control over the kingdom.

The queen rolled her eyes. "Fine, but she still needs certain qualities. Princesses should be delicate and soft." Her mouth turned up, and a gleam jumped into her eyes. "I've got it! I will place a pea under the princess's mattress. If she feels it, that means she is the one for my son."

Izla turned away to hide a grin. The queen did not appear delicate. She would find it difficult to pass her own test. How could anyone think it was a fair test? A pea under a mattress would probably get squashed, and no one would feel it even if it didn't.

"No, no, that's not good enough," the queen muttered. "I will pile twelve mattresses on top of the pea. That should do it."

Izla turned to the queen and nodded. "You must be fair in this."

"I'm always fair."

"You will tell the prince and let him know he can marry Princess Rosamond if she feels the pea."

The queen clasped her hands together. "Yes, I'll do that. I would appreciate you staying to be a judge on the matter."

"Of course."

"I don't understand this," Prince Lewyn said, as he and Thane pushed a seventh mattress onto the growing pile. "I know my mother is up to something, but she won't tell me exactly what it is until we finish in here."

Thane grunted and pushed the mattress into place. "I don't see any reason for this, but Izla won't tell me anything, either." He brushed off his tunic and sighed when two servants brought in another mattress. "How many more? We aren't going to be able to reach, and the bed frame might break."

"I don't see why my mother won't let you use magic. She said she was putting something into motion and no magic can be used. She also won't let me see Rose until tomorrow. My mother doesn't like Rose, and I'm worried about what she might do."

"I wouldn't worry too much," Thane said, picking up one side of the new mattress. "Izla's entire purpose in life seems to be getting people to fall in love, so I don't think she will let anything stand in the way of you and Rose being happy."

Lewyn lifted the other side of the mattress. "I hope you are right. Mother has always been a little overprotective." They lifted the mattress above their heads and pushed it onto the pile.

"I figured as much when you came on a quest with a dull sword. Still, the weirdest thing about this whole thing is the pea under the mattresses. What is the point?"

"I have no idea. Mother has always been peculiar, but this is strange for even her."

The two servants came back carrying small step ladders.

Lewyn's shoulders slumped. "Does that mean there are more mattresses?"

"Yes, Your Highness," one man said. "We will bring them shortly."

After a few more mattresses, it seemed they were done. The servants hadn't come back, and the mattresses were so high they wouldn't be able to get another one on, even with the ladders.

The door burst open, and Queen Maylene entered the room with Izla on her heels. She studied the pile and smiled. "Marvelous." She went to one ladder and climbed to the top step.

Lewyn stood behind her and put his arms up. "Careful, Mother."

"I just need to feel the top mattress and make sure it's soft enough for Princess Rosamond."

Lewyn scratched his head. "I doubt Rose will want to sleep up there. How will she even get up?"

"We will get a taller ladder."

"What is the point?"

The queen ran her hand over the mattress. "Perfect. Come feel it, Princess Izla. It's the softest mattress I've ever felt." She climbed down and motioned for Izla to take her place.

Izla climbed to the top and felt the mattress. "It is very soft."

"Wonderful," the queen said. "No one may enter this room until tonight when Princess Rosamond sleeps here."

She ushered them all out into the hall. Lewyn was frowning. The queen locked the room with a key and smiled.

"Now will you tell us why we did this?" Lewyn asked.

"It's a test to see if Rosamond is good enough for you."

Lewyn's head turned sharply to his mother. "What? I'm not good enough for her!"

The queen waved her hand. "Nonsense."

"What is the test?" Thane asked.

"The pea."

"The pea?"

"Yes. If Rosamond is a delicate princess, then she is right for Lewyn. If she feels the pea, she passes the test."

"I don't need Rose to be delicate. I like her the way she is, and no one would feel that pea. It's probably flattened, anyway."

The queen shook her finger in his face. "You only have my permission to marry her if she feels the pea."

He narrowed his eyes. "That isn't fair."

"Princess Izla agrees it is. If the girl feels it, you may marry her whenever you wish." She turned and sauntered away.

Lewyn opened his mouth to respond, but Thane touched his arm and shook his head. He didn't know what Izla was about, but he was sure she had a plan. He knew his sister.

The next morning, Izla sat at a table with Queen Maylene, Prince Lewyn, and Thane. Prince Lewyn had a sister, but the queen didn't want her around them, so she was forced to eat elsewhere. Rose hadn't joined them yet. The queen was full of smiles and was eating with an enormous grin on her face. Lewyn was pushing his eggs around his plate.

The door opened, and Princess Rose entered. Her blonde hair hung loose down her back, and she looked tired. Lewyn jumped from his seat and rushed to her. He took her arm and led her to the table.

"Did you sleep well?" the queen asked, as Rose sat.

She pushed a lock of hair behind her ear. "Not really. I couldn't get comfortable."

Lewyn's eyes widened with what Izla assumed was hope. "Really?"

"Something kept poking me throughout the night," Rose said, showing them a bruise on the back of her arm. "I bet my back is covered in these."

The queen's face had gone pale. Thane glanced at Izla, and she shrugged. When the queen had told her to feel the mattress, Izla had put a spell on it. She might have overdone it a little if it left bruises. It was only supposed to gently poke her throughout the night.

Lewyn laughed and grabbed Rose's hand and kissed it.

She pulled it away and frowned. "You think it's funny?"

He shook his head. "No, sorry. It was a test. My mother had a pea placed under all those mattresses. She said we couldn't marry unless you felt it. You obviously did."

Rose's brows came together. "No one would feel a pea under all those mattresses."

"But you did," Izla said, putting her fork on her plate. "Now the queen must keep her promise."

Queen Maylene's mouth formed a tight line, but she nodded. Izla was relieved. She had expected the queen to protest, or at the very least to go inspect the mattress.

Rose stood and faced Lewyn. "What would you have done if I hadn't felt it?"

Lewyn glanced at his mother, then back at Rose. "You felt it, so we don't have to worry about it."

She placed her hands on her hips. "I want to know."

He took a deep breath and let it out slowly. "I love you, Rose. I would give up my kingdom to be with you."

Izla placed a hand on her heart and held back tears. Thane looked at her with a half smile and shook his head.

Queen Maylene glared at her son. "Don't be ridiculous, Lewyn. No one is worth giving up a kingdom."

He didn't take his eyes off of Rose. "She is."

Rose smiled, and Lewyn leaned in and kissed her. Izla forced herself to hold in a squeal of delight. She didn't care what anyone said. Love was the most wonderful thing in the world.

Chapter 24

Izla's heart raced as she was bumped and pushed around a busy street. She clutched a pile of books in her hands and smiled. Her plan had gone far better than she had ever imagined. Years ago, Izla had come to this mortal world and told her stories to as many people as would listen. She stayed away for a long time and then came back to see if any of them had been passed down to future generations.

It had been hard to stay away for so long, and when she first came back, she found that there were several versions of the stories being told. They had changed drastically from the version she had told, but that was expected with time. She asked around and was referred to some brothers by the name of Jacob and Wilhelm Grimm.

Izla met with the brothers and asked them if they were familiar with the stories. They were, and she asked them if they wanted to know the true stories. They had looked at her like she was crazy, but they said yes, probably to be polite. In the beginning, they appeared bored, but after she started talking, they had begun eagerly taking notes.

A few years later, she had gone to another place in that world and met a man named Hans Christian Andersen. She did the same with him. She could do without ever meeting him again. He was strange, to put it politely. Still, if he could improve her stories and share them with his world, it would be worth it.

Now, years later, she had come back and found more than one version of each of the books.

Someone bumped her, almost knocking her over, so she took herself back to her castle and into her room. The mortal world was a mess. The smells were enough to turn a person's stomach. She was almost positive the people there didn't care about hygiene, or possibly know anything about it. The man who sold her the books smelled like he hadn't bathed in a year.

Izla sank into her bed and carefully placed the books next to her. She picked up the first book. The cover was a bit frightening, but she could look past that. She ran her hand over the lettering. *"Grimm's Fairy Tales,"* she muttered to herself. "This better be good."

"MALLIE!" Thane yelled, as he ran down the hallway of his castle. Egg dripped from his head, and he had no doubt his daughter was behind it. A maid smashed herself against the wall when he ran in her direction. The staff was skilled at getting out of his way when he was looking for Mallie. "Have you seen Mallie?" he asked, as he passed her. He didn't stop for an answer. She didn't even look surprised by the egg running down his face.

He rushed up a large stone staircase and threw his bedroom door open. Ava sat on their bed with Mallie cuddled up on one side of her and Melix on the other. She looked up from the book she was reading to them.

Mallie grinned, her deep brown eyes sparkling as she studied him. She giggled. "Look, Melix. Father found the eggs."

Melix just looked at Thane and sucked on his thumb.

Ava smiled. "What happened to you?"

"I sat on the throne, and before I knew what hit me, I was covered in eggs." He glanced at Mallie. "You know you aren't supposed to play with eggs. I am supposed to be meeting with people."

"I don't think she can reach the top of the throne," Ava protested.

Mallie grinned. "I can if I use the small ladder. It was an experiment. I balanced the eggs on top of the throne. If you sat soft, they wouldn't fall. You must have sat down hard."

Thane sighed. "Five is too young to be wandering around the castle doing whatever she wants."

"I know, but you see what she's like. Keeping an eye on her at all times is impossible."

"That's what Grandfather said when I visited," Mallie said, pulling on her long black braid. "That's why I got a maid all to myself that had to play with me the whole time. She was fun."

Melix lifted his arms, and Thane picked up the toddler. "You can't go visit Grandfather if you misbehave."

"Aunt Izla said it's not misbehaving if you are just curious."

"Aunt Izla should get married and have her own kids to mess up."

Ava climbed off the bed and straightened her dress. "It's good for them to be around Izla. She's fun."

Mallie looked thoughtful. "Izla can't get married. She isn't old enough yet. She told me so."

Ava took Melix and kissed him on the head. "You're going to get egg on him."

A pounding on the door startled them all.

"Who is it?" Thane called.

"Izla!"

"Come in."

Izla came bursting into the room, her arms full of books. Her long red hair was a mess, and she looked tired.

"What's wrong?" Ava asked.

"These books!" she said, dumping the pile on the bed. "You know I talked to some men years ago and asked them to write the stories? Well, they absolutely ruined them! They changed them so much, I can barely see the truth!"

Thane grabbed a small towel and wiped the egg from his face. "I'm not surprised. People who write often change things to fit their fancy."

"In the story of Snow White, the description of the seven dwarves' house is completely wrong. It says that it was clean! Clean! I can still smell that place if I think about it."

Thane shrugged. "That doesn't sound too bad."

Izla grabbed one book and waved it in his face. "He turned me into an evil sea witch! Instead of making me helpful, he made me ugly and evil! He called me a disgusting old hag! Most of the stories are morbid and not suitable for anyone, especially children. I had hoped to read them to Mallie, but that is out of the question."

"Perhaps no one will read them," Ava said.

"That's my hope. I hope no one remembers the Brothers Grimm and Hans Christian Andersen. I have half a mind to go give them a talking to that they won't forget. They need to fix them. My shadow world is ready, but it won't work well unless the people I take there know the stories. I'm going to have to add these horrid tails until someone makes better versions."

Ava smiled. "Your world is finished?"

"Yes, and it took forever."

"I can't believe Father is letting you go through with it," Thane said. "I still think it's a bad idea."

"It's a great idea. After I go talk to these *authors,* I will start looking for my first—"

"Victims?" Thane suggested.

Izla put her hands on her hips. "Beneficiaries."

"So, you are going to put the people in the shadow world, make them act out your stories, fall in love, then you send them home?" Ava asked.

"Exactly." Izla smiled, clasping her hands together. "I am so excited. I'm going to start slow so I can keep everything straight. Maybe only have five or six stories going at a time."

Thane frowned. "That sounds like a lot to keep track of."

"It will be fine." She walked up to Thane and touched his head. "What's in your hair?"

"Egg!" Mallie said happily. "I was doing an experiment."

Izla dropped the book and held out her arms. Mallie jumped into them and gave her aunt a hug.

Thane shook his head. "I wish you hadn't taught her to do experiments. If she grows up like you, I don't think I will survive."

Izla laughed. "I'm sure you will be fine."

"I've got to go, Princess," Izla said, kissing Mallie's cheek. She placed her on the floor and gave Melix a kiss and a head rub. "I'll let you know how things go." She disappeared in a puff of smoke.

"Do you think she'll ever do that without the pink smoke?" Thane asked.

Ava smiled. "Probably not."

Izla sipped her tea and watched Hans Christian Andersen over the brim. He kept switching off between brushing his wild curly hair back with his hand and stirring his tea almost frantically. The sound of people conversing from the other tables interrupted her thoughts, and she had to concentrate to block them out.

The inn she had agreed to meet him at was clean enough for a brief conversation. Thankfully, she didn't have to sleep here. Even though it was only early evening, the room was too dim, and the smell of burned food assaulted her nose.

Mr. Andersen nervously turned his cup in a circle. "I was surprised to get your message," he finally said. "It's been ages since we first spoke. I thought you would come see my work long ago."

Izla set her tea on the table and crossed her hands on her lap. "I wanted to give you enough time to do a satisfactory job."

He jiggled his knee. "Ah, I see."

Izla wanted to jump in and accuse the man of ruining her stories, but he looked nervous enough as it was. "Are you well, Mr. Andersen? You seem uneasy."

He put his hands to his leg and stopped the jiggling.

"I am nervous," he admitted.

"Oh? Why is that?"

He glanced around the inn, then leaned forward. "It has been a very long time since we spoke, and you don't appear to have aged a day."

Izla forced her expression to go unchanged. That was what she had forgotten. She should have made herself look older. She laughed softly. "Oh, Mr. Andersen, you are quite the flatterer."

"Not at all," he said. "I am not saying it to compliment you, but because it is not natural. You don't look a day past eighteen. To be honest, it is unsettling."

Izla chewed on the inside of her lip and racked her brain for anything that would settle his mind. "My family ages slower than some. It is a blessing and a curse."

His knee started jiggling again. "I find that impossible to believe, but I have no other answer."

Izla sighed. "Well, I didn't come here to discuss my age. I came here to discuss your writing. Especially the writing about the stories I told you."

"Oh? You've read them then?"

"Yes."

"And?"

"They are utterly disturbing."

He frowned and tilted his head. "How so?"

"Just one example. In your version, the little mermaid had her tongue cut out. How is that for children? And she never found love. I distinctly remember telling you she fell in love with the prince's friend, and they lived happily for the rest of their days."

He leaned back and crossed his arms. The uncertainty left his eyes and only irritation remained. "Everyone does not get a happy ending, and so I do not believe all stories should have a happy ending."

"Happy endings inspire people."

"Or depress them if they never get their own."

Izla narrowed her eyes and drummed her fingers against the table. "I do not see any reason to read something that doesn't make a person feel hopeful in the end. I've come to ask you to change the stories to closer versions of what I told you."

He frowned. "When you came to me, you said they didn't have to be written exactly. The stories are beginning to make me a decent income, and I will not change them for anyone. They are perfect as they are."

"I disagree. I regret choosing you for this task."

He slammed his fist down on the table. "Do NOT criticize my work!"

Izla arched her brow and took another sip of tea. She wanted to throw it at the man, but that wouldn't accomplish anything. "Perhaps you are defensive because you have never been in love?"

His face turned red, and he gritted his teeth. "I have been in love. More than once. I do not see what my life has to do with my writing. My writing will live on forever. I have that much faith in it."

"Not unless you change it."

He jumped to his feet and threw his cup against the wall. Izla cringed when she heard it shatter. Izla kept her composure and didn't bother looking at the other people in the room. There was no doubt they were staring at them.

Mr. Andersen pointed a shaking finger at her. "People need to appreciate a good story, not criticize it! Are you a writer? No, you are not. Therefore, you have no right to judge. Those that judge are always the least qualified to do so!" He kicked his chair, sending it flying into another table. The two men at the table stood and moved to another, shaking their heads.

Izla began rethinking her plan to visit the Grimm brothers after this. Writers were clearly unstable creatures in this world. No, she couldn't judge them all by one person's behavior. She sighed as the man grabbed a table and tipped it over. She had really hit a nerve.

The other patrons began standing and moving toward the walls to avoid the man's tantrum. Izla noticed they weren't leaving. They all wanted to witness the scene. Mr. Andeson threw or kicked everything he could.

A large bald man came into the room, a huge frown on his face. Another man whispered something to him and pointed at Izla. The bald man came to her table, which was going to be the only one standing soon. "Did you criticize Mr. Andersen's work?"

Izla shrugged. "I might have."

The man ran a hand over his bald head. "I can't handle this anymore." He turned to Mr. Andersen. "HANS! STOP IMMEDIATELY!"

Mr. Anderson pointed at Izla, his face purple with rage. "Remove that woman from my presence. I am almost certain she is a witch!" He stomped over to the corner of the room and leaned his head into the wall. His shoulders shook. Was he crying?

"That was your last change, Hans," the innkeeper said. "I can't have you breaking my things every time someone upsets you. I don't want you staying here anymore. Get your things, and go home."

Mr. Andersen turned and glared at the man. "You get my things. You may bring them to me." He rushed out of the room, and the other guests began fixing the tipped tables and chairs.

"Who is going to pay for this?" the innkeeper muttered.

Izla stood and reached into her pocket. She pulled out more than enough gold to fix the damages and handed it to the innkeeper. "I'm sorry for the trouble."

He looked down at the gold in his hand, and his eyes bulged from his head. "This is too much."

"Take it," Izla said. "And if you show me to Mr. Andersen's room, I will gather his belongings and take them to him."

"Of course, follow me," the man said, pocketing the money. She followed him up a wooden staircase and into a dark room. He lit a lantern and placed it on a bedside table.

"He isn't very clean, is he?" she asked, scanning the room. Clothes were thrown everywhere, and the bed was unmade. The smell of body odor and old cheese entered her nose.

"He isn't predictable. Sometimes he keeps it neat, but it's usually like this."

"He has a house?"

"Yes, but he likes to stay here occasionally. I've been very tolerant of him, but he has pushed me this time."

Izla picked up a piece of paper on the pillow. "I only appear to be dead," she read aloud. "That is odd."

"He worries about being buried alive. The note is supposed to delay anyone proclaiming him dead."

"That is peculiar."

"Very."

Izla hurried and stuffed all Mr. Andersen's things into a bag. It would have been nice to do it with magic, as all of his things smelled, but she couldn't do that in front of the innkeeper. She rushed down the stairs and out into the cool evening air. Mr. Andersen sat on the ground in front of the inn, his hands resting on his knees.

"Here are your things," she said, placing the bag next to him.

He glared up at her.

"I'm sorry I upset you, but you need to realize you've upset me as well."

He sniffed. "You shouldn't be upset. I fixed all of your silly tales."

Izla pursed her lips and held in the insults that wanted to escape. She didn't want the man to go into another rage. "I wish you would rethink the stories. Give them happy endings, and make the sea witch less hideous."

"Witches are hideous."

"Perhaps, but it wasn't a witch that helped the mermaid. It was a fairy."

He snorted. "Why is that so different?"

"Because the fairy was beautiful, and she wasn't evil." She leaned toward him. "She had bright green eyes and long red hair."

Mr. Andersen's eyes widened. Izla snapped her fingers and disappeared. She wished she could see his expression.

Chapter 25

Izla took a deep breath through her nose and let it out slowly. The bright sun shone on her head and she smiled. Her world was the perfect place. Shadow world was such a poor choice of name to call this place. It was beautiful, safe, and full of love.

"You have to admit, it's a great place," she said to Thane.

He scanned the trees and stared at the small village in the distance. "It is nice, but so is the real world."

"Yes, but here I can have control. I don't have to worry about things going wrong."

"What is that village up ahead?"

Izla smiled. "That is the village where Cinderella happens. It is one of my favorites. I like to start most people there."

"So, you stick someone there and make them pretend to be Cinderella."

"Yes. It's gotten more interesting over the years. Now that the mortal world is full of technology, the people I bring here don't know how to do things they need to do here."

"Such as?"

"Cook using a stove they have to light. Some of them can't even start a fire. They don't know how to ride horses or how to dance. I have to use magic sometimes to give them memories of how to do it."

"How many people actually leave happy?"

"Everyone who leaves is happy. They don't even need magic in their world, and they have made some of the most clever things. You should go see it sometime. They have things they call vehicles that take them from one place to another. They can put food in a thing called a microwave and push a button, and it heats in seconds."

"That sounds like magic."

"I'm surprised you aren't telling me to give this up. You usually do."

"You've been doing it for so long, I've given up. I suppose you aren't doing any harm." He ran a hand over his reddish brown goatee. That was new.

"How are Ava and the children?"

"Good. They miss you. You don't come around a lot anymore."

She nodded. "I know. I've been too busy. I'm going to the mortal world today, just to see if anyone needs me. Tell them I will come visit in two days."

"Promise?"

"Yes."

"Alright. See you then." Thane disappeared, and Izla smiled. It was time to go find someone to help. She didn't like any of her stories to be empty, and she had an opening.

⸺ ell ⸺

Izla liked to find people in big cities because there were so many people it wasn't hard to find someone that wasn't happy. This time, she decided to try a smaller place just to add variety. It always took more time, but people in small towns deserved love as much as people in big cities. So far, she had found no one, but she had eaten a delicious lunch at a local diner.

If she didn't find anyone soon, she would go to a movie. She loved movies. Maybe Thane would let her take her nieces and nephews to one someday. Fairy tale movies were the best thing about this world. Izla could see her stories come to life in a beautiful way. Sure, *The Little Mermaid* still portrayed her as evil, but the stories had improved dramatically over the years. She wondered what Thane would think about that one.

Izla wandered into a small grocery store and thought about buying a candy bar. That was another thing she liked about this world. Rounding a corner, someone slammed into her and knocked her backwards. Strong arms grabbed her and pulled her forward before she could fall.

"I am so sorry," a man with sandy brown hair said. "I wasn't watching where I was going." He picked up the small basket he must have dropped. Izla hadn't heard it hit the floor.

Izla nodded as she peeked into his light brown eyes. She had never seen eyes like his. They had flecks of green mixed in with the brown. She wouldn't mind staring into his eyes forever.

She shook her head to clear her mind and rid herself of that foreign thought.

"Are you alright?" he asked.

"Yes, fine. Thank you."

He nodded and walked away.

Izla put a hand to her heart and tried to still her breathing. What was wrong with her pounding heart? No one had ever affected her like that, especially a mortal. She took a few steps forward before she realized she was about to follow the man. Leaning against a shelf of bread, she put her hands to her cheeks and cursed them for feeling warm. She wondered if her face was pink.

The man came back into view, and he paused when he looked at her. His mouth turned down, and he moved toward her. "Are you sure you're okay? Did I hurt you?"

Izla was sure her face was red now. She fanned her face with her hand and thought about going invisible. "Just a little dizzy," she said. "I'll be fine."

"You might need some air."

Izla nodded and allowed the stranger to lead her out the front doors. She took a deep breath and smiled. "Thank you. I'm not sure what came over me."

"It can be stuffy in that store. Is there someone I can call? A husband or grandchildren?"

"Grandchildren?" Izla muttered. Her face flushed. She had forgotten she was disguised as an old lady. She glanced down at her long silver hair and sighed. It figured. The first time a man had made her heart pound like this and she looked like a grandmother.

"Do you have grandchildren?"

"No... I'm fine. I can get myself home."

"Are you sure?"

She stifled the urge to roll her eyes. "Yes, I'm sure."

"Alright, then I better get back to my shopping."

"Are you here with your wife?"

The man laughed bitterly. "No, I'm not married."

"Oh, I'm sorry."

"Don't be."

A young couple walked by, and the man frowned at them. The woman smirked at him as they walked into the store, and the man gave them a grin and a wave.

"You know them?" Izla asked.

"I know everyone in this town. Except you. Are you new to town?"

"Just passing through."

"Alone?"

"Yes. That woman that just passed. She didn't look friendly."

He turned and looked at the door the couple had disappeared behind. "She's not."

"I sense a story," she pried.

"Not a good one. I dated her for a while."

"And it didn't end well?"

"No."

"What happened?"

"That guy she was with owns the town. Well, his dad does. Once he noticed her, she couldn't waste any more time with me."

Izla frowned. "I'm sorry. Don't let that sour you on love, though."

He sighed. "I'm over trying to find love. I have more important things to do with my life."

"You can't let one unpleasant experience dictate the rest of
your life."

"It wasn't just one. I've had multiple. Anyway, I need to get
back to my shopping. Sorry again for knocking into you."

Izla watched him walk away. He would be perfect in one
of her stories. He might make a good beast, but *Beauty in the
Beast* already had a person working through it. She could see
him as a prince. He could definitely pull off that look. She
turned and looked in the store window, trying to get another
glimpse of him.

Thane's arms were crossed, and he leaned against the side
of the store, invisible. He had followed Izla to see how she
worked. What he hadn't expected to see was the look on Izla's
face when she'd looked at that man. He never thought he
would see the day a pretty face would turn her head. Thane
watched her stare into the store window, and he grinned. He
couldn't wait to tell Ava.

Izla turned from the window and shook her head, whispering something to herself. This was the first time he'd seen
Izla in her old lady disguise. That made the entire thing even
funnier. She took a few steps away from the store, and then
she glanced around quickly and changed back into herself.
Pushing her hair over her shoulder, she turned to stare at the
store. She took a deep breath and went inside. Thane's smile
grew as he followed her in. Izla ducked down beside an aisle

and watched the people around. When the man came into view, she plowed forward and bumped into him as she passed him.

The man looked at her and narrowed his eyes. "Hey, watch where you're going." It appeared his kind nature was reserved for old ladies.

"Sorry," Izla said, her face turning red.

The man mumbled something and stalked off. Izla stood staring after him.

Thane appeared beside her. "What a jerk."

She frowned. "What are you doing here?"

"I thought I would watch you work."

"You chose a poor time."

"I don't know. That man looks like he could use your help."

She glanced at the man. "I suppose. I was thinking about it, but I had to make sure."

"Or maybe you could invite him for dinner. He isn't bad looking. You would just have to see past his personality."

Izla rolled her eyes. "You know I'm not looking for something like that."

"But that's usually when it finds you. At least that's what you always say."

"Don't be ridiculous. I have the perfect place for him in my world. I'll have him happy and believing in love in no time."

Thane grinned. "I'm sure you will."

Izla and Thane were invisible, standing against the wall at a lavish castle. The man from the grocery store slept peacefully in an enormous bed, covered in a heavy blue blanket. Izla hoped he would wake up soon. If he didn't, Thane would get bored and leave, and she wanted to show him how her world worked. She had been helping people for so long, and this was the first time Thane had taken an interest.

"So, we just sit here until he wakes up?" Thane whispered.

"Yes," she whispered back. "I usually stay around for this part because they always wake up confused. I don't want them doing anything rash, so I wait until they understand what is happening. If they don't catch on in a week or two, I tell them what they need to do. Most of them recognize the fairy tale and play along after a while."

"So, you watch them for a few weeks? That sounds a little creepy."

She rolled her eyes. "Not constantly. I just pop in a few times a day to make sure they don't come unhinged. Occasionally, I send Axel or one of my other animal friends."

"Axel is here?"

"Of course. Where else would he be?"

Thane shrugged. "I imagined he died a long time ago."

"Nothing ages in this world, so I brought him here. He's such a magnificent wolf. He leads people to the places they need to go if they get lost."

"He should have died long before you made this world."

Izla shrugged. "I might have brought him here when I first started making the world."

The man yawned and sat up. Izla froze. This part was always exciting. There was no way to guess how the person would act. His eyes widened as he scanned the large ornate room. Izla smiled as he climbed out of bed and ran to the window.

He looked out and frowned. "What the... where am I?" He rushed to the door and yanked it open. Izla followed and hoped Thane did as well. Keeping track of someone when they were invisible was almost impossible.

The man went into the hall, and his head jerked from side to side. He didn't seem to care about the fact that he was in a fuzzy pair of red pajamas.

"You!" he called.

A maid in a calf length black dress and cream apron rushed toward him and bowed.

"Where am I?" he asked.

The young girl looked up with large brown eyes. Her forehead was creased in confusion. "In the hallway, Your Highness."

The man tilted his head. "Highness? What are you talking about? Who do you think I am?"

"You are the prince, Your Highness."

The man ran his hand through his hair and sighed. "I'm losing my mind."

Izla smiled. She knew she shouldn't enjoy people's confusion, but it was always a little funny when they first came here.

"Am I dismissed, Your Highness?"

The man grunted something and walked away from the girl. She sighed with relief and went back to dusting. Izla followed the man down the red carpeted hallway and then some steps. He was handling this better than most people. They always asked the same questions, but some panicked a lot more.

Something bumped into her, and she twisted around.

"Sorry," Thane said quietly. "I didn't see you."

Izla grabbed his arm and pulled him with her. The man found the front door and exited into the sun. He placed his hands on his hips and peered around the countryside. He rubbed his chin, and his mouth turned down. Izla pulled Thane around the castle and away from the man and made herself visible. Thane followed her example.

She smiled. "He's going to be fine. He'll be confused, but I think he's smart enough to figure it all out. I doubt I'll even have to come explain anything to him."

"I still think it's all wrong. The poor man probably thinks he's out of his mind."

"They all do at first, but it's worth it in the end."

Thane shrugged. "Whatever you say. So, if they don't get it, you appear as an old lady and tell them to follow the stories?"

"Yes."

"And they obey?"

"Usually. Once they know it's the only way to get out of here, they try harder. By the time they are done, they believe in happily ever after. It's quite fulfilling."

Thane chuckled. "It's funny your idea of a perfect world is you running around disguised as an old woman."

She touched her silver hair. "It's not my favorite way to look, but people don't take me seriously when I look like myself. So, when I'm here, I always appear old."

Izla peeked around the corner. The man was walking away from the castle and heading down a dirt road. He didn't seem to care that he was in his pajamas. She didn't need to follow him. It didn't matter how far he walked, he would wake up tomorrow in the castle, and soon he would meet a princess.

That thought usually cheered her, but not this time. The thought of watching this man fall in love with someone didn't give her the usual thrill she got when she imagined people's happiness. Still, it was her job to help him find love and she would do it.

Thane smiled. "What do you have people call you? Grandmother?"

"When I am here, you can call me Nancy."

Also By Kristy Dixon

Akkron (The Silver Eclipse Series Book 1)
Boztoll (The Silver Eclipse Series Book 2)
The Other Continent (The Silver Eclipse Series Book 3)
The Amethyst Crown
More Than Once Upon a Time
Trapped In Once Upon a Time

About the Author

K risty Dixon started writing stories when she was seven and never stopped. She enjoys writing fantasy books for middle grade and teens. At home, she spends her time playing board games with her husband and kids and writing. Occasionally she takes part in a Super Mario marathon. She has six chickens and a cat that help keep life amusing. If she isn't playing with her kids or writing, she is usually eating cookies, or wishing she was eating cookies.